I0581505

Chapter 1

Zen stared up at the curved screen, the helmet tucked under her arm. She still wore the lightweight flight suit. A 10k-laser digital image surrounded Stuart Auditorium, one part of the training center. The space station Star Flight hovered overhead. Beyond it the newest one, Hyperion, appeared as a much smaller dot. In fact, it would not be visible from Star Flight. Hyperion orbited Mars while Star Flight remained a moon satellite.

"You have another assignment, a new exciting murder case?" a man's voice said close to her ear.

Too close. Zen turned toward the sound with a scowl because the voice was familiar. She blew out a sharp breath. The reporter smiled back. His suit had the Global Associated Press logo on the chest.

"Clairmont. What the hell are you doing here?"

"Training like you. Gotta stay in shape for space travel," he said and executed a series of stretches. "I could ask you the same. You work out, standard for maintaining muscle strength and bone mass while off Earth. But you were in the section typically used for longer trips."

"Stop stalking me. No new story for you. Maybe I like a challenge. And stop stalking me," Zen shot back. She exited the auditorium before the curse words in her head came out of her mouth.

"I know what you're thinking. Damn reporter. We're always on the job, like a cop," Clairmont said as he followed her.

"I'm not a cop. I'm a—"

"Criminologist and forensic social worker who specializes in mental health. And pioneered the field of studying social structures in space communities. With an emphasis on crime." Clairmont rattled off Zen's career details with precision.

"What's my favorite dessert, if you're so smart," Zen retorted without looking back at him.

"Bread pudding with praline sauce." Clairmont jumped back a step when Zen whirled around to face him. "Okay, that was a lucky guess. Your family is from Louisiana and your great-grandmother's cookbook has that as a specialty."

"I don't eat bread pudding."

"Great cookbook though. My girlfriend loves it. Wonderful recipes from your great-grand's café in Baton Rouge. Or was it Lafayette?" Clairmont affected a slight frown.

"Gold stars for doing your homework. The Star Flight story is over. Digging into my background is a bit, I don't know... obsessive is the word that comes to mind. Should I be worried?" Zen stared at him hard. "Space habitation for long periods can affect people in unexpected ways. Especially someone who has an anxiety disorder and tends to be claustrophobic. I'm surprised you chose off-world as your beat."

Clairmont gazed back at her for a few moments and then nodded. "Well played. You won't get me shipped back to Earth because I'm unstable."

"Who the hell do you think I am?" Zen snapped and turned to walk away.

"Someone who's got more pull than she'll admit publicly. You know where the bodies are buried. Metaphorically speaking. You find out who leaves real dead bodies around and why. I mean the government—"

"Look, if you're trying to make friends with me this ain't the way. As for power, you have me mixed up with my boss."

Zen marched into the locker-room. The name didn't fit. By most standards the "locker-room" was luxurious. One section did include thirty wide closets for personal items. Another area had a steam room. The exercise gym had advanced equipment and a juice bar. Clairmont leaned against the wall as Zen retrieved her smartwatch, computer tablet, and other times. She stuffed her pockets and then headed off to turn in her helmet.

"Oh, Clive Anderson is a powerhouse. No debate there. But you've caught killers on two worlds. You're the future when it comes to cops."

"I'm not a—"

Clairmont held up both palms. "Fine. The future of criminology then."

Zen went to the unit to check space training tools. Clairmont followed but stopped talking as they approached the entrance. An attendant took the helmet. It would be sanitized and checked before use again. The woman eyed Clairmont with a slight smile. When the woman left, Zen rolled her eyes at Clairmont. Then she tapped the screen to register her return of the helmet and walked off.

"You've been keeping busy socially, I see," Zen said.

"Better than on earth actually," Clairmont replied.

"Yeah, not much to choose from in the men department out here." Zen turned down a wide hall with Clairmont on her heels.

"Ouch. I happen to be quite a charming companion. If I didn't think General Ramirez would tear my head off, I'd invite you out for drinks."

When Zen stopped and faced him, they almost collided. She grinned when Clairmont jumped back. "Okay, what do you want?"

He looked around at the steady stream of colonists, scientists, and even a small group of tourists led by their guide. "Not here."

"Seriously?" Zen snorted when he jerked a thumb in dramatic fashion for her to follow him.

But she did. Clairmont was annoying and self-righteous about his journalistic responsibilities. He was also damn good at ferreting out information five steps ahead of other reporters. She was curious, as he knew she would be. Zen felt like prey following breadcrumbs into a trap. He wouldn't find her so easy to trip up though. Clairmont led her to the restricted area for NASA personnel and those with special access. A hallway held one large lounge and six smaller pods. Zen's eyebrows went up when he tapped a code that opened the door.

"We can talk here. Coffee?" Clairmont moved to a coffee and beverage station tucked into a corner.

"A bottle of that juice will do. Speaking of having pull and privileges," Zen murmured and accepted the blend of mango and banana juice.

"This is reserved for the media. They think I don't know it's been shielded so I can't hear a thing or tap into digital phones." Clairmont stirred cream into a steaming mug and turned back to Zen.

"Boo-hoo. The hard life of a highly paid crybaby." Zen popped open the bottle and found a paper cup. "Let's play the game then. You'll pretend to know more than you do. I'll keep saying 'No comment' until we both get bored and go on our merry *separate* ways."

"Why are you back on the moon? As you pointed out, the Star Flight investigation was completed long ago. It's been almost two years. There are no new deaths on the moon or the other three space stations. Unless... there's something I don't know about."

"My job entails space travel, and training out here is optimal. Fewer need for simulations like back home. As you say, I do consult with Commander Okoro on counseling and social outlets for colonists. We don't want them to begin to feel like zoo animals on display as more tourists are allowed to visit." Zen gave him a professional smile as she laid on her spiel.

Clairmont waved a hand as if brushing off her attempt at obfuscation. "You went back to Earth almost two years. Doing routine stuff. Psych profiles, background checks, consulting on making life in isolated colonies more bearable. Yawn-worthy stuff for a dynamic crime fighter like you."

Zen laughed and unzipped the front of her jumpsuit with one hand. She wore an olive green long-sleeve t-shirt and matching pants underneath. "Dynamic crime fighter? Good Lord. You've been reading too many of those twentieth-century comic books. You'll get bored if you keep dogging my footsteps."

"I very much doubt it, Dr. Zen," Clairmont shot back. He stared at her as though trying to solve a puzzle.

"Sure, we've handled a couple of unusual cases, but 'routine stuff' is an accurate description of what our unit has been up to since then. It might sound mundane to you, doesn't bump up your digital subscriptions. But working to make space communities mentally healthy for long-term stays is just as critical as physical health. I'm sure you can agree. A lot a money is at stake. Your own news agency is owned by a corporation that has heavily invested in at least three projects." Zen maintained her smile as she spoke.

"I have complete freedom to follow stories wherever they lead. My agency has a firewall between corporate and us," Clairmont said in an even tone.

"Oh really? How lucky for you," Zen drawled. She sipped more juice, gazing at him over the cup's rim.

"You turned over some mighty big moonrocks here and on Star Flight. Hero to some, villain to others. At least two trillion-dollar corporations weren't happy, and three governments. Including more than a few in the US power ranks." Clairmont lifted his mug at her and drank. "Let that sink in."

"You like that word a lot. Power. Is that what gets you going, Jacques?" Zen shook her head in mock disappointment. "I thought you were interested in truth and justice."

"Power, people who have it and people who want it, have led me to some of my biggest stories. There used to be an old saying, "Follow the money." Well, I've found following who has or wants power will point to truth. Sometimes even a bit of justice."

"Wow. Such depth in a guy who writes cheesy headlines like, 'Zero Gravity Sex and Death.' I've misjudged you." Zen finished her drink and tossed the cup in a recycle bin.

"I do go deep. For example, I know the story didn't end with your murder case on Star Flight getting wrapped up. Or even the secret mining operation you discovered. What's really kept you coming back to the moon? You have a daughter, a life on Earth. It must be something pretty big—"

Zen started to answer when a tone from her smartwatch sounded. The trill of piano keys told her it was an incoming call. She retrieved her noise-canceling earbuds and inserted them. "You'll have to excuse me. I need to take this."

"Sure." Clairmont started to sip from his mug but stopped as she continued to stare at him. "Oh, you mean... Right. I'll wait for you outside."

"No need. We're done," Zen replied. She nodded at the door.

Clairmont chuckled as he strolled out. "For now, Dr. Batiste. For now."

The door whisked shut, leaving Zen alone. She let out a satisfied sigh. "Perfect timing, Wyvette. You saved me."

Her new assistant's face appeared on the screen of Zen's smartwatch. She wore an intense expression. "Ma'am, I can be there in five minutes."

"No need. I didn't mean literally. Relax and have another cup of coffee." Zen smiled back at her.

Wyvette Anita Young was Zen's recruit to the OSI, Office of Special Investigations. She'd been a member of the Lunar Military Police Department. The twenty-five-year-old had been invaluable to the Star Flight investigation. Zen recommended they offer her a special agent position. Clive hadn't needed much convincing. Especially since Zen's partner, Peter Navarro, was placed on suspension after the case. An OSI agent stationed in space made sense, a decision Clive planned at some point anyway. Finding Wyvette simply pushed up the move.

"I'm on my fourth cup and keyed enough up as it is. And don't tell me to swear off caffeine. Not gonna happen. Training brutal this morning?"

"Went fine until your pal Clairmont showed up. Sniffing around for his next big story." Zen grinned at Wyvette's pained expression at the mention of Clairmont. Their on and off affair turned permanently off after his reporting on Star Flight.

"Is he gone gone? Check outside," Wyvette said low.

Zen's pulse picked up the tone of her voice. She went to the door and it slid open at her approach. After a look out into the empty hallway, Zen went back inside. "He left. What's up?"

"Come back to the station. Mr. Anderson wants a meeting."

"Hold on. I'm getting a message from him now," Zen said before Wyvette could go on. The double ringtone assigned to Clive told who it was.

"Wrap up your training session and make sure you've ditched Clairmont. We need to talk," Clive said without preamble. "Thirty minutes. Your office."

"Yes sir. How did you—" Zen barely got out before the beep signaled that he'd ended the connection.

"I heard," Wyvette said. "And naturally he didn't tell me what it's about. I'm way down the power food chain."

"There's that word again," Zen muttered as she exited the pod.

"What?"

"Never mind. I'll tell you about it later. See you in a few."

Zen kept an eye out for Clairmont. She worked to shake off the paranoia that everyone seemed to be tracking her movements. Imirah Suri's sudden appearance at her side didn't help. The trip from the training section had taken just under ten minutes. Imirah was waiting outside the LMPD main station. She watched as Zen parked her small rover.

"Special Agent Suri," Zen clipped by way of a greeting. "Or whatever title they gave you. Hell, I still don't know exactly who *they* are."

"The good guys, I assure you," Imirah said with a smile that lit up her lovely face. Clear brown eyes seemed to observe everything at once. She turned in a circle and scanned her surroundings, then faced Zen again.

"Hmm." Zen noted she didn't answer the question.

Imirah, a hybrid humanoid, told her what she needed to know. Although she received direction, Imirah had full authority to ignore orders and make up her own plan.

"You'll eventually figure it out," Imirah said in a good-natured tone as she matched Zen's stride entering the station.

"You're here to see me? Only I have a meeting and can't—"

"Yes, I'm here by invitation," Imirah said.

Her reply brought Zen up short. She stopped so fast that Imirah was five steps ahead before she realized Zen wasn't beside her. The mysterious agent doubled back. Imirah stood feet apart, hands folded in front in a military stance.

"Clive called you?" Zen gaped at her as Imirah gave a slight shrug. "Do you know why?"

"We're both about to find out. Shall we?" Imirah jerked a thumb in the direction of Zen's assigned office.

"Why can't anything be straightforward." Zen heaved a sigh and resumed walking.

Minutes later they reached the long hallway that led to Zen's spacious office. Wyvette waited outside. The size and location were enough let station officials know Zen's importance. She wouldn't have chosen it but Hadley Truman, Clive's assistant, had made the arrangements. Hadley was no glorified secretary. She had been an intelligence operative in the past. She had a genius for digging up facts and extensive contacts. Her counsel on all things related to assignments was not to be taken lightly.

Imirah let out a slow whistle when the double doors slid open. Wyvette shot a questioning look at Zen when Imirah's back was turned. Zen shook her head. B0th looked at Imirah when she faced them again.

"I like. You have a window. Meteorite silica glass. A big perk reserved for top officials. I'm impressed."

Imirah swept a hand at the view. One of two European Space Agency colonies was visible in the distance. The rocky landscape between stretched in colors of soft beige and gray. A large surface rover kicked up a small trail of dust as they drove. The vehicle traveled along the road, headed for another colony, no doubt.

"Hadley says I need to be taken seriously here. Appearances matter. I thought that kind of superficiality would be left behind on Earth." Zen laughed. "I sound stuffy."

"No, you're on target." Imirah made herself comfortable in a chair. She crossed her long legs. "Your boss's able assistant happens to be both wrong and right. Appearances do signal authority. But you'll find that those of us who have been off Earth don't respond the same."

"Meaning?"

"We have more autonomy. After all, if we violate the 'rules' how will your leaders penalize us?" Imirah looked from Zen to Wyvette. "Officer Young understands."

"We have laws and ways to enforce them," Wyvette said.

"Only if other nations and big business consortiums cooperate," Imirah replied in a mild tone. "And then there are the lone wolves. People who act on their own authority beyond the reach of official confines. It's space. There are no true borders. Jurisdictional limits mean nothing."

"You mean we're in the wild frontier? I don't think so. We've both sent people to prison," Zen said.

"She's right, boss," Wyvette put in. "On the main colonies, LMPD, Space Command, and Black Rock Security maintain control. But when you start talking about other planets and the private space stations? Not so much."

"Not at all. And don't get me started on the Mars, Titan, or the space station a group of criminal gangs plan to launch," Imirah added with a grim expression.

Zen gaped at Imirah. "Wait, what?"

"Yes. They're very well financed by their illegal businesses. They're looking to cash in like other big companies. Which may be why Mr. Anderson called this meeting." Imirah looked around. "I could use a nice cup of espresso right about now. You got a machine?"

"This is an office, not a coffee shop," Zen muttered, her thoughts still on gang activity in space.

"Um, yeah. Over here at the beverage station," Wyvette said. She went to a cabinet Zen hadn't paid attention to before. "One of Commander Okoro's staff sent this over. I thought it would be great when you have meetings."

"Seriously?" Zen shook her head.

Imirah laughed as she strolled over to the beverage bar. "I can prepare it myself. Hey, you've got a bag of Turkish blend. You know, I grew up in a suburb of Istanbul. My mother is from South Africa. Papa is from Findikli, a town a few miles from Istanbul—" She stopped at the silent glower from Zen. "A few luxuries aren't a crime, Dr. Batiste.

"Let's circle back to the criminal gangs setting up shop in space, please," Zen said with forced patience. "Your coffee break can wait."

"Okay, okay." Imirah heaved a sigh as she glanced back at the machine. She walked over to Zen, who stood with her arms crossed. "Listen, Dr. Batiste..."

"Zen. Since we're in the wild no need for formalities."

"Well, Zen, your country and the ESA are well aware of the gang's activities. One from North Africa has joined forces with an offshoot of a Russian gang. Call themselves *Vlast*; roughly translated, it means to grip or gain dominion," Imirah said.

"That's not good," Wyvette said. She poured fresh coffee beans into the espresso portafilter. A soft whirring came as beans were ground.

"Thanks, Ms. Barista," Zen quipped.

"We're all going to need a shot of something after Mr. Anderson drops more bombshells on us," Wyvette replied.

Zen looked at Imirah. "So, you're still on the moon to deal with Vlast?"

"I can't go into details. But maybe soon." Imirah breathed deep and sighed at the scent of the coffee brewing.

"I sure as hell hope Clive has more answers than you're willing to give," Zen said.

She faced the screen again as if willing it to come on. Instead, the door to her office whisked open. Zen spun around to bark at whoever had come to interrupt them. What she saw snatched the words right out of her mouth. She gaped at Clive dressed in a light gray space jumpsuit. He stood for a few seconds examining the interior before he strode in. Wyvette almost dropped the cup she was about to hand Imirah.

Imirah took it from her and sipped. "You must have been a barista indeed in a previous life. Welcome, Director Anderson. Officer Young will fix you a cup of your preferred beverage."

"Sir, you... you're here," Zen managed to stammer after a few seconds.

"My doctor cleared me for the trip. I'm not that old or decrepit yet, special agent. I'll be heading back to Earth soon anyway," Clive replied mildly. He walked to the wide desk and placed the bag he carried on it.

"I didn't mean to imply—"

Clive waved away her attempt to clarify. "I could use a mineral water if you have it. The trip dried me out. My one-and-done trip since, as you pointed out, I'm old. Had to experience space travel at least once."

"Sparkling or regular, sir?" Wyvette asked.

"Sparkling. Thank you, Special Agent Young." Clive opened his bag as he talked. "Unlock your screen so I can sync my tablet with it. Secure?"

"Yes, sir," Wyvette replied before Zen could. "Standard protocols installed and updated every thirty days."

"Excellent. Batiste. Passcode," Clive said and stood aside.

Zen blinked at him for a few seconds. Then she shook off the shock of seeing her boss in the flesh. "Right. Of course."

She tapped a series of commands into the flexible silicon keypad on her desk. Only her unique fingerprints and body chemistry would activate three devices in her office. One being the fifty-five-inch thin video display on one wall. She entered her passcode. Six icons appeared on the screen. Clive approached to take over and Zen moved aside. He didn't need any help with the image cast function. Zen glanced at Wyvette, but she was still busy playing hostess.

Clive nodded with satisfaction after a few moments. He nodded with Wyvette handed him a glass. "Thank you, Special Agent Young."

"Wyvette is fine, sir." Wyvette took up a position against one wall out of the way of her superiors. She folded her arms in front, at attention military style.

"Nothing we discuss leaves this room," Clive said.

"Of course, sir," Zen and Wyvette said in unison.

"Naturally," Imirah murmured. Her enigmatic smile widened when Clive's thick eyebrows went up at her response.

Zen had just about recovered when another shock left her speechless. Space Command Major-General Malone Ramirez entered. Right behind him was Ewan Lewis, an agent who worked for the United Nations Security Council. At least that was what his file said. Zen didn't believe it told the whole story.

"Malone." Zen took a step forward to hug him but caught herself in time. Instead, she gave him a crisp nod.

"Hmm." Imirah's dark eyes twinkled mischief as she looked at them. She sipped from her small cup. Her expression became somber when she faced Clive. "Let's get this show on the road."

"Indeed," Clive rumbled. His fingers moved over the control pad lightly. Images popped onto the screen. "Space station Crius is above Saturn's moon Titan. Two nations funded it. With cooperation from the United States."

"The United Nations Global Space Council and European Space Agency are not pleased about it either. They only just learned about US involvement," Lewis put in.

"They had the resources, the technology, and were going forward no matter what. It's not like we could have stopped them," Clive replied with scowl. "Our intelligence learned about the project and offered our scientific expertise."

Zen felt chills at his words. Her sister had been selected as part of that "expertise." Alexis "Lexi" Batiste hadn't been a murder victim after all. Not one of the three college students at Georgetown University who had died. Not at all. Lexi seemed to be a strong suspect. Yet Zen had details on her motive. James had used his contacts to get Lexi into the advanced criminal rehab program called The Lodestone Project. With her brilliant work in the fields of astrobiology and astrophysics, Lexi was a prime candidate. Those who went through the process were deemed too valuable to lose. The conventional criminal justice system, even with advances since the mid twenty-first century, didn't make sense for people like Lexi. After all, proponents pointed out, they were in 2086 and on the brink of a new millennium. Why waste such extraordinary minds as we became a multi-world race?

Zen wondered if Clive knew and if so, how much. They hadn't discussed her family secret. Malone placed a hand on her arm. His touch was her answer. Clive had all of the answers. Her mind spun as she considered who had told her boss. What was his reaction? Someone calling her name made Zen blink out of her reverie.

"What?" Zen looked around to find everyone gazing at her.

Clive walked over to Zen and placed both large hands on her shoulders. His gruff voice had a gentle undertone as he spoke slowly. "Major-General Malone will coordinate with the commander of Crius, Antonia Gusev. Peter is already on Crius. Special Agent Young will be assigned to assist him in investigation. You'll accompany me back to Earth."

"Like hell I will." Zen glared at him and then Malone as though they were co-conspirators against her.

Malone walked over to stand next to Clive. "Zen, just listen to—"

"No, I don't need to hear the speech about me being too close to the situation. Or that my emotional state will be a huge liability. I'm going, one way or another." Zen pushed Clive's hands off her shoulders and walked to the screen. "Let's get the brief."

"Give us a moment," Clive said, his voice a quiet rumble. He waited until the door whisked shut, leaving him alone with Zen. "Not only is the investigation on Crius diplomatically delicate, it's dangerous. Your sister's role is unclear."

"Are you saying Lexi is a suspect in whatever is going on?" Zen's heart beat so fast her chest started to hurt. She clinched one fist and worked to control her breathing. The walls of the office seemed to bend, closing in on her.

"Here, drink." Clive pulled her other hand up and pressed a cup into it. "Juice filled with electrolytes and serotonin."

Zen took it, gulped down a mouthful, and exhaled. "I'm fine."

"You haven't even heard the full brief on what we know so far and—"

"I'm good, damn it." Zen drained the cup. "My father is pulling the strings. Trying to cover up his shit."

"Batiste, you're doing a poor job of convincing me you can handle this." Clive stepped away from Zen, arms crossed. He eyed her with the intensity of a doctor examining a patient.

Zen took in a deep breath and exhaled. "Sorry, sir. Obviously, this situation hits close to home for me. My first reaction was natural."

"Humph. Exactly my point. Do you honestly think you could focus after seeing your sister?"

"I've had almost twenty-four months to... process this new reality." Zen stood straight and returned his steady gaze.

"You think I don't know?"

"I don't..." Zen stopped when his thick eyebrows pulled together. The kindly uncle persona was replaced by the hard-nosed military intelligence veteran.

"You've had twenty-four months to arrange your personal affairs. Your daughter is pursuing her studies in France with her older cousin, Brianne. Astra is well established, independent. Your ex-husband and brothers will look out for her. You have a long-term house sitter service on standby. You've been cultivating informants to find out about transport to Crius. Since it isn't supposed to exist, flights to Crius definitely aren't advertised. That's even if you could get clearance to go under normal circumstances. Space flight isn't like booking a plane trip back home." Clive went to the control panel and tapped in commands.

"I've been under surveillance," Zen said.

Clive didn't look up from what he was doing. "Of course."

"You didn't stop me from coming to the moon or Star Flight. How did you know I wouldn't find my way on a ship to Crius?" Zen watched him for a few moments. Then she hissed in anger. "Because you've been feeding me false leads, controlling my informants."

"One of whom is with the UN Global Space Security Council. Undercover. It seems they don't trust the US any more than they trust Russia, China, or any other players," Clive said with good humor.

"Crius is one huge chunk of evidence that they're right," Zen retorted.

Clive tapped the keypad twice and then looked at Zen. "The decision has been made. I'm telling you because the news about Crius will be released soon." He glanced at the digital time-zone map on his screen. "Actually, the first press statement should be out in a few minutes. Six o'clock AM Eastern Standard Time. No more secrecy."

"I'll bet the press release won't include tidbits about Vlast. Or the real details of what kind of research is being conducted," Zen said.

"I meant secrecy about its existence. Limited information will be for security reasons. Standard procedure." Clive's cool façade would be perfect for a news conference.

"An entire space station being built and deployed is hardly standard. I'm sure the UN won't see it that way."

"The secretaries of the UN Security Council and the UN Space Council are being briefed as we speak. Thankfully, I wasn't included in that task," Clive said with a dry chuckle.

"No. You were sent to reign in your rogue special agent in space."

Clive grimaced at Zen. "No one 'sends' me anywhere like a damn errand boy. The work being done on Crius is critical to Earth and future space exploration. Even more so than Star Flight. I need boots on the ground with no personal agenda at stake. Otherwise, people could die. Is that clear enough for you?"

"You're saying my sister is in danger. I should ignore that fact, pretend she doesn't exist. After all, I thought she was dead for years. It's not like I haven't gotten used to her not being around." Zen felt the anger building like a fire in her chest. She paced and talked. "My father made the decision about lying to me all this time. You're making the decision about what's best for me now. I'm a minor annoyance to be dealt with after I stumble onto the truth."

"No, you're a seasoned investigator who knows the risk of being emotionally involved in a case. Look at me," Clive barked.

Zen stopped to face him. "Yes. I know the risk. I also know about the social structure of gangs, isolated space communities, and crime occurring in both."

Clive blinked. Puzzlement replaced his frown. "Wait, what?"

"Jacques Clairmont is already sniffing around. He's going to put the pieces together."

"We can handle Clairmont." Clive waved a hand as if dismissing her point.

"He'll write speculative news articles about the 'top space cop' when the Crius news breaks. How will you explain to NASA and the White House that you won't assign me?"

"You'll continue to consult with Commander Okoro to stabilize community life here and on Star Flight. You work will help the other space stations as well."

Clive's response sounded well-rehearsed yet natural. Even reasonable. Zen's Star Flight investigation had revealed cracks in the social structures of the moon colonies. Malone and Commander Okoro had worked to root out compromised LMPD officers. Okoro also continued to deal with black market activities, underground parties involving designer space drugs, and other issues.

Zen gazed back at him as seconds ticked by. Then she affected a tight smile. "Well, that's it then."

"You're up to something, Batiste," Clive muttered. His blue-gray eyes narrowed. He stared at Zen as though trying to see into her thoughts.

"Like you said, the decision has been made. Feel free to use this office for your briefings. And whatever else top-secret stuff you need to do. I can set up in the one down the hall." Zen walked to the door. Malone, Imirah, and Lewis spun around when it slid open after her approach.

Ewan Lewis raised his eyebrows at Zen when the door opened. He'd worked for her father on more than a few operations. "You're going to call Director Batiste. About Crius. Not advisable."

"Former director. He's an occasional advisor on diplomatic affairs. Nothing of national or international security concern. Simply a private citizen." Zen rattled off the sanitized version of her father's role in federal government matters.

"Before you do anything rash, let's talk," Malone said.

Zen turned to him. "Let's have dinner later. There's a wonderful Indian café that just opened in D sector."

Malone glanced the others. They took the hint and went back into Zen's office with Clive. The door closed, leaving Malone and Zen alone in the hallway. "Honey, I know you're upset."

"Upset doesn't even begin to cover it, Malone," Zen snapped. Then she sighed. "Sorry, it's not you."

"So, what next?"

"I'm going to say hello to Daddy."

Chapter 2

Two hours later everyone except Imirah was back in Zen's office. Clive had called them to a final briefing before his departing flight. He was behind Zen's desk working the control panel. Wyvette alternated between checking her tablet and gazing at Zen for clues. They hadn't had a chance to talk since Clive's dramatic arrival earlier. The screen had an image of a spring day in the country somewhere on Earth. Wild flowers, sunflowers, and blue bells swayed in the breeze. Every few minutes birdsong trilled.

Out in space, seasons meant nothing. Research showed recreating the familiar in space aided adjustment and emotional health. Cultivated gardens and even a small park in one sector of the moon colony had been built. Every home had video "windows" with a variety of nature scenes.

"Pretty." Ewan swiveled his chair around to face them after enjoying the view. "I feel serene now."

Clive gave him an irritated glare. The field of flowers winked out. "Change of plans. Special Agent Batiste will join Navarro on Crius. Special Agent Young, you're still going."

Wyvette glanced at Zen. "Yes, sir."

"So will Lewis." Clive fixed his famous freezing stare on Zen as if daring her to object.

"And the gang's all here," Zen quipped. She gave Lewis a playful wave. He winked back.

Malone leaned close to Zen and whispered, "You won this round. Don't gloat."

"I'd never."

"Speaking of gangs... May I, Clive?" Lewis stood when Clive nodded. "From what we've gleaned from our sources, Vlast has embedded at least four agents on Crius. Their planning started fifteen or twenty years ago. Paying off employees within the Russian space program and the African Union."

"So, they learned about the space station from their own spies. Forward thinking," Wyvette put in.

"They're not the only criminal enterprise wanting in on profits from space. But they're the most ambitious. They want to make an entire colony or space station their turf. Take control. They're smart and patient," Lewis went on with a nod.

"Long-term planning like you describe sounds uncharacteristic," Zen said. "They tend to choose crimes with a quick turnaround. Drugs, identity theft, prostitution. Even groups like the Mafia or Gangster Disciples kept it simple."

"Welcome to the new age of thuggery." Malone gave a grunt.

"Malone is correct, Batiste," Clive grumbled. "The prospect of billions, even trillions, of dollars is too tempting for them to ignore. They have a leader who looks ahead."

"Former Russian strongman. Family ties to a twentieth-century oligarchy. Vladimir Putin's great-grandson. Putin pioneered cementing ties with outlaw groups in northern and eastern Africa. Publicly, the Russians have had investment agreements with governments there and the Middle East for decades, "Lewis continued.

"Playing both sides against the middle," Zen said.

"Exactly. So, Vlast leadership is using official and black-market resources. Our reports say there's growing tension between Vlast and the current Russian president Elizaveta Rozova. Which is significant because one of the Russian agents helped us get information on Vlast. Otherwise, we wouldn't know much. Talk about the old 'Iron Curtain.' We lost two people trying to get close to Vlast." Lewis frowned.

"Lost, as in…" Wyvette blinked at him.

"Dead before they could give us anything useful," Lewis replied. "They'll kill their own if they become useless or fail one too many times."

Wyvette shook her head. "Working against them is risky. Working for them is dangerous."

"We have to tread carefully on Crius. Navarro has done great work preparing the way for us. He's getting help from an insider. She's sleeping with one of the Vlast members. And yes, she volunteered to help. We won't share her name or picture. The fewer people know who she is, the safer she'll be. For now." Lewis left his chair and crossed to a control panel. He tapped keys and the Crius administrative chart appeared. "Vlast could be any one of these."

"Either on the payroll or Vlast members," Clive grumbled. He squinted at the photo display.

"And then there's the murder. A process engineer took a long fall," Lewis said in a mild tone as he brought up another photo.

"Not an accident, I'm guessing," Wyvette said.

"Meet Mikhail Navalny," Lewis went on. "He wasn't an inside member of Vlast as far as we can tell. He might have been what they call a 'useful idiot.' Someone not that smart but in a job or position to help."

"And our way in at Crius." Clive turned to Zen and Wyvette. "You're going to join Navarro for the investigation into his death. We're not calling it a murder officially."

"Won't it raise questions with so many of us for one death?" Zen looked at him.

"Lewis isn't going with you," Clive replied.

"I leave in a couple of hours. I'm the new confidential assistant to the head of facility maintenance. The other guy decided to return to the moon. A new job, I think." Lewis wore a wolfish grin.

"Paid off or scared off?" Zen asked.

"No comment," Lewis replied.

"Right. So, the story is Peter needs help doing what? I mean, it's still a pretty iffy cover if you ask me." Zen turned back to Clive.

"That's just it. Everything is shady and shifty on Crius. Even the mob leaders are nervous. Petty crimes have increased. They're afraid of losing control," Clive said.

"Wyvette will liaison with Space Command substation officers," Malone said. "I'll keep in touch with her and their colonel from here."

Zen nodded at the explanation for his presence. "Got it."

"They're so distracted, I doubt you and Wyvette showing up will cause a ripple. And Crius is big." Clive gestured to Lewis, who changed the screen. "You're quite familiar with the system, Ewan. You wouldn't have hacked into the secure server, would you?"

"You had the files open and labeled. I just touched the right screen icon. Sir." Lewis smiled at him.

"Humph." Clive eyed him as if plotting to investigate the Brit's activities.

"Looks comparable to Hyperion." Wyvette pointed to the image of the secret space station.

Clive rose and marched over to replace Lewis at the panel. "This official photo will be released at the press conference unveiling its existence. Crius has a flight crew of sixty-five people. Another fifty are facility workers. Space mechanics, plumbers, and more. There are five scientific research units with eighty more between them. The rest, a hundred, are humanoids. But reports show a good fifty unofficial human residents."

"Undocumented residents?" Wyvette looked at Zen with a shocked expression. "But how—"

"Lots of ways for people to come and go undetected," Lewis said with a glance at Clive.

"Wait, that can't be possible." Zen looked around at the others.

"Crius is actually three separate sectors. It has the benefit of tech developed from space research over the last five decades." Clive swiped a small screen on her desk.

Zen gasped at the new image. A multi-level wheel within a wheel hovered over Titan, Saturn's largest moon. "How did they pull off such a massive build?"

"They started small in 2055. It was called a research satellite with probs sent to both Saturn and Titan. Most of the world forgot about it. Even the media ignored reports about rock compositions and inert gas percentage. Pretty damn clever to be honest," Clive said.

"And thirty years later you have a massive secret space station. Crius gives Africa and America a solid claim to Saturn and Titan." Wyvette's assessment caused the others to look at her in surprise. "I can add two and two, you know."

"The kid is on target," Lewis said with a wink of appreciation at Wyvette. He chuckled when she glared at him.

"I'm no teenager," Wyvette complained.

"Which is why we're going to weather an international storm for months. Special Agent Young isn't the only one doing the math. Despite assurances that every nation will benefit from the research and discoveries," Clive said.

"Sounds like you helped craft the wording," Zen said.

"Your father did." Clive's intimidating frown included James Batiste and Zen.

"Well, if anyone can pull off soothing international outrage it's my father. His years as a diplomat and professor will help. He has friends around the globe." Zen looked away from his intense gaze.

"Humph." Clive's response rumbled like thunder from deep in his chest.

Lewis clapped his palms and rubbed them together. "So, onto the details of our operation. As I said, I leave in less than two hours now. You two will leave in the morning. Navarro is at the local cop station."

"Space Command headquarters," Wyvette clipped.

"As you wish, milady," Lewis replied with a slight bow. "You'll join Peter at *headquarters*. We also made another substitution at Crius. Two new medical doctors, one with forensic certifications, swapped out physicians whose assignments ended. Nothing we arranged. As luck would have it, their contracts were up."

"We'll have an untainted autopsy and other forensic results. First encouraging news about this case," Zen replied.

"Indeed," Lewis replied with enthusiasm. "As your investigation progresses, we'll turn up the heat. Drip details to push things along. First, you'll announce that poor Mr. Navalny was murdered. That will shake up the factions."

"Whoa, whoa." Zen leaned forward to make her point. "We don't want to set off a gang war. They don't have enough of a police presence to deal with a surge in violence. Criminal groups function on loyalty and demonstrate zero tolerance when attacked."

"Yeah, dude. You'll get a lot of folks killed. Including maybe us," Wyvette added. "I don't have your *decades* in the field. But even this *kid* knows a real bad idea when she hears one."

"We're at risk the minute our ship docks at Crius," Lewis countered. "And time is of the essence, as they say."

Clive nodded with a grimace. "Lewis is on target about time. The UN meets in six weeks to decide on action about Crius. They could send a security force to take over. To ensure that no activities there violate international space treaties. Having a serious crime problem will give them more justification."

"The only reason they're waiting that long is to give their attaché time to reach Crius, review the situation, and report," Malone added. "They could act sooner depending on what he says. Ambassador Abramov will be on the ship with you. We didn't have a choice and neither did the UN. They don't have a ship to make such a long trip with EmDrive yet."

"And the US couldn't afford to ramp up global tensions by not letting the UN hitch a ride," Clive added.

"I don't think saying no seats left would have worked," Wyvette murmured.

"Hardly," Clive said with a grin that vanished into a frown fast. "UN Security General Blanc was sent ahead months ago. Diplomatic negotiator as well. International cooperation on security and crime investigations is his job."

"Fallon Blanc, age thirty-seven. Married for ten years with two kids. He isn't dumb, but he is a plodder. Meticulous to a fault, in my humble opinion," Lewis said.

"Because naturally you have a file on him down to his favorite breakfast cereal." Zen gazed at Lewis.

"He prefers eggs and toast," Lewis quipped and then grew serious again. "He trained as an intelligence officer but went with the UN early on."

"Which means he knows how to get information, dig for answers," Wyvette put in.

"Yes. But his slow and steady approach is in our favor. He has three to four weeks to get his report in." Lewis stared at the image of Crius.

"The UN Global Space Council will digest his findings and list possible actions," Clive said.

"Fallon is expeditious when required. I'd say we have seven to ten days to find the killer, neutralize Vlast, and give the UN reasons to keep hands off Crius." Lewis turned around to face them all again, fists on his narrow waist.

"Which they're inclined to do based on my sources," Clive said. "They don't have staff or expertise to run a space station, manage multiple research projects, and time to deal with the logistics of a takeover."

"But make no mistake, Clive. They'll marshal resources if needs must," Lewis said.

Zen turned to Lewis. She gave him a head-to-toe glance before gazing into his grayish-green eyes. "Who exactly are you working for now, Agent Lewis?"

Lewis let a charming smile light up his handsome features. "Ewan, please. I work for the UN Global Security division. On loan from British intelligence. I had the honor of being assigned to your father's section for a time when he was a diplomat."

"Lewis has a certain degree of... autonomy," Clive murmured with a side glance at Lewis.

"And you freelance for him from time to time." Zen heaved a sigh. Her father would have eyes on her.

Lewis seemed to read her thoughts. "Not at present."

"Yeah right," Zen mumbled.

"I'm going to have my hands full with Vlast, fending off Jacques Clairmont, and pretending to do my job. The director of facility management doesn't know who I am. I'm just a new engineer to assist him," Lewis replied in a mild tone. He didn't appear overwhelmed by what he had to juggle.

"Wait, what's this about Jacques Clairmont?" Zen asked, thoughts of her father vanishing for the moment.

"In a gesture of transparency, the US State Department agreed to allow one member of the press on our fact-finding mission. His boss at the Global Associated Press agreed he could have an exclusive on the murder investigation. He can't release reports until we're done and he's back on Earth," Clive said.

"Holy sh—" Wyvette gaped at Zen.

"He's going to get himself killed," Zen blurted out. "Not to mention be underfoot while we're trying to do an already tough-as-hell job."

"He's signed a release of liability. He knows the risks." Clive held up a palm that cut off another outburst from Zen and Wyvette. "Clairmont already has information on Vlast. I have no idea how. Sometimes I suspect the guy has more sources than me."

"His boss dropped a few hints about 'organized crime' in a meeting with the UN information office. He didn't say Vlast but then he didn't have to." Lewis shrugged.

"Jacques is super smart. Not much gets past him. I'm sure he started digging the minute the official statement hit his inbox," Wyvette said."

"I believe Special Agent Young is familiar with all of Clairmont's talents," Lewis said aside to Wyvette in a stage whisper.

Wyvette's brown eyes narrowed to slits. "Don't start with me, *Ewan*."

"Alright, kids. Let's all just get along," Zen said before full-scale war could break out between them. She glared at Lewis. "You specialize in provoking conflict."

Lewis grinned back, unaffected by angry stares from both women. "A bit of lighthearted teasing to ease the dark mood. If you don't want to let out information to move things along on Crius, I'm open to another idea."

"I say we play it by ear. It's not like we're starting from scratch. Wyvette can assess the state of local policing. Give me a report on security. At least we can be prepared *if* we go with your plan," Zen said.

"Yeah. Space Command combined with Black Rock Security officers can go to sectors most likely to pop off," Wyvette added with a nod to Zen.

"Assuming those two don't have Vlast infiltrators in their ranks," Lewis said with a scowl.

"I've had two video calls with Colonel Smith and the head of Black Rock. They'll have reports and stats ready for Wyvette when she gets there," Malone said.

Clive stood. "Let's hope Peter has identified likely suspects. We agreed that he would keep contact to a minimum. We don't know if Vlast or their informants have hacked into voice or digital systems. We set up dummy texts that look like he's sending messages to his family and a close friend. They're coming to me instead."

"Good. Sounds like we have our strategy in place. Sir, here's a message from my command on Earth." Malone turned the screen of his tablet so Clive could read it. They moved away and talked in low tones.

Lewis gave a jaunty wave with one hand. "I'm off to the final frontier, mates. I hear there's a great pub on Crius with authentic Earth spirits. I'll treat you to real English ale, Special Agent Young."

"A date? With you? You gotta be kidding," Wyvette said with a grunt.

"I'm not as old as you think. And I'll lay bets I've got more *talent* than Clairmont." Lewis leaned close to her with a wink. He strolled out before she could reply.

Wyvette watched him leave and rolled her eyes. "So full of himself."

"He's a couple of years older than me, Wyvette. Not exactly ancient. And good-looking." Zen spoke to Wyvette but her gaze stayed on Clive and Malone.

"What, he started being a spy when he was in middle school? I wouldn't doubt it though."

Zen faced Wyvette again. "You could do worse."

"You mean stay away from Jacques. *Or* I could find out what he's up to." Wyvette raised both her dark eyebrows at Zen.

"While enjoying his company as an added bonus. You like him more than you'd like to admit. Clairmont must really have all-round skills," Zen said with a giggle.

"I don't usually kiss and tell, but he does this thing where he—"

"I don't need to know the details, Special Agent Young."

"Hey, I'll sacrifice to get the job done, boss. You know how dedicated I am. Besides, you might want to try teaching Major-General Ramirez his technique."

"Oh, stop. But on second thought..." Zen and Wyvette dissolved into laughter like two high schoolers.

"You two are happy because you have good news on the case?" Malone looked them with a puzzled expression.

"No, it's just..." Zen scanned Malone's toned body and imagined him in an impossible position. Naked. She smothered another giggle.

"I get the feeling I should be in on this joke."

Clive's deep voice boomed across the office before Zen could reply. "I need a few minutes with Special Agent Batiste. Alone."

"Yeah, I got to pack and get stuff done." Wyvette blinked at the severe expression that wrinkled Clive's brow. She backed to the door and mouthed "good luck" to Zen. Then she was gone.

"Clive—" Malone stopped when Clive raised a palm.

"This is between us, general," Clive said in a quiet rumble.

Malone turned to Zen. "I'll see you later. Rafa's Greek Café. Seven."

"Yes. Don't worry," Zen said softly and patted his arm. Malone shot a glance past her at Clive and then strode out. She faced Clive, ready for the blow-back. "You talked to my father."

"Basically, you blackmailed the man. How did you find out? Oh c'mon, Batiste. Don't waste my time with the clueless act."

"I put together bits and pieces. Then I guessed the rest. So, while the White House and cabinet members talked a hardline about criminals..." Zen shrugged and sat down.

"The government supported an advanced program to treat brilliant but dangerous criminals. Who also happened to be either rich, valuable to the government, or to large corporations." Clive rubbed his jaw.

"Members of the infamous 'One Percent' tribe. And the administration talks a good game about alleviating income inequality. All the while the influence of millionaires and billionaires stays the same behind the scenes. Soon we'll be talking about trillionaires. Those folks want to be so ahead of the rest of us that by the time we figure it out, there's not a damn thing we can do. Eighty years and they're still in control."

Zen shook her head as she thought about the Black History classes she'd taken. The first African-American president of America had tried to address income inequality. Despite two terms, Barack Obama had made no headway. The powerful and rich elite had simply dug deeper.

"You would have snitched on your own father?" Clive frowned at Zen in disapproval.

"He's pretty much bulletproof. We both know it. Daddy has backup plans for his backup plans. He doesn't care about approval from top officials, not even the President of the United States," Zen replied.

Clive nodded slowly and studied Zen for a few seconds. "Your mother, brothers, and grandparents don't know the full story about Lexi."

"Who does?" Zen stood. "I don't want them hurt. But I can handle whatever the ugly truth is. I've pretty much imagined the worse for almost two years. I gotta go call my kid. Astra doesn't know I'll be gone longer yet. I need to pack, talk to Peter before I get to Crius, and get some sleep. Is that all, sir?"

"You sure you *want* the whole truth?" Clive said quietly.

Zen let out a slow breath. "No."

Three hours later Zen sat across from Malone in a booth at Rafa's Café in the newest part of the US moon colony. Early buildings were embedded partially in rock formations. Their design gave them protection from the constant onslaught of meteorites. Newer buildings were constructed in caves and built with polymers that blocked radiation. Once inside, lighting and décor made Sector U seem almost like Earth. Mostly commercial, Sector U contained shops, restaurants, and business offices.

Rafa's Greek Café buzzed with activity as wait staff delivered orders to tables. Zen and Malone sat in one of four booths that lined one wall. A flameless candle in the table center gave off a soft romantic glow. Turkish pop music flowed from a speaker set in the wall of their booth. Malone ordered lamb with Greek potatoes. Zen got a vegetarian platter. They maintained a comfortable silence in between accepting their food, getting Lebanese tea refills, and people watching. Their waiter appeared.

"Here is the bill, but no hurry, General," the young man said with a wide smile for Malone.

"Thanks, Caius." Malone accepted the dinner bill. "We're still thinking about dessert."

"None for me. I can't load up on that wonderful baklava before my flight," Zen said with a shake of her head.

"Oh, but it is light as air," Caius replied.

"Don't tempt me. Thanks, but not this time. Next visit." Zen smiled at him as he nodded and left.

Malone waited until the waiter was a few feet away. Then he leaned forward. "Are we going to talk about how you pulled it off?"

Zen pretended to arrange the sweater that matched her skirt. She'd decided to forgo pants one last time for their dinner. She mostly lived in them while in space, as did most women. Wearing dresses made a pleasant change.

"Pardon?"

"You applied pressure to your father. Only you could have moved that mountain. But then, you're a daddy's girl." Malone grinned at the scowl his observation brought.

"Please. Lexi had the privilege of being his favorite," Zen said. "And no, this isn't about sibling rivalry. We all kind of spoiled Lexi, except mama. Maybe that was the problem."

"You're trying to figure out how your sister became a... you know." Malone glanced around at the other diners.

"Three degrees, Malone. And my sister turning to crime is a mystery to me." Zen's voice was low but intense.

"Hey, you always tell me the brain and human behavior are incredibly complex." Malone massaged the back of her hand as he spoke.

Zen nodded but felt no comfort. Her stomach twist as the word "killer" came to mind attached to a mental image of Lexi. "I keep wondering if she suffered some trauma I don't know about. Our childhood seemed normal. She was headstrong. Clashed with our mother from the time she could talk, it seems. They were too much alike, I suppose."

"Have you asked your parents?" Malone said.

"Daddy said nothing happened to her. Mama insists he let her get away with too much. Beauty and brains. Lexi could charm her way out of anything. But she wasn't cruel, certainly not violent. Not the little girl I remember." Zen rubbed her forehead as if that would help her troubled thoughts.

"You told me she took your mothers BMW for a joyride three times. Hacked the private school computer system when she was thirteen. She was a rulebreaker." Malone shrugged when Zen looked at him.

"What looked like typical kid stuff was more, you mean. We missed the signs that Lexi would go on to bigger and worse things." Zen leaned against Malone's strong shoulder for comfort and support.

"All the expertise in the world doesn't mean you have a crystal ball into the future. The same kid that drives everybody crazy can become a Nobel Peace Prize winner. Solve problems that have plagued the world for generations," Malone said.

"I don't think we'll ever get the point where we know precisely which direction people will take. There are so many environmental factors that affect genetics and biology. Two people can experience the same thing and have completely opposite reactions."

"Yeah. Life's still a mystery even now." Malone sipped from his glass of red wine. "How pissed was Clive that you went around him?"

"He wasn't. Not that he'll admit it. I mean, maybe a little on general principle. He's genuinely worried about me facing off with Lexi. But he feels a lot better knowing Peter and Wyvette will be on Crius."

"So, Peter survived almost helping a killer escape," Malone said, referring to their case on Star Flight.

"Hell, she fooled me, too. He also helped catch her." Zen took the goblet from Malone and drank before handing it back.

"You said heavy meals and alcohol do you in on long flights." Malone moved the glass out of her reach.

"I needed a drink just thinking about...everything. My mother's symptoms of dementia are coming back. The magnetic brain treatments aren't a cure, apparently. She's forgetful, tires easily, and gets irritated at odd things. Not that being irritable is out of character for her," Zen quipped and tried to smile but failed. Enola Batiste—independent, smart, and accomplished. Imagining her as frail and confused scared Zen.

Malone signaled to their waiter and ordered a glass of wine for Zen. "You think she even remembers the events surrounding Lexi leaving?"

"Daddy didn't tell her the whole story, Malone." Zen stopped when Caius returned. She accepted the wine with a smile. Then she leaned closer to Malone when the waiter left. "She thinks Lexi knew too much about the murders and some bogus secret operation. Daddy arranged for her to work on a valuable project to keep her safe."

"And she bought his story?"

"She probably could tell there was more to it but chose not to force the issue. Or maybe she was just willing to believe Lexi had gotten mixed up with shady people. My little sister had a talent for finding the 'wrong crowd.' She usually ended up being the ring leader."

"Basically, you'll be free to chase down Lexi while Peter and Wyvette look into the murder." Malone raised both his dark eyebrows as he gazed at Zen.

"Hey, I'm going to do my job," Zen shot back with a scowl. "Can't believe you think I'd leave them hanging."

"Peter and Wyvette are loyal to you, Zen. They'll most likely shoulder the load knowing the situation." Malone shrugged at the heated look she gave him.

Zen stared into her wine glass for a few seconds and then sighed. "You're right. If I'm being honest, I kinda thought they would. Made me feel less guilty about being on a personal agenda."

"Mikhail Navalny getting himself killed came at just the right time."

Zen winced. "I don't want to think of it that way, Malone. He was a person with a family that cared about him."

"He hooked up with criminals. If you run with wolves, you risk getting eaten."

"Yeah."

Malone studied her for a few seconds. "You stopped pushing hard to get on a ship to Crius after a while. You knew something."

"I studied space communities." Zen ticked off points on her fingers. "A highly secretive mission, isolation, and the prospect of making huge sums of money. Perfect ingredients for corruption. I pulled info on Crius."

"Your pal Chloé did a digital dive into someone's secure server," Malone interjected.

Zen grinned at him. "No comment. Anyway, six years ago a report from Crius security cited concerns about possible criminal infiltrators."

"You figured it was a matter of time before something happened. A reason for the Space Crime Team to be called in." Malone laughed at the way Zen rolled her eyes.

"Damn Jacques Clairmont for those colorful names. But yeah, I decided to be patient. Of course, daddy had a Plan B. Ways to keep me occupied here."

"Well, he's right. The moon colonies ain't exactly paradise. A disorganized police force hasn't helped. I've had a job getting things in order," Malone said, referring to the LMPD corruption Zen's last case had uncovered. "Add to that a spike of domestic violence and... Frankly, we could use your expertise."

"My former colleagues from Columbia University arrive in two days. They can consult on behavioral health treatment and preventative services. My friend Abbas Nasir has been eager for a chance to visit the moon," Zen said.

"Ah-ha. Your Plan B."

Zen nodded. "He and I co-wrote two articles on social dynamics in closed communities. He's been fascinated with my work on space communities ever since."

"You're leaving Astra behind for an extended period though."

"Not too long. The EmDrive has changed everything. Flight to Titan from Earth takes weeks instead of years. Getting there isn't a problem, especially from the Moon," Zen said. She sipped from her glass. The Tempranillo went down smooth. "I know it's just in my mind, but this helps."

"Red wine has less acid than white. So, you likely won't get indigestion," Malone said.

"It's not food or high-speed space ships that will twist my stomach in knots," Zen retorted.

Malone's only response was to take her hand. They finished dinner. On their way out they saw Wyvette at another table with Jacques Clairmont. He had his back to them. Wyvette looked past Clairmont in time to see Zen and Malone. She gave Zen a slight nod. Wyvette's left eyebrow lifted when Zen pivoted to head their way. Focused on his bowl of lentil soup, Clairmont didn't notice Wyvette's attention had shifted.

"She didn't waste time," Zen drawled as she studied the couple.

"I don't think baiting him is a good idea," Malone muttered. Still, he trailed behind Zen.

"I'm just going to say hello," Zen replied as she kept going.

"So, I told my bureau chief—" Clairmont finally registered that Wyvette was staring over his shoulder. He turned around. His handsome young face lit up when he saw Zen and Malone. "What an unexpected bonus to see Special Agent Batiste and Major-General Ramirez. Join us."

"We finished dinner and are on our way out. Lots to do," Malone said before Zen replied.

"I'd think you would be busy preparing for the trip as well," Zen added.

"I'm so looking forward to learning about the science of this special space station. I hear it's filled with groundbreaking technology. New medical research that will extend life, mitigate climate change, and more." Clairmont's dark eyes sparkled with excitement. He glanced at Wyvette and then back to Zen. "And of course, there's the death of Mikhail Navalny."

"Stick to the science projects, Clairmont. I'm sure there is plenty for you to report on besides our case. We won't be releasing statements. His death could be an accident, maybe even natural causes."

"Yes, well, that's why an investigation is warranted. Don't worry. Wy isn't talking about the case. She's the consummate professional officer of the law."

"Oh, I know. She's not the one I'm keeping my eye on, *Jacques*," Zen said with a glacial smile at him. "Enjoy your evening."

"Thanks." Clairmont lifted his glass of wine at Zen and Malone. Then he gave Wyvette a sexy grin.

Zen led the way out of the restaurant. "Too damn smug this early in the game. He's already got a source on Crius."

Malone looked back at them. "You think so? I'd say he's trying to milk tidbits out of Sergeant Young."

"Special agent. She's with us now," Zen replied.

"On *loan*. I'm still annoyed you poached my most promising LMPD officer. Young could be headed for big things in colony policing," Malone said.

"Face it, Malone. She's gotten a taste of cases with global importance. Wyvette won't go back to chasing petty thieves on the moon."

"Humph, we'll see." Malone stepped out to wave down a ride share cab.

The large rover rolled to a smooth stop. Equipped with life support, the vehicle could do short hops on the surface between colonies or sectors. Two other couples were already on board. Malone and Zen didn't talk during the ride to the main and largest portion of the NASA colony. One couple spoke Chinese in low tones. Zen guessed the taxi would take them twenty-five kilometers to the Guójiā Hángtiān Jú colony. Zen and Malone got out in the atmosphere-controlled hangar. Malone paid for the ride with his agency digital payment app. More vehicles, some private, others with various company logos, arrived and left around them.

"I've got your favorite herbal tea," Malone said as they strolled onto the main boulevard. The smooth walls covered surface of the rocky entrance part of the building was built into. He took her by the hand and steered them toward his residential section.

"I should check my messages, call Astra one last time, and go to bed early," Zen murmured. Yet she continued to follow him. She'd left her things at his spacious apartment.

"All of which you can do at my place." Malone wrapped one arm around her waist.

He was right. Astra was happy to hear from her but pouted at the lack of details Zen shared. Zen's messages contained only logistical details Hadley had arranged related to her trip. Then Zen and Malone went to bed, not sleep. At least not for a while. Then her dreams were filled with disturbing images of her sister and dead bodies. Zen woke the next morning with a sense of foreboding that she tried to shake as she headed for the launch sector.

Chapter 3

"**W**elcome aboard, ladies," the smiling flight attendant said with a nod to Zen and Wyvette. She wore a Space X logo on her crisp light blue shirt tucked into slacks. Her icy-blond hair was pulled back into a bun. "You're in row two of cabin number one."

"Thanks. Wow, I've never flown premium class before. Look at these comfy seats. They recline back to beds. Oh! They've got old episodes of my favorite shows on the entertainment menu." Wyvette grinned like a kid at her favorite theme park. Her seat was across the aisle from Zen's.

"Perfect environment for the trip. And an entire section where you can walk around, even exercise." Zen enjoyed watching the young agent take such pleasure in the trip.

"The entire ship is outfitted as Premium First Class. We mostly fly executives, government officials, and VIPs," the flight attendant put in.

Wyvette squared her shoulders and grinned. "I feel hella special."

We have nutritionally balanced yet delicious meals for you. Your agency sent over your food preferences." The flight attendant handed Wyvette and Zen packets with moist wipes, travel-sized lotion, and lip balm.

"Cool." Wyvette stowed her carry-on in the bin beneath their seats. Then she settled in and immediately put on the headphones.

"Glad I don't have to reassure you about flying across space at warp speed," Zen quipped.

"I'm good." Wyvette bobbed her head to the theme song of her show.

"Good morning," a second flight attendant said in a soothing tone. His voice came through speakers. "I'm Ben and I'll be with you for our journey. Delmar is my colleague. Together we'll answer any questions you might have."

The blond flight attendant's image popped on the compact screens overhead. She gave a cheerful wave. "Welcome again."

"Our craft is the *Phoenix Star Ship* from Space X. *Phoenix SS* is the latest model outfitted with the most efficient and fastest propulsion system yet developed. We have up to a maximum of fifty-seat capacity. Though we have a bit less than half that number of passengers for this trip. We should arrive at Crius in six days, give or take a few hours. Our outer shell is made up of the latest polymers to protect us from radiation and impacts from meteorites," Ben said in an airy tone.

"Gee thanks, Ben," Wyvette said. "Now I'm thinking about giant asteroids flying toward us at the speed of light."

Zen laughed. "I'm sure the pilot will have plenty of time to get out of the way. Asteroids are the size of mountains. Can't miss 'em."

"Hell, I'm feeling better already," Wyvette quipped. Despite her words, she looked relaxed.

Ben finished his safety speech and other instructions. A light overhead would signal when they could remove their helmets. After another twenty minutes, the signal to put them on flashed. The ship hummed to life, surprisingly quiet. The electrically powered EmDrive engine had no moving parts or heavy fuel. Soon the ship pulled away from the docking area. With another jolt that shook the cabin, they were on their way. Though Zen had plenty of time, she decided to review her digital files on Crius and its organizational structure. For the first twelve hours, she watched videos Hadley had included with text summaries.

Wyvette had gone to check out the activity cabin. She took to the fitness equipment with the enthusiasm of youth. She returned to her seat and craned her neck to look at Zen's tablet.

"Jacques is in cabin three," Wyvette said. "He says hi."

"Humph. What a pain." Zen wasn't pleased to be reminded he was along for the ride.

"He's not a bad guy. Just passionate is all." Wyvette took out her own digital reader.

"Yeah, so you keep telling me."

"I meant about his *work* and the importance of a free press to democracy," Wyvette shot back with a chuckle.

She glanced around, her expression turning serious. She took the empty seat across from Zen. The ship had been built with super-rich business execs in mind. Zen raised a panel, creating an enclosed pod. Wyvette tapped her wireless earbuds and waited for Zen to put her on. Seconds later they'd synced for a conversation.

"You were right. He's got a source on Crius feeding him information."

"Shit. He told you that?"

"Nope, but Jacques couldn't resist testing out how much I know. He's clever, but it's obvious his questions weren't random," Wyvette said, her voice low.

"So, what does he know or think he knows?" Zen stared at the screen of her tablet. She wouldn't be able to download updates for now. It would be another twenty-four hours before they passed a communications satellite.

"Well, word is out that Navalny's injuries may not have been because of an accident."

"That's not exactly breaking news. OSI sending me to Crius is like a press release his death was suspicious," Zen replied.

"Like the stories say, murder dogs your footsteps." Wyvette quoted from salacious tabloid reports about Zen.

"I thought you had better sense than to read trash," Zen said with a grunt of disgust.

"You have to admit they do a great job of making you look like a superhero." Wyvette giggled at the sour expression her comment inspired.

"Easy for you. Wait until they start zoning in on *your* life. Let's see how funny you'll think it is then."

Zen mumbled a few more curse words as she thought about the press coverage. Clive and Hadley hadn't been perturbed by the attention to Zen. Hadley pointed out that OSI controlled the narrative. Meaning Hadley seeded the stories to take a direction they wanted. A young Black woman who not only investigated crimes, but had a doctorate provided rich bait for reporters. Her publications on the sociology of space colonies had been widely quoted and misquoted.

"Yeah, well." Wyvette let out a sigh. "I have a feeling my day is coming, especially after Crius. Jacques is trying to find out about organized criminal activity out there. He even brought up this article you wrote. It's inevitable that humans will show some dysfunctional reactions in closed societies. A secret space station is a breeding ground for such behavior."

"I didn't say inevitable; highly likely given the dynamics of isolation, alien environments, and adjustments to the conditions. Much of which can be mitigated with proper planning," Zen countered as if Clairmont was sitting across from her instead of Wyvette.

"Like my Pop-Pop says, 'People be peopling all over,'" Wyvette replied with a headshake.

Zen let out a short laugh. "Your grandfather is a wise man. He summed up my academic work in five words. The same resentments, stressors, greed, and more travel with us. Doesn't matter if we're exploring Earth or going to other planets."

"Including gang activity." Wyvette whispered the words despite their precautions to prevent being overheard.

"Hmm. Two of them collaborating across national boundaries and going into space. I gotta admit, even I didn't see that one coming." Zen scanned a summary on her tablet for the third time.

"Yeah. Sure as hell wasn't on my bingo card," Wyvette said.

"Huh?" Zen glanced up at her.

"Pop-Pop and his buddies like playing new versions of this old game. One of them has future events. Match them on your card and win. If it comes true, you win an even bigger prize. Mostly it's about sports scores or championship games. But sometimes it's about politics or the outcome of a criminal trial."

"Your Pop-Pop has interesting hobbies." Zen went back to re-reading her intel reports.

"My grandmother says he's going to hell for gambling," Wyvette joked. "Anyway, I don't think Jacques knows about Vlast. But... I can tell he figures there is way more to what's been revealed or learned."

"Of course he does. He's a reporter," Zen complained with a deep sigh.

"I can't believe the powers-that-be agreed for him to come along. Jacques is known for breaking stories other reporters miss. Especially about *you*, boss."

Zen thought for a few seconds. "The UN doesn't know the whole story. You really think the US and African Union were totally candid?"

"I could just imagine that convo. 'Oh, by the way, we think the Russian and Algerian mobs are taking over our advanced space station.' Yeah, no." Wyvette let out a dry laugh.

"The White House, NASA, and the State Department are hoping we clean up this unholy mess so they don't have to explain. *Ever*." Zen looked at her tablet again. She scrolled through the summaries. "Which is why so many cooks are in the kitchen."

"What—" Wyvette blinked at her and then her expression cleared. She snapped the fingers of one hand. "Peter is there working with an insider. Ewan is on the scene. We're going and... Yeah. They're trying to cover all bets. Otherwise, why not just have the two of us investigate a suspicious death?"

"Exactly. And..." Zen stopped at the series of taps on the panel of her pod. She slid it open.

Imirah Suri, impeccably dressed in a slate-gray and dark red flight jumpsuit, smiled down at them. The knit fabric, made for ultimate comfort on space trips, hugged her curves. "Hello there. Just thought I'd do the polite thing and check in with you ladies."

"What the actual hell?" Wyvette's mouth hung open as she gawked at her.

"If I may..." Imirah tilted her head to one side as she looked at Zen.

"Sure. Plenty of room." Zen waved her in.

"Thank you."

Imirah slid into the spacious seat next to Wyvette's slim frame. She pressed a button and an armrest slid between them. One wide seat became two smaller but still-comfortable spaces. The enigmatic international agent wore a congenial smile as if she was reuniting with two old friends. They might have been on a transatlantic airplane on Earth about to catch up on old times. Except they were zipping at light speed into space. The "old times" they shared included murder on another space station, police corruption on the lunar colonies, and a secret humanoid settlement. Add to that, Imirah Suri was the one of the first experimental human/humanoid hybrids. Her published personal history said she was half Turkish and half South African. Very few knew she was a hybrid. Even fewer knew she was an intelligence officer.

"How has your trip been so far?" Imirah glanced from Zen to Wyvette and back again.

"Screw small talk," Wyvette blurted. "How did you... Who sent... Girl, you know all the questions. Now spit them answers."

"Her St. Louis, Missouri, street vernacular comes out when she's stressed." Looking at Zen, Imirah let out a soft chuckle. She wiggled her hips on the soft imitation leather. "Premium class is so decadent. Imagine having one of these all to yourself. Well, you don't have to imagine it, Special Agent Batiste."

"Hmm. I see you're fully recovered from your adventures on Star Flight," Zen said mildly. She ignored the way Wyvette gaped at her for being so nonchalant. Zen knew full well the implications of Imirah being on the ship to Crius. Now she was curious as to what Imirah would reveal to them.

"Modern medicine is a marvel. My iridium and titanium components help though. Yes, I'm doing fine, thanks. You no doubt want to know why I'm here. I could have concealed my presence. You didn't see me board. If I'd wanted to, you wouldn't have seen me exit on arrival to Crius."

"Right. We get it. You're a ghost. So secret even your bosses don't know what you're up to. I'll bet they prefer not knowing," Wyvette tossed back at her.

Imirah's dark brown face broke into a delighted smile. She looked at Zen. "I like her more and more."

"Get to the point of this big reveal," Zen clipped.

Her amused expression faded. "The UN Security Command has information that Lewis could be in danger soon. A certain group already knows who he is. Which means the UN has at the very least a leak, maybe even an infiltrator."

"Vlast?" Wyvette asked, her voice low.

"Or one of the big companies. Vlast isn't the only one fighting for control of Crius and a jump on trillions in space profits," Imirah replied with a scowl. "The things flesh bags do for money."

"Hey, watch the insults." Wyvette bristled at the pejorative description advanced AI humanoids used for biological humans.

"Sorry. At least I didn't say rotting or rancid flesh bags. Besides, I wasn't talking about you two." Imirah laughed when Wyvette rolled her eyes.

"Has Lewis been attacked?" Zen cut into their budding feud.

"No, and I wouldn't give anyone dumb enough to try chances of survival. Don't let that genial British gentry act fool you. Ewan Lewis is lethal. He trained me," Imirah said and sank back in the seat.

"So, he doesn't need you to protect him. Why are you here?" Zen chafed at having to wait more hours for an update and to send messages to Hadley.

"I'm going to find out who is working with a bad actor. We think it's someone already on their way to Crius."

"On this flight? Damn, Vlast works fast." Wyvette looked at Zen.

"Don't jump to conclusions. I'm not sure Vlast is on to him," Imirah replied. "Anyway, that's what I know so far. Only a bit more than you. Let's order drinks and appetizers."

"You mean breakfast," Wyvette retorted.

"Whatever you want to call it," Imirah replied with a wink. She slid the panel into the pocket.

Ben approached with a tense face before Imirah could signal for him. He addressed Zen. "Ma'am, the captain requests you join him in the cockpit."

"Another nice perk for VIP American government officials." Imirah studied his face for a second. "Or... something is wrong."

"This way, Agent Batiste." Ben gestured for Zen to follow.

A passenger, a woman dressed in a blue pantsuit, stomped down the aisle. "I demand to know what is happening. A man has taken ill and was whisked off with no explanation. If there is some kind of infection—"

"Please return to your seat," Ben cut in sharply. "Both Delmar and I are trained emergency medical techs. There are no indications the passenger's distress is a risk to others."

"We have a right to be fully informed," the woman snapped, her Russian accent growing sharper as her face flushed with anger.

"Ma'am, please return to your cabin." Ben's voice went up as he took a step toward her.

Imirah moved past him in the aisle. "The crew has everything in hand. I'm sure they have ruled out infections.

They have rapid tests that detect a range of viruses and bacteria."

"And who are you?" The woman gave Imirah a head-to-toe glance.

"I'm trained to assist the flight crew. Let's not cause a panic. It's not like we can pull into the nearest port to catch another ship now, can we?" Imirah used her statuesque five foot, eleven-inch frame to herd the woman down the aisle.

The flight attendant waved to his female colleague, who stood at the other end of the aisle. Delmar took her cue from Imirah and began talking in a soothing tone. From their position, Zen couldn't make out what she and Imirah were saying. The passenger gestured toward the cockpit, but both women were immovable forces.

Ben turned to Zen and Wyvette. "This way, please."

He led them in the opposite direction toward the control room of the ship. They passed through the galley kitchen where the flight attendants prepared meals. Two seats were folded up against a wall. Before Zen could notice any other details, they were in the control room. A man with silver hair but a young face greeted them.

"We just got one pilot?" Wyvette looked around at the panels of lights and screens with data.

"I'm Captain Travers. Delmar is actually a trained pilot as well. So, she's my human backup. We're also equipped with the best flight AI developed in the last fifty years. But I'm not going to get sick. Which brings us to our problem. The passenger who became... incapacitated wasn't sick earlier." Captain Travers swallowed hard.

"Seriously ill?" Zen glanced at Ben.

"He's dead! Oh my God. I've never seen a dead body before." Ben clapped a hand over his mouth.

Holy shit." Wyvette turned to Zen with wide eyes.

"Lower your voice and remember your training." Captain Travers had a sheen of sweat on his forehead. His voice shook even as he tried to shock the flight attendant into getting a grip.

Zen turned to Ben, a hand on his shoulder to get his attention. She spoke in a level tone to help calm him. "Go take Delmar's place helping Ms. Suri. Wyvette, you get Delmar's statement. Ben can tend to the other passengers as usual."

"Done," Wyvette said. "I'll get my tablet to do a video record." She hurried back toward their seats.

"What's next on your duty schedule, Ben?" Zen asked.

"Um, serve water or juice—you know, snacks. Offer pillows or blankets for people who want to sleep. Check life support levels." Ben seemed steadier talking about his regular tasks.

"Good. We'll talk later." Zen nodded to him and then exchanged a glance with Wyvette. The young agent understood to keep an eye on him. Then Zen faced Captain Travers. "Where's the body?"

"We have a below-deck medical pod. He's there for now. Later I can place him in a special body bag. We keep them just in case. They inhibit rapid decomp during flights. I mean no smells or unpleasant fluids leaking." Captain Travers walked away as he explained.

He led the way through Section Two of the ship to a set of stairs that led to a lower level. The passengers in the

Business Class cabin appeared at ease. Some munched on snacks or napped. Others sat reading. Apparently, word hadn't spread yet. Then Jacques Clairmont appeared in the aisle two sections away. He waved to get Zen's attention. She ignored him and followed the pilot down the stairs.

"Lock these doors behind us," Zen said. "There's a reporter on board."

"I'd forgotten about Mr. Clairmont." Captain Travers tapped in a code on the door's entrance panel. "Delmar and Ben will be able to enter if needed."

"You know Clairmont?" Zen looked around as he led her down another aisle that led to the compact medical unit.

"I have full dossiers on every passenger. I have limited security clearance. Standard for pilots licensed for longer flights. Especially to secret space stations." Captain Travers stepped through a doorway and let out a long sigh. "Here we go."

The long cabin looked like a hospital emergency room. Four beds, two on either side, were surrounded by medical monitoring equipment. A cubicle functioned as what would be called a nurse's station. A figure covered completely lay on the first bed. Zen accepted a pair of disposable gloves and mask from Captain Travers. She walked over and carefully pulled back the white sheet. Zen studied the man's slack face.

"Who is he?"

"Roman Bocci, forty-seven. One of the three UN staffers on board."

"Right, right. I recognize him now."

Zen had a profile of the other passengers as well, which included photos. Hadley had sent it over. The plan was for

Zen, Wyvette, and Peter to concentrate on solving the murder. The UN people would deal with diplomacy and heading off an even bigger international firestorm.

Captain Travers studied the man a few moments and then glanced at Zen. "You didn't know him? I thought all you government people were together."

"Nope," was all Zen said. She wasn't about to explain the complicated circumstances.

"Humph, beyond my clearance level. I get it." Captain Travers went back to studying the body. "Glad all I need to do is fly you folks.

"Believe me, you're way better off," Zen replied. She bent closer to look at the man's clothing. He wore the usual attire of space travelers, a zip-front jumpsuit of lightweight but strong fabric. "What about his belongings?"

"Ben is bringing them." Captain Travers stepped back and crossed his arms, a frown of concentration on his face. "What a mess. Makes me wonder if I should go back to flying planes on Earth."

Delmar, the female flight attendant, entered the cabin carrying a bag. "Here's Mr. Bocci's luggage."

Zen eyed the hard-shell gray suitcase. "That's it? He must have had a tablet or laptop."

"Maybe it's inside." Delmar produced the device flight personnel used to access sealed luggage.

"We all have clearance to access all bags in emergencies," Captain Travers said.

Zen took the unlocked bag to a metal table nearby. Once open, Zen took out items one by one. "The usual clothes and personal care items. Here's his UN badge."

"He has another one in an inside pocket of the suit he's wearing," Captain Travers said.

"Extra toothbrush. Extra everything. He was a meticulous kind of guy," Zen murmured.

"He questioned me about the water filtration system before he ordered a cup of tea. Ben and I joked that he might have smuggled his valet on board. We could tell he was used to the best things in life." Delmar glanced back at the supine figure. "Poor man. He was just here to do his job."

"We want to keep his death quiet until the ship docks. We've got a load of jumpy business heavies," Captain Travers said to her.

"Ben and Ms. Suri told Ambassador Abramov Mr. Bocci took ill and had to be moved. She's expecting to be told more soon," Delmar said.

"Did you check around his seat?" Zen pressed on the bag looking for concealed compartments.

"Ms Young is searching it now. Keeping it low key. Most of the other passengers are in their own world. They don't know anything out of the ordinary has happened. Thank God," Delmar said.

"That might not last," Zen mumbled. She left Bocci's personal items out. She and Wyvette would go over them more thoroughly with digital tools later.

"If you've got this in hand, I'll get back to the controls. AI autopilot is fine, but for regulatory and insurance purposes..." Captain Travers backed away from the body.

"Ah yes, the anti-robot lobby," Zen said.

"Nonsense based on movies and sci-fi comic books about killer smart machines. Anyway, I'll check back later." Captain Travers nodded to them and left.

"Anything else you notice about him physically?" Zen said to Delmar. They both walked back to the corpse.

Delmar pulled the zipper of his suit down. He wore the usual microfiber t-shirt and fitted pants beneath. "I'd need help getting all of his clothes off. We'd have to cut—"

Zen grabbed her hand reaching for large surgical scissors. "No. He might have smart tech built into his clothes. You could damage evidence."

"I didn't think of that." Delmar put the scissors back on a side table of other instruments. "I read about you. I mean, when I saw your name on the passenger list."

"Don't believe everything in the news."

"Speaking of that, the reporter is making himself a nuisance. I had to get the air marshal to handle him. He wouldn't stay in his cabin, kept trying to nose around Mr. Bocci's seat and come this way." Delmar clicked her tongue in disapproval.

"Good. I'd forgotten at least one air marshal is standard on all flights, even those in space." Zen went back to staring at the victim.

"Hmm, this one happens to be with UN Security. Bill—Captain Travers—knows her. She'll have an easy job since we won't have passengers for our return trip to pick up more officials."

"No?" Zen looked at her.

"All other departures have been delayed indefinitely. Ben and I figure it has something to do with all the government people making a special trip. Now this." Delmar frowned at Bocci as if the trouble was his fault.

"We won't be able to contain the news for long," Zen said with a sigh. Keeping the lid on Navalny's death was tricky enough. But two?

Imirah strolled in and stood next to Zen. "Roman Bocci. Age forty-three. Italian by birth, but grew up in Nice, France. He's been a UN legal logistics staffer for six years. An expert on international and space law."

"So, the UN sent a lawyer to Crius?" Zen said.

Imirah glanced at Delmar. "We've got this locked down. I have forensic medical training. So…"

Delmar blinked at them for a few moments. "Oh, right. I should help Ben anyway. I mean, so things look normal up top."

"Great." Imirah beamed at her with a nod.

Despite her agreement, Delmar seemed reluctant to leave. "You'll need forceps, swabs, and of course sterilizers. We have a bioclave here."

"Excellent. I'm sure we'll find everything we need," Imirah cut in before Delmar could keep talking.

"Okay then. Just a reminder that I do have security clearance. Four years experience flying with VIPs of all kinds, so confidentiality is in my DNA. And I love a good mystery," Delmar said, her eyes bright with excitement.

Imirah walked to Delmar and nudged her out of the clinic. "We'll keep it all in mind. You've been a tremendous help to us so far."

"She's eager to play detective," Zen joked when Imirah returned alone.

"You mean get in the way. Murder isn't an electro-game," Imirah replied with a snort. "She has her uses."

Zen studied her. "Like everyone else?"

"We all have our roles. N'est-ce pas le cas?" Imirah grinned at her. "Ewan and I have duties with a global scope of a very secret nature."

"Global and now extraterrestrial," Zen replied.

"I'm here to help him neutralize all threats to peace on Crius."

"I wonder how you decide who is a threat though." Zen raised one eyebrow as she continued to stare at Imirah.

"Let's not quarrel, my friend. You and I are on the same side."

"Uh-huh. You have a suspicious mind. We don't know how this guy died." Zen glanced at Bocci one again.

Wyvette returned with a petite woman with red hair in braids. She had a tight grip on one of her arms. "We got a confession."

"So, let's go over this once more, Ms. Riley," Zen said. "You knew Mr. Bocci was having trouble breathing, maybe a heart-related crisis, but you left him anyway. And didn't alert the flight crew."

Theodora Riley hiccupped through more sniffles. With her heart-shaped face, she looked younger than her thirty-one years. Zen scanned Riley's profile on the tablet Wyvette had handed her. Imirah stood guard at the door to shoo away anyone, including Captain Travers, who tried to enter. Zen and Wyvette waited patiently for the woman to settle enough to speak again. Her confession had streamed out in a jumble. It was time to get a more coherent account.

"How close were you?" Wyvette pressed. "You don't work in his department."

"Um, I suppose you've accessed his phone by now…" Theodora balled up the wad of tissue she held in one hand.

"Hmm," was Wyvette's noncommittal response.

"It's not against the rules. Especially if you're not in the same division. I'm Ambassador Abramov's top aide. We frequently consult legal about laws in different countries. It's critical information diplomats at her level use on almost a daily basis." Theodora smoothed down the front of her knit shirt.

"You were having an affair," Wyvette said, cutting to the chase.

"He told me he and his wife led separate lives, married on paper only," Theodora protested.

"Damn, that old line still works?" Imirah chuckled after delivering her commentary.

Zen shot a hot glance at her with a frown that clearly encouraged Imirah to shut up. Imirah shrugged and leaned against the wall near the door. Zen faced Theodora again.

"Mr. Bocci told you his marriage was over." Zen used an empathetic tone.

"He showed me the papers on his computer. The lawyer sent them for his electronic signature." Theodora's sorrowful expression switched to one of anger. "Then I found out he was sleeping with another woman. An intern for Senator Jordan. Can you believe it? A child barely out of school!"

"And he's not getting a divorce," Wyvette added.

"Another lie. His other lover showed up to see him off on this flight—a surprise. She even had on a ring he'd bought her. I couldn't confront him then and there. We were getting ready to board, going through check-in, and suiting up. Ambassador Abramov kept demanding my attention to last-minute details. It's not like he could get away, right? But he did a great job of avoiding me in the first few hours."

"You worked up a big head of steam all that time. Going over the times you'd spent together. Replaying every conversation. When you did get to him, you let Bocci have it. Tell us how." Wyvette's quiet voice urged her to go on.

"I thought he was faking, pretending to have an asthma attack. I knocked the rescue inhaler from his hand and stormed off. I said he could choke to death, but I didn't... I mean, I was so furious. I calmed down. Then I went back to tell him exactly what kind of no-good half a man he was, and that's when..." Theodora went back to being grief-stricken. She smothered a sob with the damp tissue.

"Here." Wyvette offered her a trash bin for the used paper and handed her several fresh sheets from a dispenser.

"Thank you. I didn't kill him on purpose. I was so sure he was playing sick to avoid taking responsibility. Is that... Could I be convicted of murder?" Theodora looked from Zen to Wyvette, her hazel eyes wide with fear.

"Let's not get ahead of ourselves, Ms. Riley," Zen replied. "As you said, not being a medical professional and given the circumstances, your reaction was reasonable."

"Oh, thank you. Thank you so much for understanding." Theodora grabbed both of Zen's still-gloved hands.

"Our investigation isn't complete, of course. And I can't make promises on behalf of the court system," Zen added.

"But you just said—" Theodora blinked as the dose of reality sunk in.

"Special Agent Young will escort you back to your seat. You're not to discuss this conversation with anyone. Absolutely no one," Zen said firmly.

Theodora wore a look of pure dread. "Ambassador Abramov will have to know. I should—"

"Keep it shut, lady," Wyvette clipped.

"I'll inform the ambassador when I know more. Special Agent Young will stay with you." Zen looked at Wyvette. "Anything else?"

"I should take her to our cabin until you get a chance to have a chat with Abramov." Wyvette gazed at Zen with a silent message in her dark eyes.

"Good thinking. Get her some tea or something from one of the flight attendants." Zen signaled past them to Imirah, who approached. "We'll check in with you in a bit."

"Done. Come with me, Ms. Riley." Wyvette ushered the woman to the exit that led back to the passenger sections.

Imirah looked over at Bocci's body with no trace of sympathy. "Well, that's that. Problem solved. A slight diversion into reality show drama. Cheating husband and all-around lowlife learns about karma the hard way."

Zen walked over to the clinic bed where Bocci was laid out. She pulled back the sheet. "Except I doubt he died of natural causes. Look at his chest."

"Shit." Imirah frowned down at him. "He's a troublemaker even dead."

Chapter 4

"No one knows I'm not in the control pit. I can access below deck through a door." Captain Travers said. "Figured it would be easier if you had help moving him and taking off his clothes. I brought Ben along." He nodded to the male flight attendant right behind him.

"Very thoughtful," Imirah said with a winning smile and the captain puffed out his chest.

Zen pressed her lips together to smother a snarky comment. Imirah had a lot of humanoid power in her runway-model body. However, her hybrid status was classified. Being seen as a human female gave her an advantage. Imirah stepped aside as the two men efficiently stripped the clothes from Bocci. Ben draped the sheet over the body from the waist down.

Captain Travers tapped his gloved fingers on Bocci's chest. Then he lifted first one arm and then the other. "Hell."

"Problem?" Imirah peered at the body and then looked at Captain Travers.

"See the bruises here? They're burns, actually." Travers clucked his tongue as he looked around. He grunted in satisfaction when he found what he wanted on a nearby tray—a tiny measuring tape. "Yeah, the spacing fits."

"We better check our pissed-off mistress and find it," Imirah muttered.

"Find what?" Zen leaned closer to stare at the dead man's chest.

"A stun gun of some kind," Captain Travers replied with a grimace.

"We, we're not sure though, right, Bill? I mean, he could have had an underlying health condition that kicked in." Ben's words tumbled out as he rubbed his hands in agitation. The strain of maintaining calm in front of the other passengers had taken a toll.

"I served in the UN Troops. I know what they look like." Captain Travers crossed his arms and stood back.

"Sonic electroshock device or stun gun in street language. Very effective in neutralizing a subject," Imirah said.

Zen glanced at her. "Personal experience, huh?"

"Hmm." Imirah either didn't notice or chose to ignore the implied judgement. "Of course, the modern version has improved on the old devices."

"Exactly. Two small bruises that will fade soon. His death will look like heart failure. It has happened during space flights, but only three times in the past twenty years," Captain Travers said.

"Del got to him first. She loosened his shirt to help him breathe and... Well, he fell forward. The bruises could have come from that." Ben looked from the Captain to Zen.

"Delmar tried to resuscitate the man, listened to his heartbeat. The irregular pattern, the burns, twitching muscles. What she describes fits." Captain Travers pointed to the corpse.

Zen looked up at Imirah. "I didn't think she was lying."

Captain Travers looked from Zen to Imirah and back again. "Who?"

"Theodora Riley." Imirah gave him a quick summary. "Cheating husband cheats on mistress with another mistress, she gets mad and tops him mid-flight. Lucky us."

"She seems so... nice," Ben blurted. He blinked as if life confused him.

"Yeah? Well, *nice* people murder other people all the time," Imirah retorted. "We better tell your baby agent what to look for—a shock wand or gun. It can look like either."

"She's got her earbud on. I can get her." Zen stepped aside to call Wyvette using her smartwatch.

"It might look like an ordinary object by the way. Something compact. Maybe a fashion color to make it looked like a cosmetic tool," Imirah said.

"You sound so familiar with using the thing. The UN brokered an international ban on the use of such devices." Zen squinted at Imirah.

"Who can keep up with all of the nitpicking. I sent her pics." Imirah slipped her smart-com, a combination phone and tablet, back into an inner pocket of her jacket.

"How did you get my agent's direct message—" Zen heaved a sigh. "You know what, I shouldn't even bother asking."

"I was given both your contact points when I was assigned. Do I have to keep reminding you we're on the same side?" Imirah lifted both dark eyebrows at Zen.

"Probably. Never know which boss you're serving," Zen shot back.

Ben let out a shaky breath as he stared at the dead man. "Wow, this flight has gotten way too complicated."

"Calm down, kid. You can't exactly get off at the next stop, can you?" Imirah gave a soft chuckle.

"Holy shit. Management will lose it if this gets out." Captain Travers rubbed a large hand over his face. "They didn't want to be the carrier for this flight. They refused but three governments pressured them."

Zen yanked Imirah by one arm and pulled her into a corner. "Ben is already on the edge. Now you're winding up the captain. Smartass comments aren't helpful. We need to keep the crew steady."

"Okay, okay." Imirah shook free of Zen's grip. "I forget not everybody lives for the thrill of 'complicated' like me."

"Thank you." Zen glared a final warning at her and walked back to Ben. "Please go up and help Delmar. She can babysit Ms. Riley while Special Agent Young does a thorough search."

"Yes, ma'am. I don't mind getting out of here," Ben murmured. He gave a last look at the dead man as he rushed off.

"Captain Travers, we'll communicate with your senior management together. After I explain the situation to my boss at OSI. I'm sure they were made aware of the special nature of this trip. Only an autopsy can confirm what we suspect," Zen said in a level tone.

"Yes. Yes, of course. We don't know for certain what killed him. Even so, who could predict a crazy woman would lose it and kill her lover?" Captain Travers let out a long breath. He looked a bit more relieved.

"We've got another thirty-six hours until we get to Crius. Right?" Zen tapped his arm to draw his attention from the corpse. She didn't want him getting worked up again.

"Closer to forty-eight." The captain's frown returned.

"Plenty of time for more..." Imirah's voice trailed off at a sharp look from Zen. She cleared her throat. "We've got the one suspect contained. Special Agent Young will no doubt find the weapon soon. So, we have time to gather more evidence. Maybe wrap up this soap opera so it won't distract us from the real mission."

"Considering the circumstances, we've got things under control. As much as possible, obviously. Delmar and Ben have made sure the other passengers aren't alarmed. I'll get back to the controls, check our data. Our EmDrive has been updated. We could reach Crius faster than I estimate." Captain Travers removed the gloves and dropped them in a bio-disposal bin.

Zen glanced at her smartwatch. "We'll be at the next sat-com in another two hours. We'll probably have even more information to relay by then."

"I'll re-emphasize to Del and Ben to make the flight seem routine. Everything on schedule." Captain Travers squared his shoulders like a man back in charge.

"Excellent," Imirah called out with a smile. She watched the captain leave and then snorted. "Everything routine except for a dead man and a killer side-chick."

"You had to let out another zinger, didn't you?" Zen clipped and shook her head as she went back to examine Bocci's body again.

"Hey, I waited until they were all gone this time. Give me points for restraint." Imirah followed her.

"Humph," was Zen's only response. "Why would Theodora Riley have a stun gun on a diplomatic mission? Sounds like attacking Bocci was planned."

"Sonic stun guns have made their way onto the black market. We don't know for sure Riley killed him." Imirah walked slowly around the bed with Bocci's corpse, looking at him from all angles.

Zen studied Imirah. "A second suspect? I get the feeling there's something you're not telling me."

"Now, really. Would I keep secrets?" Imirah picked up one of Bocci's stiffened arms and put it back down.

"You damn well better not be, Imirah. I'm sick of you and Ewan playing James and Jane Bond games," Zen snapped.

Imirah looked up at her with a frown. "Who?"

"James Bond. A twentieth-century fictional spy. They're making movies about him except now he's going to other planets and..." Zen sighed at the befuddled look still on Imirah's pretty face. "Never mind. Just don't screw with me again."

"Wouldn't dream of it. Besides, this assignment has too damn many moving parts for my taste. We need to collaborate. Bocci didn't die a natural death. His heart wasn't enlarged or otherwise damaged." Imirah crossed her arms and continued to gaze at the corpse.

"How do you know?"

Imirah held up her hands. "I have biometric sensors in my fingertips. Sort of a simple body scan. I can give medical aid to humans and hybrids. It also helps with quick postmortems in the field."

"You need those a lot in your job?"

"Not usually. I don't investigate murders. And if anyone is dead after an encounter with me, I don't have to question the cause." Imirah's smile lit up her face in a dangerous way.

Wyvette strode into the clinic. "Whew, this is some start to our case, huh, boss? I got Ms. Riley settled down. Then Ambassador Abramov kicked up, demanding to speak to you. I don't think you can put her off much longer. She's used to getting her way. The captain dodged talking to her, saying he had to keep the ship steady. Something about meteorites. Bull, he just didn't want to get stuck listening to her rant." She took a breath and looked from Zen to Imirah. "What'd I miss?"

"Nothing, just more indications Bocci didn't die of natural causes," Zen replied. "Found the shock device?"

"Nope, and I searched all over. The other passengers grumbled, but cooperated. I just told him I needed to find missing equipment. We'd need to dock this thing to thoroughly search. So many panels where something could be stuck," Wyvette said.

"Yeah. I figured." Zen thought for a few seconds. "Look at the passenger list. See if anyone has experience in space flight, ship engineering or anything. Somebody with knowledge of the best hiding places on a starship."

"And a connection to Crius, the Russians, or anything that jumps out at you," Imirah added.

"Gotcha. Oh, I did find Bocci's rescue inhaler. It was lodged between a seat and the wall. Riley's fingerprints weren't on it, just his. Makes sense if she slapped his hand hard enough to make it fly off." Wyvette made notes on her tablet as she talked.

"She doesn't seem like the type to plot revenge with such detail," Zen said.

"I scanned my file on her. Ivy League education. Parents are professors. No suspect connections or anything shady in her past. One failed engagement. A past affair with a married man," Imirah said.

"Bad judgement but not a killer. Unless she's finally been pushed to the edge. She's gotten her heart broken one too many times." Wyvette looked at Imirah.

"Eh." Imirah wore a skeptical expression.

"Yeah. Unless she's a good actress, Theodora Riley doesn't strike me as the cold, calculating type. I mean, her emotional reaction to Bocci's betrayal and her confession argues against it," Wyvette replied.

"Astute observation." Imirah smiled at her.

"Thanks," Wyvette said with a smile back at her. "I'll keep checking backgrounds. By the way, the ambassador moved fast to retrieve his tablet and mobile phone."

"Good. I'll go up and talk to Abramov. Any other of the VIP passengers I have to pacify?" Zen asked Wyvette.

"Flashing my agency ID impressed them enough. They know having a UN ambassador and her staff onboard means this isn't a typical trip. They expect hush-hush goings-on." Wyvette went back to reading the text on her tablet.

"The captain has remote access to secure the clinic. There are cameras he can activate as well to keep an eye on it." Zen pointed to an unobtrusive circular lens set in the corner of the ceiling.

Wyvette looked up. "I fiddled with the audio, so he can't hear us. He'll just think it's an equipment malfunction. Ben told me it's happened before."

"You continue to impress, Agent Young. What about our reporter friend?" Imirah looked from Wyvette to Zen.

"I managed to keep him away from the UN folks. Instead, he's trying to get interviews with the executives onboard. All big mining and tech conglomerates. Some with questionable ties to governments. I think he's distracted for now," Wyvette said.

Zen blew out a long sigh. "Okay, I can't put it off any longer. I'll talk to the ambassador."

"I'll come along. She knows I'm with UN Security. My presence will assure her we're taking her seriously and not leaving her in the dark," Imirah said.

"I thought you were the UK's MI6, working with Lewis." Zen faced Imirah with her arms crossed.

"We're both with the UN Global Security Service. But we collaborate with MI6 and the CIA, and other acronyms I won't need to mention. It's... complicated. International intelligence has evolved in the past one hundred and sixty years."

"One thing hasn't changed; Russia and China keep challenging anything the UN and US want. Do you think

Russia enables Vlast? They might not care if criminals cause problems for other countries," Zen said.

"At the very least they turn a blind eye. The current Russian government will use any method to further their goals. Not that they need Vlast. They have their own hackers, dark web operators, and more to cause trouble. Let's go tackle the ambassador."

"I'll be in our cabin doing research. First, though, I'll check on Jacques to see if he's still preoccupied. Del is babysitting Ms. Riley. She took an anti-anxiety pill her doctor gave her, so she's napping for now," Wyvette put in. "And I thought this trip would be boring. Except for having Jacques along."

"Thought you'd have some alone time with him in a sleeper cabin, did you?" Imirah wiggled her eyebrows at Wyvette.

"I don't know what you're talking about. See you later, boss." Wyvette scowled at Imirah and strode off.

Imirah chuckled as she watched her. "Touchy subject, I guess."

"You like poking people. It's going to get you in trouble one day," Zen clipped.

"Trouble is my specialty, Special Agent Batiste," Imirah joked.

Zen sighed. "I'll take the lead with Abramov."

"As you command." Imirah swept a hand out, a gesture for Zen to go first.

"You make me actually miss Lewis."

Zen marched ahead of her. Imirah's soft laughter at her back didn't help her mood. Minutes later she'd composed herself to face an agitated Ambassador Abramov. They met in the ambassador's large cabin. At one end, Theodora Riley reclined in a seat, softly snoring. Imirah let out a whistle as she looked around. Although the cabin had been reserved for the UN staff, one section had been divided with a partition. The ambassador had privacy. The other staffers with her, Riley and the now deceased Bocci, had seats at the other end. Abramov had just finished dinner. Del came in to remove the tray with the remains of grilled fish, avocado salad, sparkling water, and a custard for dessert. Zen and Imirah waited for the flight attendant to complete her duties. Del tucked the blanket closer around Riley. Then she pushed the serving station down the aisle to take the dishes away.

"She's less upset now that she's eaten," Del murmured to Zen and Imirah as she passed them on her way out.

"Hope you slipped a sedative in her food to help us out," Imirah whispered.

Del's eyes went wide. "Oh no, I'd never—"

"Joking, dear. Just joking." Imirah patted her arm and walked on.

When they reached the ambassador, Zen gave Imirah a fierce warning glance. Imirah pressed her full lips together to gesture she intended to keep quiet. Zen pushed down her irritation as she faced Ambassador Abramov. The middle-aged woman had pulled her reddish-blond hair into a short ponytail. She wore a tan pullover sweater and matching pants. She tapped the keyboard of a slender laptop on her tray table.

"Ma'am, I—"

The ambassador held up a palm to cut her off and then went back to typing. Minutes ticked by as Zen and Imirah exchanged glances. Zen clenched her teeth to keep from making a very undiplomatic remark. Imirah seemed more amused as time passed. She walked around the cabin as if taking in every detail. Abramov's gaze flickered up to Imirah a few times. Finally, she closed the laptop.

"I'm sorry to make you and your colleague wait. I needed to get notes in my report down while they were fresh. According to Captain Travers we'll be in range of a communication satellite soon."

"Yes, ma'am. In about ninety minutes. He maximized speed for that purpose," Zen replied with a nod. Captain Travers had explained to her and Imirah that he could only increase speed twice for limited periods.

"Which means we'll reach Crius sixteen hours faster than we would have otherwise. I suppose a murder onboard qualifies as an extraordinary event requiring extra speed," Ambassador Abramov said, her tone mild as she gazed up at Zen.

Zen took a seat across from her. "We haven't established that Mr. Bocci was murdered, so please don't repeat—"

"Theodora told me everything. Silly woman thought I'd be shocked to learn about her affair. Of course, I knew. I make it a point to be informed about my staff." Ambassador Abramov looked over one shoulder at the sleeping woman.

"You spy on your own people?" Zen raised both eyebrows at her.

"I've had two delicate missions screwed up because of unwise personal choices by employees. So, the answer is yes.

I keep tabs on people in my employ. Not that she was all that discreet. You'd think everyone would know not to send sexy text messages on their work devices, wouldn't you?" Ambassador Abramov clicked her tongue in disapproval.

"And this mission is definitely *delicate*," Imirah said. She smiled when both women looked up at her in surprise.

"Please have a seat, Special Agent Suri. I'll have neck pain looking that far up." Ambassador Abramov waved at the aisle seat next to her row. "And you're correct. I'm not overstating the situation when I say we're trying to avoid a war. Accusations are flying hot and fast about Crius. But then what the hell did the US expect?"

"Not to mention the nasty complications," Imirah murmured as she sat.

Ambassador Abramov fixed her with a piercing gaze. "What complications are *you* referring to?"

"The death of Mikhail Navalny. It's in your report," Zen broke in before Imirah replied.

"Most likely an accident as described to us." The ambassador transferred her laser gaze to Zen. "He was working on the water filtration system or some such and was killed. An unfortunate industrial malfunction."

"His friends contacted his family on the moon. That's how word got out about Crius. My department investigates all deaths in space. Routine procedure." Zen kept her voice neutral, like a good government employee following the rules.

"The Office of Special Investigations. Space cops." Abramov smiled when Zen winced at the sobriquet. "Crius isn't considered US territory. Or maybe it is and the other countries are just a ruse. Establishing sovereignty means any benefits from Titan would be controlled by the US. Then there's Europa, not to mention Saturn."

"You've been doing your homework," Imirah put in.

"The Saudi government denies they did anything but help fund the space research programs of two nations, Kenya and Rwanda. They would, of course." Ambassador Abramov shrugged.

"Now that the shit has hit the proverbial fan," Imirah retorted. "Leaving the African nations to defend themselves."

"Now Bocci is dead. Another *complication* as you put it, Agent Suri. Does anyone with a brain believe his death is a coincidence?" Abramov looked from her to Zen.

"Ms. Riley admits to knocking Bocci's rescue inhaler from his hand. He has a medical history of asthma attacks. He was hospitalized twice in the past six years. Maybe the stress of their argument and being in space compromised his ability to recover," Zen said, keeping her voice level.

"I checked. His admissions coincide with his wife finding out about two previous affairs," Ambassador Abramov said dryly. "She forgave him both times. Silly woman."

"Which supports what your assistant says, that she thought he was faking," Imirah said.

"Technically not confirmed as murder. Maybe manslaughter, assault at the very least. An autopsy is the only definitive means of knowing the cause of death. Until then, we'll treat it as death due to a medical crisis." Zen glanced at Imirah.

"Agreed. Based on the information we have from Ms. Riley," Imirah said promptly with an impassive expression.

Ambassador Abramov waved a hand when Zen started to speak. "Investigating two deaths is your job. Mine is brokering peace between nations in space. That's all the information I have that might be relevant in that regard."

"Um, thanks, ma'am," Zen said.

"I expect you to be as forthcoming if you know anything that might make my job difficult."

"Naturally, ma'am," Imirah piped up before Zen could reply. She gave the ambassador a crisp nod.

"Hmmm." Ambassador Abramov's eyes narrowed as she studied Imirah's impassive face. Then she looked at Zen. She opened her laptop again when both women stood and walked away.

"I don't think she believed me," Imirah whispered close to Zen's ear.

"Wonder why?" Zen retorted.

They arrived back at Zen's and Wyvette's cabin. The other passengers gave them furtive looks filled with curiosity. Jacques Clairmont stood in the aisle as they walked in. Wyvette sat in her seat frowning at him.

"Can you comment on the medical issue onboard? I'm told the sick passenger is a UN legal employee. What's his status?" Jacques held up his smartwatch to record the response.

Imirah slapped his wrist down, turning off the app in the process. "No comment."

"Hey, watch the equipment. This thing cost serious coins. Now I'm even more curious about Mr. Bocci's condition." Jacques frowned as he checked the smartwatch.

"We can't comment on the record. Besides, how do you know it's a man and not a woman?" Zen played for time before answering.

"He's the only passenger I haven't been able to find in the past six hours or so. Two execs saw him sleeping. Then the flight attendants put up the divider. Poof! He was gone. I'd like to visit him in the ship's clinic. I know there's one below." Jacques looked at all three women in turn. "Okay, look. I'll keep everything off the record. File a low-key report when we get to Crius."

"Ever heard of protected medical information? HIPPA?" Zen leaned against her seat but didn't sit.

"Ever heard of public health saftey taking precedence?" Jacques countered. "If he has some kind of infection—"

"We've ruled that out. Plus, necessary precautions were taken before the flight staff were satisfied contagion wasn't an issue," Zen said in a crisp tone as if she was at a press conference.

"The public has a right to know if the EmDrive has harmful effects on the body. We're traveling at unprecedented speeds. That and the fact that Crius has been kept secret... It doesn't inspire trust in governments. Transparency goes a long way toward combating conspiracy theories and hysteria," Jacques argued.

"An official statement will provide information when we have all of the facts. Since no one else has taken ill, it seems unlikely the EmDrive is a problem," Zen said.

Jacques hissed in frustration. "I guess this is the government version of cooperation with the press?"

Wyvette stood, her nose inches from his. "Jacques, you know damn well we won't compromise privacy or an investigation to give you a statement. If we release information and then have to backtrack, you'll have us looking like we're dumbasses."

Imirah smirked at him. "As usual, Agent Young cuts to point in her own colorful way."

"I'll get back to you on the 'official' statement then," Jacques said. He gave Wyvette a last long look before he strode away.

"That should add spice to your next date," Imirah quipped with a grin at Wyvette.

"I'm completely professional," Wyvette said, her voice rising with each word.

"I know, Agent Young," Imirah replied evenly. Her brown face had a serious expression.

Wyvette blinked at her. "Oh, okay. Good."

Zen looked at them in turn with a sigh. She retrieved her OSI-issued tablet. "Now that we've got that settled, let's go talk to Captain Travers. We need to know how long we'll be in range of the satellite."

Ben bustled around the service cabin. He seemed less anxious as he entered the security code to open the control room doors. "Everything seems to be going smoothly. Del is making those corporate people feel really special."

"You're both doing an excellent job," Imirah replied with a winning smile that made him blush.

Captain Travers greeted them without turning from the screens before him. They didn't disturb him with questions for ten minutes. Instead, Zen took the time to walk around taking in details. Imirah and Wyvette sat in comfortable leather command chairs and engaged in a low conversation. Zen kept an eye on them in case hostilities flared again. The two must have reached détente. Wyvette nodded as Imirah spoke quietly.

Zen walked around to a large screen set in a semi-circular panel. Data on the status of each cabin scrolled by. Temperature, oxygen levels, gravity levels, and other metrics were reported every thirty minutes. Zen sat down and studied the panel for a few moments. She pulled up the virtual keyboard. In seconds, she figured out how to access historical readings. Zen started with the UN cabin. Then she compared the readings to the rest of the ship.

"You found something?" Imirah bent low to peer over Zen's shoulder.

"I looked for a heat signature or some kind of reading for Bocci's cabin about the time we think he died," Zen said, her fingers still gliding over the keypad.

"An ultrasonic stunner wouldn't generate much heat. Maybe a spike in magnetic levels? Not sure the ship would be equipped to detect sonic waves though. We're don't know exactly what was used on Bocci." Imirah sat in the chair next to Zen. She glanced at a screen next to Zen's and started her own search.

"I thought you were an expert on all things lethal." Zen gave Imirah a brief side-eye.

"I do my best to keep up. The bad guys have unlimited imagination when it comes to ways of killing people," Imirah said.

"Here's a note. The AI flagged a peak of... something. I have no idea what this means but red is usually a sign of trouble."

Zen looked over at Captain Travers. He and Wyvette were talking in a relaxed manner. She got his attention and gestured him over. Wyvette followed him as he crossed the space to join Zen and Imirah.

"I'm going to ignore the fact that you shouldn't be touching my controls," Captain Travers said.

"Sorry." Zen didn't stop staring at the screen.

"No, she's not," Imirah said in a stage whisper. Wyvette smothered a chuckle.

"Look, at nineteen hundred hours." Zen scrolled through the screen and pointed at it. "Mean anything to you?"

Captain Travers studied the readings for a few moments. He rubbed his square jaw. "Somebody have a shaver or one of those fancy hair curlers going? Some of those cosmetic tools have gone high tech. We warn passengers not to use them in flight. Though the risk is minimal to be honest. In fact, the S-FAA is close to issuing guidelines that allow them. Our ships have really advanced when it comes to—"

"That's Bocci's cabin within forty-five minutes of Theodora Riley visiting him," Zen broke in to head off a lecture on space flight tech.

"A rescue inhaler wouldn't give show up. Too bad we don't have video," Imirah said.

"No way. Our business passengers would object. Not to mention we have you government folks and the UN on this flight. Discretion is part of our service," Captain Travers said. He leaned closer to read the display. "Yeah, AI recorded sonic waves at two frequencies. I'll have Ben or Del make an announcement reminding folks about prohibited personal devices."

"Humph, that ship has sailed. Pun intended. Anyway, the killer wouldn't care about following your rules." Imirah frowned at the screen. Then she sat forward and brought up a second virtual keypad.

"Those readings are from Bocci's cabin about the time we think he was killed," Zen said.

The captain stared from Zen to the screen as her words sank in. "Damn."

"With a device we still haven't found," Imirah added. "I don't see any additional red notations."

"You don't think someone else is in danger?" Captain Travers raked blunt fingers through his dark, straight hair.

"Abramov is a high-value target. If someone wants to sabotage the UN mission, cause more chaos and paranoia among nations?" Imirah rocked her chair back as she thought. "Assassinating her would make more sense."

"Yeah, and they could have done it before now. Like, why wait days into the flight? Th perp couldn't get the word out to trigger a crisis," Wyvette added.

"Bocci was a minor official compared to Abramov. And his murder seems... I don't know, less political." Zen grimaced at the bank of data as if the answer would appear to her questions.

"More personal, which puts Riley back in the frame?" Wyvette looked at Zen.

"Huh." Zen shook her head.

"Yeah, something about her being the killer doesn't fit to me either. Though I'm sure she was pissed enough cause him harm. Bocci led her on about a big wedding. She blubbered a good hour after we talked to her. She'd take the guy back if he was alive," Wyvette said.

"Strong passions can inspire deadly rage when one is betrayed. I think she would have found a way to poison him, something to cause an agonizing death. Or she would have inflicted more damage on him physically. In a fit of violence fueled by said passion. Stab wounds to the heart, scratches on his body. Something like that," Imirah said in a matter-of-fact voice.

Captain Travers cleared his throat. "We're close to the satellite. I'll just, uh, check our position and let you ladies get back to your—" He glanced at Imirah and away quickly. "Yeah. Let me know if you need me again."

"I seem to have made the captain uneasy." Imirah grinned at his retreating shoulders. Then she faced Wyvette and Zen again.

"Wonder why?" Wyvette shook her head when Imirah let out a throaty laugh.

Zen tapped the screenshot of data. "Back to the case, please."

"So far, the only person onboard who has an obvious motive is Riley." Imirah frowned at the myriad of tech around them. "But we don't have CCTV to show who might have visited him."

"Major stumbling block," Wyvette agreed.

"Yes, but we have witnesses to interview," Zen said.

Imirah turned to Zen. "I thought you wanted to avoid alarming the other passengers."

"No choice. Without video and a significant lead, we have to talk to them. Which means... we'll also be talking to our killer. So, proceed with caution. Don't give away anything." Zen spoke low as she glanced over at the captain.

Wyvette followed her gaze before facing Zen. "The captain is a suspect, too?"

"And the air marshal," Imirah put in.

"Everyone." Zen nodded slowly as Wyvette's eyes went wide and Imirah let out a soft whistle.

Chapter 5

Two hours later Zen and Wyvette linked to the satellite as the space ship came into its range. Captain Travers slowed their speed to allow communication. They would be in range for about three hours. Optimal connection would last for the first ninety minutes at least.

Zen took the opportunity to give Clive and Hadley a live report. Wyvette sat behind her as the video feed connected. She waved to the boss she hadn't met in person. After Zen's summary, Clive shot a series of incisive questions at her. Wyvette took notes as he made observations after Zen answered. After thirty minutes of the intense exchange, Zen called Malone. His reaction was predictable—anger at himself for not going on the trip. Still, Malone calmed down quickly because he was a professional. He didn't waste air time on complaints about what couldn't be changed. Once she ended his call, Wyvette left to give Zen privacy. She sent a recorded message to Astra. Just to let her daughter know she was fine. That call was filled with details about trip itself and what it was like flying through space. By now reports about Crius and the global tensions it was causing would dominate the news cycle. Even the death of their first victim had probably gotten out. Zen didn't want Astra to worry about her. By the time she ended her last call, Zen felt drained. She sank against the seat in her flight pod with a sigh.

"Here you go, boss."

Wyvette returned with a tray. On it were two paper cups of hot coffee. Café au lait for Zen and black coffee for Wyvette. A plate had two large bagels with cream cheese. Round slices of deli meats, cheese, and veggies were on another plate.

Zen lifted the cup with "Z" on it. She sipped and gave an appreciative groan. "Smooth and sweet, just the way I like it. Thanks, Wy."

"I figured you needed sugar and protein after those calls. I know I do and I didn't have to call my kid." Wyvette set down the food on a tray table. "Not that I have a kid. But I can imagine what's going through her head. I've been reading the news stories. Jacques gave me links. Earth and the moon are lit up with talk about Crius."

"Lord. How bad?" Zen gulped more café au lait for comfort and to brace herself.

"Just about everybody is pissed at the US. Again. Our government leaders must put in overtime cooking up ways to make the world mad," Wyvette said with a snort.

"Anything that might give us a lead or information for our case? Correction, our *cases*." Zen grimaced.

"Jacques has been true to his word. He hasn't leaked anything about Bocci," Wyvette said with a nod.

"He doesn't know the guy's dead though." Zen picked up a bagel and bit into it.

"But he's pretty much figured it out, boss. Bocci hasn't returned to his seat. His UN colleagues aren't visiting the clinic or talking about him."

"Yeah. Our luck to get the really sharp reporter. The Global Associated Press must have a dummy they could send into space. A fluff reporter interested in fashion or something," Zen grumbled around chews.

Wyvette grinned at her. "No chance. Hadley sent me additional background on Bocci, along with everyone else. That lady dug deep. Remind me to stay on her good side."

Zen let out a short laugh. "She only uses her powers for good."

"I've got a lot more details about Bocci and his cheating ways. The man jumped on any warm female he could find." Wyvette placed pepperoni between two layers of cheese and munched on them for a few moments.

"Plenty of people who wouldn't mind seeing him dead. But they're all on Earth." Zen licked cream cheese from one thumb and then pointed at Wyvette. "Unless..."

"I checked. No jilted lovers or vengeful husbands onboard. Far as I can tell, Bocci didn't know any of the NGO guys riding with us," Wyvette said.

"Where's Imirah?" Zen asked.

"Pretty much doing what we've been doing. She sent a message to her headquarters and she's reading up on all of the passengers. You know she can scan a digi-page in thirty seconds?" Wyvette said.

Imirah slid open the divider that separated Zen's cabin from the rest of the ship and stepped through. "Twenty-five. And no, I haven't been eavesdropping. Enhanced audio reception with a range of twenty feet. I switched it on to pick up chatter. I can also turn it off. We're trained to follow privacy laws."

"Oh, yeah. Right," Wyvette said.

"Quite true. Besides, the noise pollution would drive me nuts after a while. You wouldn't believe the inane conversations humans seem to adore." Imirah grimaced as if the thought pained her. She sat in Wyvette's seat in the row next to Zen. She stretched out her long, shapely legs.

"So, we can conclude that you haven't heard anything useful." Zen moved over so Wyvette could slide in next to her.

"Not a freakin' thing. Though those execs are looking to cash in on emerging tech developed on Crius. One company actually has six employees already there. His competitors don't know it yet. She's quite smug about how they pulled it off." Imirah eyed slices of cucumber. She grabbed a few and crunched on them.

"Connections to Vlast?" Wyvette asked.

Imirah continued to chew as she shook her head no. "Hayir. Nothing."

Zen wiped her fingers on a napkin. "Naturally it couldn't be that easy. Let's get to it then."

"Hey, let's at least finish lunch, or whatever meal this would be Earth time. It's not like they're going to escape before we talk to 'em," Imirah quipped. She polished off carrot sticks, a handful of nuts, and more. When she noticed Zen and Wyvette staring at her, she shrugged. "Hey, I'm part human. I need fuel like you."

"Okay, but leave some for us. Sheesh." Wyvette swung the tray away from Imirah, who only laughed.

The three women split up the passenger list between them. First, they came up with an explanation for Imirah asking questions. Imirah was supposedly a UN demographer specializing in documenting space communities. Perfect for Zen's purposes. They could say she'd been deputized informally to help interview the passengers.

Zen took the executives. As Imirah pointed out, they wouldn't have missed that Zen took the lead in talking with the ambassador. People at the top expected access to whoever was in charge. Wyvette and Imirah interviewed staff that had accompanied them. An assortment of engineers, CFOs, and tech experts rounded out the list. They slogged through getting statements over the last thirty-six hours of the flight. When Captain Travers announced they were four hours from docking at Crius, a cheer went up. Everyone had cabin fever.

Imirah, back from a nap in her seat, sat across from Zen. Wyvette walked down the aisle with a large cup. She settled in for their meeting. Zen accepted a bottle of sparkling water from Delmar with a distracted "Thank you." Imirah watched the flight attendant leave. She got up a few seconds later, checked both partitions, closing off the cabin, and sat again.

"Making sure we don't have extra ears," Imirah said. She tapped her smartwatch.

"I already activated white noise in case anyone is using a listening device," Wyvette said.

"Note to self; get a partner with brains like Wyvette Anita Young," Imirah quipped.

Zen had her tablet before her on the tray table. Results of her interview were in a modified word processing application. Text to speech recorded interviews. Her notes and comments were entered in the margins.

"Imirah, go first with the UN folks and flight staff. Get them out of the way since we've talked to them the most," Zen said.

"Won't take long because they didn't tell me anything we haven't heard from them."

Imirah gave a meticulous report all the same. Wyvette described her interviews with as much detail. Then Zen went through what she'd learned. For almost two hours they compared statements, looked for conflicts, confirmations, or holes that might be leads. At the end they looked at each other in frustration.

Wyvette blew out air. She stood and rubbed the back of her neck. "Basically, we're saying nobody killed Bocci."

"No obvious opportunity or motive, other than Theodora Riley's. I couldn't find any obvious connections to anyone onboard. Not even a distant relative." Zen stretched her legs out.

"Which means..." Imirah raised both dark eyebrows to her braided hairline.

"We're dealing with a pro. One with a damn good cover," Zen replied.

"But we've gone through everyone's personal details. Down to their favorite color, food, third-grade crush, the works." Wyvette threw up both hands. "I even know one guy has hyperhidrosis, a fact I could live without thinking about."

Imirah blinked at her. "Hyper what?"

Wyvette's nose wrinkled. "Seriously sweaty feet. He wears extra absorbent socks."

"Ah. Well, we didn't find a puddle of sweat next to our victim. Would have been helpful for forensics," Imirah joked.

"No one is ruled out. Were there any passengers added at the last minute? You know, someone had to be replaced or something?" Zen looked at Wyvette for the answer.

"None that I found. Though I didn't specifically ask during the interviews." Wyvette frowned as she grabbed her tablet again.

"When we get to Crius, I'll have Hadley check their companies. Maybe someone at one of the corporations can tell us if they had to substitute an employee. Someone who couldn't make the trip for any reason." Zen typed a message to send automatically when they had wireless comms again.

"Last-minute changes to the approved passenger list would be an obvious red flag. Security would have dug deep into anyone added," Imirah said.

"It's a long shot, I agree. But might as well make sure. I'm guessing our guy, or woman, has been in place for a long time. Keeping a low profile, living a life that doesn't set off alarms," Zen replied. "Someone skilled at blending in and playing a role for however long necessary."

Imirah gazed at Zen with a slight smile. "I agree. This person is intelligent, charming, and probably damn good looking."

"And excellent at carrying out a hit," Zen murmured.

"So, we should look for someone who reminds of us of... me." Imirah pointed to herself with a chuckle. "In that case we'll have one hell of a job. Such a person rarely makes a mistake when they're undercover."

Wyvette snorted. "Every crook I ever grabbed eventually did something that tripped them up."

"You mean in your long years of being a cop, youngster?" Imirah said.

"Being old isn't much of an advantage," Wyvette shot back with a smirk.

"You just called your boss old."

"Hey, I never," Wyvette protested.

"I feel ninety after this damn flight. So much for arriving fresh to Crius, ready to sort through the case and find my sister." Zen stood and stretched, leaning first right and then left.

"Any news when you linked with the satellite?" Imirah asked.

"No, Lexi isn't waving a sign with 'Fugitive' printed on it." Zen's muscles went rigid talking about her sister and what she might be up to on Crius. She continued the range-of-motion exercises to work the kinks out.

"Ahem. There's no reason to believe she's involved in Navalny's death," Wyvette said after a few moments.

Zen stood still. "No reason not to either. Lexi is very intelligent, charming, and damn good looking, to use Imirah's description of a killer."

"Well, we know for sure she didn't kill Bocci. And because she's smart, she wouldn't draw attention to herself. Or do anything that would risk her new life."

"Plus, she was just a college kid when... you know. People change, learn from the past," Wyvette added.

"She's a stranger to me. Matter of fact, I don't think I ever knew Lexi. Not really. I have no idea what she's capable of now." Zen focused on her training as an investigator. She pushed aside emotions, the feeling of loss. Her sister seemed more shadow than real. "I need to find Lexi and check her history since she left Earth. Hadley couldn't do one of her deep dives for obvious reasons."

"She's been living on a place that didn't exist as far as most of the world knew." Imirah shook her head.

"I'm looking for someone who's become an expert at hiding. And had help from someone with the resources to make her disappear completely." Zen's anger at her father flared.

Imirah gazed at Zen for a few seconds. "An interesting challenge for sure."

"People who assume new identities, who fly under the radar via the black market, have ways to make it. And ways to send messages." Zen smiled at Wyvette and Imirah. "And I know someone who jumps into the Dark Net rabbit hole on a regular basis."

"Good evening. We're approaching our destination and will dock in twenty minutes." Captain Travers's deep voice came through speakers set in the cabin walls. His deep voice sounded confident, steady. "It's June Fourth, 2086, thirteen hundred hours Earth time. The atmosphere on Crius is a steady seventy-four degrees. Humidity levels are maintained at forty percent, optimal for human habitation. All systems operating normally. Please remain in your seats, safety restraints fastened, until all lights turn green on the indicator panels."

"Thank God we're here." Wyvette squirmed in her seat as if eager to get off the ship.

"There are no connecting flights, so I can skip that speech. We're at the edge of the known universe. Unless of course there's something else they're keeping from us." Captain Travers chuckled into the speakers. His joke seemed to have fallen flat. Low mumbling came from those onboard instead of laughter. "Have a safe and productive stay on Crius, everyone."

A series of ship movements jarred the passengers. Ben spoke on the intercom system to reassure them it was normal. He explained the need to get in position for a safe docking process. Soon they were gathering their luggage just as they would on an Earth airplane. Captain Travers and both flight attendants lined up at the exit port.

"Good-bye. Thanks for flying with us," Delmar chirped as passengers filed past them.

"Like we had a range of choices," one woman said.

Delmar flinched but maintained her professional smile. "Thank goodness for a smooth flight."

"Define smooth," Ambassador Abramov retorted, her voice low. Then louder, "Thank you for doing your best to make us comfortable."

"Um, yes." Theodora Riley avoided looking everyone in the eye. Head down, she scurried after her boss.

"Hey, should we just let her leave." Wyvette jerked her head at Theodora's rapidly retreating back.

"Where's she going to go?" Imirah stepped up, a colorful backpack slung over one shoulder. She pulled a wheeled compact duffle bag as well.

"Imirah's right. We can put our hands on her easily enough. She doesn't know how to hide here or know anyone who can help," Zen said. The three of them brought up the rear, leaving last by design.

"Right. I'm off to shower, change, and meet up with Lewis. See what's what." Imirah nodded to them and strode down the long ramp.

"Well, boss. The adventure begins." Wyvette gazed down the exit tunnel leading to the terminal.

"Yeah." Zen's heart pounded at the thought of her first encounter with Lexi. She didn't move to follow Imirah and the others. Instead, she turned to Captain Travers. "You and the crew have been very helpful. We appreciate all you did under the circumstances."

"All part of the job." Captain Travers looked more relaxed now that their journey was over.

A tall man wearing a Space Command uniform approached. "Captain Travers? I'm Officer Schwartz, here to get the body."

He stood aside for two more officers who approached with a folded gurney. Zen, Wyvette, and the captain followed them to the clinic cabin to observe. Peter Navarro arrived a few minutes later. He wore a grim expression as he greeted Zen.

"What's that old saying about trouble coming in threes?" Peter muttered.

He nodded to Officer Schwartz, and the officers placed Bocci's corpse on the gurney. A black body bag was attached, so all they had to do was zip it closed. Captain Travers let out a long sigh when the officers pushed their tragic load away. They would unload it from a cargo exit.

"Threes?" Wyvette looked at Peter.

"Two murders and an international crisis," Peter replied.

"Let's look on the bright side. Our suspects can't flee and shots haven't been fired on Earth yet." Zen turned to Peter. "So, where are we?"

"The officers are taking the body to our medical examiner. Don't worry. They're fully vetted. Black Rock Security will escort them, make sure they don't get sidetracked."

"Things that bad you got to double up?" Wyvette asked.

"Let's call it an abundance of caution. I'll explain when we get to my office. I'm set up at Space Command headquarters." Peter jerked a thumb for them to follow him. "Here, let me help. I'm parked outside the terminal."

Peter took the heavier bags Zen and Wyvette carried and easily handled them as they left. They went back up to the exit ramp. Once in the terminal, they went through a routine security check. Their credentials had been sent ahead so the process went quickly. Ten minutes later they walked to a parking area. A line of six utility vehicles, or UTVs, were lined up in spaces. Peter led them to a four-seater with the Space Command seal on both front doors. As he arranged their bags so they all fit, Zen glanced around. The terminal, unlike airports on Earth, was quiet, with sparse foot traffic.

Wyvette was obviously thinking the same. "Not much action around here."

"People don't leave. Crius is—correction, *was*—a big secret. Anyone accepting an assignment signed a contract for a minimum stay of forty-eight months. Ships coming and going too frequently would arouse suspicion." Peter loaded the last of five bags. "I'm guessing you want to stop at your apartments first. Rest, freshen up, eat?"

"Apartments?" Wyvette looked at him in surprise.

"This place has really evolved over the years. There are family neighborhoods in Quadrant Six. You're near Space Command headquarters, Quadrant Two. Mostly for singles and couples with no kids. You have studio units across from each other."

"I'm hungry." Wyvette rubbed her flat abs and looked around as if searching for food.

"I took the liberty of stocking your quarters with refreshments. Water, fresh fruit, crackers, stuff like that," Peter replied as he climbed behind the wheel.

"Drop us off and then we'll meet in three hours." Zen got in the passenger seat beside him.

Wyvette jumped into the rear seat next to the bags. "I might need more than snacks though."

Peter smiled at her. "Okay. I'll show you a little deli I like. The food there is good and not expensive. Check your smart devices. I've sent you station credits."

"Say what now?" Wyvette leaned forward between their seats up front.

"Credits are the monetary system developed on Crius over the years. A kind of crypto currency out here. Residents can earn real Earth currency when they return home. If they ever do."

"That sounds ominous." Zen took in their surroundings.

Peter pressed a button. The electric engine hummed to life. They went through a large exit for vehicles and onto a street of sorts. "As I said, stays here have been necessarily long-term. And space habitation was risky in the early years."

"Not just the early years," Wyvette retorted. She propped her feet on one of her duffel bags, yawned, and leaned back.

"Yes. Current events were not what the builders of Crius had in mind. We can meet in the morning. Looks like you both could use a nap," Peter said when Zen yawned as well.

"Maybe give us a little more time," Zen agreed. Still, she doubted her eyes would close.

She turned out to be wrong. A warm shower, a sandwich, hot herbal tea, and a change of clothes did the trick. Zen stretched out on a sofa in her studio apartment to unwind. Six hours later she woke up to knocking. She slid onto the faux wood floors when she tried to stand.

"Whoa." Zen sat with her back against the sofa. She rubbed her forehead as the dizziness subsided.

Wyvette came in with a worried frown. In case of emergencies, they shared the access codes to their twin apartments. "I came to check on you. Need a doctor?"

Zen looked up at her. She blinked hard to focus. "I'm okay."

"Space lag, like jet lag back home. It's best to hydrate and keep moving. A short nap is fine, but sleep too long and—"

"You wake up feeling drunk and crazy."

Zen gagged, stumbled to the small bathroom, and threw up. She pressed a cold wet washcloth to her face. Then she rinsed her mouth twice before going back to the living area. Wyvette handed her a cup when she sat on the sofa.

"This will settle your stomach. Peppermint tea. I made it while you were... recovering." Wyvette sat on the matching chair. Wearing thick slipper socks, she tucked both feet under her.

"Thanks. I see you've acclimated better than me," Zen muttered. She sipped the tea slowly. The sweet drink went down smooth, leaving a cool sensation on her tongue.

"According to the booklet in my room, older travelers have a tougher time adjusting. You should take it easy." Wyvette eyed her as if ready to be Zen's caretaker.

"I'm only eleven years old than you. Hardly a senior citizen. Though I'm feeling like one right about now."

Zen drained the cup. She sat still for a few minutes. Wyvette wisely decided not to comment again. Instead, she concentrated on reading the screen of her tablet computer. She shot side glances at Zen as she stood up and did stretching exercises. Zen was sure the younger woman was ready to rescue her if she stumbled. Zen began to feel better after five minutes or so.

"I should have come by sooner, sorry. Lost track of time walking around our quadrant. And to think, this is just one section of the place. They have hydro-ponds for seafood and three greenhouses. It's pretty much a city in the sky. They're developing tech to eventually build a colony on Titan. In fact, humanoids and robots will construct buildings. Then they'll set up oxygen and water-generation plants." Wyvette's voice became more animated as she described all she'd learned.

"Did you get any sleep? Conserve some of that energy for two murder investigations." Zen went to the kitchen. A basket contained the supplies Peter had described. She prepared a banana-flavored protein shake.

"I'm good," Wyvette said, not looking up from her tablet.

"Now I really do feel old," Zen mumbled. She hit the button for the small blender on the countertop. Peter had really thought of everything.

"I didn't hear you."

"Nothing. After I get more in my stomach, we'll go find Peter." Zen perched on a stool at the breakfast peninsula. The dizzying queasiness was gone. Her need to get things moving kicked into high gear.

"We can walk from here based on the locater map. I made sure it was loaded on your devices. I sent him a message. It's seven a.m. Earth eastern time."

"Cool. I'm going to get dressed."

Zen finished her shake and Wyvette left to put on her boots. Like other space station inhabitants, they'd been given boots with weights in them. Gravity was not consistent in all parts of Crius. The maintenance techs lowered levels on occasion. Gravity from Titan or Jupiter affected the big space station at times.

Wyvette returned wearing a military green pullover and matching knit pants. Her boots had an abstract camo pattern. She wore sunglasses pushed up on her head. The twenty-five-year-old's outfit was fashionable yet functional.

Zen wore a tan shirt tucked into black leggings and a black jacket with the OSI logo. She pointed to the sunglasses.

"Really think you'll need those?"

"They simulate sunlight on a larger scale than Starflight or on the lunar colony. So, it's possible," Wyvette said. "Plus, they look good on me."

"Right." Zen grinned at her with a headshake.

The Residence Inn complex had twenty apartments on four levels. Their apartments were on the second level. They took the stairs down to exit the small building and set off for Space Command headquarters. Wyvette led the way with confidence using turn-by-turn audio guidance from an app. Fifteen minutes later they were at headquarters, an internal pod with three levels. Headquarters had a mix of Space Command officers and Black Rock security personnel moving around. Peter met them at the long, oval-shaped front desk. Once in his office, he served them drinks. Water for Zen, apple juice for Wyvette.

"So, what do you think of the place?" Peter perched on the edge of the desk.

Zen looked in front of the seventy-inch screen on one wall, turned on to show scenes around Crius. "Is that a livestream?"

"Yes. I can split it between all eight quadrants. But I didn't want to get you any more dizzy than you've already been," Peter said.

Wyvette cleared her throat when Zen squinted at her. "He was concerned about you, too."

"I'm fine. Just tell us what you know so far," Zen clipped. She stumbled a bit on her way to the chair facing his desk.

Peter started to say something but stopped. He picked up his tablet computer swiped the screen. "The preliminary post-mortem on Bocci confirms he had a myocardial infarction."

"Heart attack brought on by a stun device, a powerful one." Zen blew out a sigh. "I was so hoping the guy had a respiratory crisis and died."

"He was in pretty good health. Cholesterol a bit high, but his asthma was mild by all accounts. The local docs are doing the full autopsy this morning. Space Gen has the largest research staff on Crius. Headquartered in Alexandria, Egypt, but they have offices in Ethiopia and Madrid. And Florida," Peter replied.

"The US and African connections," Wyvette put in.

"Sí, de hecho. I'm glad we don't have to deal with the diplomacy mess." Peter looked at the video feed.

"Yeah. What about Navalny's death?" Zen asked.

Peter read from his notes. "Mikhail Navalny. Thirty-three. Born in a little city in northwestern Russia. Family moved to Moscow when he was eleven. Traveled extensively in his late teens and twenties. Mostly to the Middle East and Europe. Trained as a mechanical engineer specializing in power generation plants. Also worked for the Russian space agency. Came to Crius a year ago. He has an arrest history but nothing major."

"So, he could have been a member of Vlast," Wyvette said.

"Not confirmed. My confidential source says criminals are trying to get a foothold here. She didn't mention Vlast by name," Peter replied.

Zen did a similar mental profile of him. Peter Navarro, forty-four. A native of Spain. Considered a top physicist with a stellar future at one time. His addiction to prostitutes and rough sex, including with humanoid "bang bots", made him a murder suspect. Because of his value to the US and European space programs, he went through a specialized mental health program called The Lodestone Project. The treatment consisted of magnetic deep brain stimulation to alleviate violent impulses. Cleared of a series of murders when the real killer was caught. And... he had a history of getting too emotionally involved with female informants.

"She?" Zen studied Peter for his reaction.

Peter looked up at her, his expression unchanged. "She works at one of the agricultural outfits here. Her on-again, off-again boyfriend hangs with a tough crowd. Black Rock cops have answered several domestic calls at their quarters. Officer Turner introduced us."

"I'll talk to her," Zen said.

"The boyfriend keeps a close eye on her movements. Look, if Vlast is operating here then they'll be watching us. I don't want her to end up like Navalny. I promised to keep her safe." Peter shrugged. "Besides, I don't think she knows anything more useful."

Zen nodded after a few seconds, deciding to let it go. For now. "Okay. What about Navalny's death?"

"He got a call to check out equipment at a power unit. It's restricted to authorized personnel. He reported in that all was normal. Then three days later, his friends reported him missing," Peter said.

"Three days?" Wyvette frowned. "That's strange."

"He'd finished his shift schedule. Six days on, three days off. They just assumed he was hanging out with one of his ladies in another quadrant. When he didn't answer texts or turn up for work, then they got worried. They traced his last movements to the industrial quadrant. Two employees found his body. The first examination indicated he'd gone over a ramp. Engineers and other workers climb the equivalent of five stories to examine machinery."

"And his injuries were first thought to be consistent with a fall," Zen said.

Peter nodded. "Yes, until a closer examination showed defensive wounds on both hands and arms. He had bruises to his torso. He suffered several blows before the fall. Finally, the trajectory calculations indicate he was pushed with some force."

"Two murders," Wyvette murmured.

"Wyvette, check in with the doctors doing the autopsy on Bocci. Then do more research into his past. Look for any ties to crime or Russia, including relatives with a shady history."

"Will do." Wyvette stood after draining her glass.

"I've interviewed Navalny's co-workers and known associates. Let's go over them, see if you spot something I might have missed. Also, I have the forensic reports of the scene and his living quarters." Peter tapped commands on the screen of his tablet. "Just sent those to you. You too, Agent Young."

Zen stood. "I'd like to look around Crius first. Stretch my legs. Get familiar with the layout."

"Um, okay. But Commander Gusev is anxious to meet with us, especially now that we have two Russian murder victims," Peter said.

"Set up a time and send it to my calendar with an alert," Zen replied, her gaze on the images of Crius still on the screen.

"She wants it pretty soon, as in right now." Peter glanced from Zen to Wyvette and back again.

"Do we have anything new to tell her?" Zen looked at him briefly before looking at the screen again.

"No..." Peter admitted.

"Then another few hours won't matter. See you in a few." Zen started for the door.

"I'll show you around." Peter put his tablet down.

"No need. I have the digital map. Contact Commander Gusev and gather any loose ends before we see her. We don't want any surprises." Zen paused before the door and turned. "How much do we know about her?"

"Scoured her background thoroughly given the situation. No red flags," Peter replied.

"There are a lot of Russian players, seems like." Wyvette looked at Zen.

Peter shook his head. "It only seems that way. There are people from all over the globe here, including a lot of Americans."

"A gang with strong Russian ties has wormed into Crius, and it's a coincidence the commander is also Russian? Smells like a plan to me," Wyvette said.

Zen looked at her smartwatch when a ringtone announced a text. "A message from Ambassador Abramov. She's already met with the commander."

"Getting their stories straight maybe," Wyvette murmured.

"She wants an update before a full meeting with the Crius Executive Council." Zen tapped a reply and then cleared the screen.

"Let me be your guide. You'll get through faster—" Peter started for the door but Zen stopped him.

"I won't take long. Just a quick look." Zen waved him off.

He exchanged a look with Wyvette. "Okay. Can we talk first?"

"On my way to the medical and research sector in Quadrant Three. Check in later." Wyvette made a hasty exit with one last glance at the two senior agents.

When the electronic door clicked shut, Zen faced Peter with her arms crossed. "Well?"

"We need to stay on task. Focus on the murder investigations that could impact diplomatic relations on Earth." Peter let out a breath as if he'd been holding in the speech.

"By *we* you mean *me*. I just spent almost fifteen days on a ship with a testy UN Ambassador. I know the stakes, Navarro," Zen shot back.

Peter flinched as if her words struck like darts. "I wasn't implying you didn't. It's only... I know the danger of getting sidetrack by emotional conflicts."

"It's a tour, Navarro. Not a search for my sister. I'm pretty sure she's not just hanging out in a food court somewhere.

I need to get a firsthand feel for my surroundings." Zen pushed down the prick of guilt in her belly. She'd been staring at faces for some spark of recognition.

He studied her for a few moments and retrieved his tablet again. "I've narrowed it down to five women the right age and professional credentials that would match."

Zen took the tablet when he extended it to her. Anxiety made her hand shake. "Thanks."

Five pictures of ID tags were on the screen. Young women stared impassively back at her. None of them struck a chord. Could her sister's transformation be so complete? If so, Zen could walk past her a dozen times and not know. Peter seemed to read her mind.

"A combination of surgery and medical cosmetics can make a drastic change in appearance. Voice training goes along with it. Alexis might not be hiding from you intentionally. Deep magnetic brain stimulation can cause memory loss. In its early days, Lodestone treatments still had that side effect." Peter's voice trailed into silence. He watched Zen as the minutes ticked by and she swiped through screens with more details about the women.

"Have you recovered?" Zen looked at him.

"I'm... It's better. I went through Lodestone after Alexis would have done. They've made refinements to the protocol since then," Peter said.

Advances in the field of criminal rehabilitation started in the typical American way. High-status people who had committed serious violent acts were call "sick," in need of treatment. The approach of long-term imprisonment was suddenly unthinkable. They were deemed too valuable to lose, especially brilliant scientists. Peter, a physics and math genius, was one of them. Add the offspring of millionaires and billionaires with the unfortunate habit of killing people, and a revolutionary approach was funded.

The reality of Lexi being alive dropped on her like a rock. Zen let out a slow breath to settle her nerves. Looking into faces that could conceal her sister had shaken her. She sat down hard in a chair and gave him the tablet. "Send those to me. Thanks."

"Sure. Zen, maybe concentrating on the cases for a few days is a good thing. Meeting Alexis will be a jarring experience to say the least." Peter sat across from her.

"Especially if she doesn't even remember who she is or... what she did." Zen rubbed the tightness taking hold in her forehead.

"I understand those who had new identities created really went through intense sessions. Some didn't respond well." Peter leaned forward. "Crius is a closed world cut off from Earth. From my short observation since here, those outside the command structure have formed unique social structures."

"So, you're saying I need to get a sense of this society. Not just the physical layout."

Peter nodded. "Your field of academic study. As a young grad student, you would have been thrilled to observe this firsthand, yes? Because of you, a new name was coined."

"Astro-sociology." Zen smiled at the memory of the days when she worked on her PhD thesis. At the time the first colony had few inhabitants. Zen had become fascinated with how those communities would develop.

"We don't know what your sister went through in her journey here. Or what she's experienced since," Peter said in a gentle tone.

Zen's expression turned serious again. Lexi had presumably built a career and personal relationships. Zen could disrupt or devastate her new life by bringing the old one to Crius. Had she given enough thought to what might be best for Lexi? Zen cringed at the obvious answer. Her anger had been focused on their parents. The desire for answers, to deal with her own emotional earthquake, had dominated Zen's decisions. But Lexi was still a human being. She deserved some measure of sensitivity. Maybe even compassion.

"You've done a lot of thinking about this," Zen said as she gazed at him.

"The parallels between your sister's life and mine are striking. And remember, deep magnetic brain stimulation changes us."

Zen stood. "So, no rush to judgement or hunting her down first thing. Message received. How about that tour?"

Peter stood and nodded. "First, let me check for a message. Ah, I've heard back from her AI executive assistant. Our meeting with Commander Gusev is delayed. Seems she's dealing with other urgent matters. You've caught a break from her singular brand of grilling for a few hours."

"I hope it's nothing that makes our investigations more complicated," Zen retorted.

Peter looked at the message again. "She doesn't say, so maybe that's good news?"

Before Zen could reply, a ringtone came from the big LED-screen TV on the wall. The display flashed text that it was a classified call. Peter retrieved his tablet from the desk, opened an app, and swiped the touch screen. The electronic door lock clicked, an AI voice announcing the room secure.

"Offices are soundproof. Scramblers prevent hacking into the call," Peter explained.

"I gotta get one of those," Zen said, pointing to the app. "It would keep Astra out of my closets and my business."

They shared a laugh but it evaporated seconds later. Clive Anderson and James Batiste, her father, appeared on screen. The two men wore matching grim expressions. Clive whispered something aside to Hadley. James tapped a fist against one thigh with barely concealed impatience. The audio was on mute on their end. Her father made some comment. Clive shot a glance at him that Zen tried to decode. Something was said between them. Then the sound was unmuted.

"Hello, you two. Anything significant on where we are with both murder investigations," Clive said. Only he was onscreen.

Zen gave a concise summary on the Bocci case. Then Peter took over with known details about the Navalny murder. Clive nodded a few times but didn't interrupt. Zen tried to read his expression. Her boss seemed distracted. Peter shot side glances at Zen as he talked.

"So far we haven't connected the two, but my instincts say it's no coincidence." Peter turned to Zen.

"Peter is right. There's got to be some kind of connection. But as far as we can tell, they never met.

Ambassador Abramov and Ms. Riley assured us they didn't know Mikhail Navalny," Zen said.

The camera zoomed out and Hadley appeared. "From what I've learned, that's correct. I couldn't find where they were ever in the same locations. And I tracked Navalny's and Bocci's travels. Not that Navalny couldn't have gone underground at some point."

"Aside from being a cheating husband Bocci seems straight. No criminal ties. He even worked as an Italian prosecutor at one point." Zen frowned. "Did he ever go after any Russian gang members? I don't know if they've ever operated in Italy or the south of France. Bocci lived and worked in both countries."

Hadley consulted her tablet for a few moments. "Italian gangs and French criminals. I'll get back in touch with our Interpol liaison."

"Sounds good," Zen replied.

"There's more news. I'm not entirely sure how this will impact your investigations but..." Clive's dark eyebrows pulled together. "A coalition of the European Space Agency has negotiated an agreement with the African Union. They're threatening to take over Crius. The US has strongly objected. Russia and China have accused all three of conspiring."

James appeared onscreen. "They accuse the US of plotting to gain control of space tech and products worth trillions. The ESA doesn't have the resources to operate Crius independently. Tensions among the member countries of the African Union have been ramping up. So, the US has actually taken the lead on Crius in terms of operations."

"Commander Gusev is fifth-generation American. Her family emigrated in the early twentieth century because of the Russian Revolution in 1917. They were members of the aristocracy," Hadley put in, now offscreen.

"So, it's unlikely she has ties to Vlast," Peter said.

Clive spoke up before Hadley could reply. "But not impossible. Keep an open mind."

"Yeah. Money talks and Vlast is willing to spread it around for long-term gain," Zen said.

"The larger point being we have a growing international crisis on our hands. You need to assure multiple players no government agents killed these two men," James broke in.

"Wait, what?" Zen blinked at the screen and looked at Peter.

Her father's frown deepened. "Russia and China assert that the US or the UK sent someone to commit murders as an excuse to accelerate taking over Crius. Over the past twenty years, Russia and China have sent scientists there. With the cooperation of certain African nations. Hence the growing tensions within the AU."

"Which gave an opening for Vlast to move in," Peter said.

Clive scowled and crossed his arms. "That's a working theory."

"The African Union and Saudis are adamant that the Russians and China haven't taken over. Like the first international space stations, any developments will benefit everyone," James continued.

"The US didn't know about the Russian and Chinese scientists, did they?" Zen studied her father's expression. The way his jaw tightened and his left eye squinted answered her question. He did both when anything had gone very wrong.

"They were issued dual citizenship and passports from several African countries. Most had lived abroad for at least five years," James said.

"How did that slip by? I mean, someone must have noticed the names." Peter flinched at the heated look James shot him.

"We don't profile people based on ethnicity or country of origin, young man," James barked. "Also, only one or two traveled, and it was spaced out over time."

Zen studied her father for a few seconds. "How does it involve you, Daddy?"

"You know I still advise the White House on global space relations." James waved a hand as if brushing aside her question. "What's more important is that we get to the bottom of these murders. Naturally, the White House and the UK prime minister have issued firm denials of any kind of government-sanctioned assassinations."

Zen looked at Clive. "Ewan Lewis and Imirah Suri being here won't help. Two UN intelligence agents with nebulous explanations of why they're here. Hell, Ewan came undercover and he's been compromised. Which is why they sent Imirah."

"I understand the problem has been handled." Clive's face flushed as he spoke. His gaze flickered to James briefly and back to Zen.

Peter spoke before Zen could ask. "What does that mean?"

"He was able to explain his background with the UN," Clive said.

"His story is that he worked on humanitarian construction projects. The Russians are paranoid. They think everyone is a spy," Hadley put in. "Ms. Suri's identity hasn't been concealed as I understand it. The UN and the US wanted to send a message with her presence."

"That they're not messing around." Zen squinted at Clive. There was much more to the story, and she was eager to hear it. "Thanks for briefing us on the political implications, Daddy."

James scrutinized Zen for a few moments, his brows furrowed. "How has your trip been so far?"

"Uneventful."

"Hmm. We'll talk later. Message me and I'll be available." James looked at Clive. "Keep me informed."

"Yes."

Clive's terse reply made her father's face go blank. But his dark brown eyes narrowed, his nostrils flared. Another familiar expression Zen recognized. He was pissed but in no position to strike back. Hadley appeared suddenly.

"We'll take a break and be back in five minutes," she said. A city scene screen saver popped on with soft jazz music.

Peter stared at the screen in disbelief. "They just put us on hold. Across millions of miles, no less."

"I don't think they wanted us to hear Clive and my father going at it," Zen said mildly. "Clive doesn't like people sticking their noses in OSI cases. I can hear him now. He's telling Daddy that whatever diplomatic shit that's hit the fan is *their* problem."

"You mean the US and UK governments." Peter turned to her. "You really think they're butting heads?"

"Oh yeah. They both looked like they'd been sucking lemons." Zen grimaced as she sorted through what she'd heard and saw, puzzle pieces with answers.

"Two murders, a political nightmare, and global hostilities that could flare into armed conflict. More than enough to create a stressful atmosphere." Peter paused to rub his jaw. "But now that you mention it, they didn't seem too happy with each other."

"Understatement," Zen retorted.

"Mr. Batiste seems to be taking this crisis personally."

"I'm willing to bet he had a role in the Crius project. Which means it's a problem for him. He's being asked tough questions." Zen's eyes narrowed. She would add a string of her own when they talked.

"I know your father is influential, but he can't have been involved in everything, Zen." Peter shrugged.

"He had the connections to get my sister here. Think about it." Zen stopped when the screen winked on to Clive's office again.

Their boss stood before them with a scowl that would shake most to the core. "Focus on getting answers—who and why. Don't think about the political implications. I'll expect your updates to land in my encrypted inbox every four hours."

"Yes, sir," Zen and Peter said at the same time, and video transmission ended.

"You understand what he meant about ignoring political implications? One or more governments may have had a hand in at least one of our murders."

"He has suspicions but not enough information to point us in the right direction. He's looking for something substantial before he shares it."

"Or he doesn't want us to be biased by what he only suspects. We must have a blank slate, follow the evidence no matter the consequences."

Zen looked at Peter. "Shit. We could help spark a war on earth."

For the next two hours Peter led Zen around a walking tour of Crius. Despite their earlier discussion, Zen couldn't help staring at every female resident she passed. They managed to cover almost four quadrants. They went to the sectors with the facility maintenance department, the medical unit, the power generation unit, and finally the research complex. The last was too vast for them to cover in one tour. Not without sacrificing time on the investigation. Zen felt the weight of Clive's command that he be updated often. They finally emerged back on a main transport pathway. A variety of UTVs zipped by while pedestrians took parallel sidewalks.

"Wyvette sent direction to the medical forensic lab. Let's go," Zen said.

"I know the way. Let's grab a cab." Peter waved to a golf cart with yellow lines painted on the sides.

"You're kidding." Zen looked around in wonder as the taxi slowed to a top

"Hey, we need to get around here, too. This place is big." Peter tapped on a keypad attached to the back of the driver's seat. "My code to transfer credits. They have flat rates."

"Yeah, and we're lobbying to get that changed. You know how many fares I lose taking someone two quadrants away?" the driver complained in a heavy Scottish accent.

Zen shook her head. Crius was a microcosm of home, complete with grumpy human taxi drivers. "Well, the good news is we're not going that far."

The driver glanced into his rearview mirror to make sure they were settled. Then he pulled into the sparse traffic. He wore a mollified half-smile when they reached their destination ten minutes later.

Zen looked at the sign over the wide entrance. "The Goddard Corporation owns this?"

Peter followed her gaze up. "You're thinking of a previous case. Yes, but they have never been accused of any wrongdoing."

"Yet," Zen said as she followed him down two corridors to a third that branched off.

A security officer rose from behind the desk ten feet in. "Identification, please."

Zen and Peter presented their smartwatches in turn. He scanned the QR codes on their ID apps. They had authorization to access every quadrant and sectors within them. The guard then waved them on with directions to the forensic examination pod.

Peter spoke low even though there was no one else in the hallway. "I arrived here only three days before you. Mikhail Navalny was still alive but I never met him. No reason to. I was sent to gather intel on Vlast, to report on any criminal activity present. And possible corruption."

"And?"

"Nothing solid, but something is not right. Commander Gusev and her staff are holding back. I'm not sure what it is. There's the usual black market activity. Some designer drug use. Quadrant Eight has a sex district with a full menu of 'personal entertainment'. There are fights, petty theft—the typical small crimes humans seem to take with them everywhere."

"Yeah. I wrote a dissertation on it." Zen followed him around a corner.

Wyvette stood a few yards away. She waved to them. "Hey, guys. You're right on time. Dr. Simeon is finishing up his report on Bocci."

"Good. Any surprises?" Zen smiled at her youthful enthusiasm.

"He wouldn't say until everything was complete. And he wanted to speak to the 'senior investigative agent in charge.'" Wyvette executed her bad imitation of a snooty accent.

"Glad you've made a friend," Zen quipped.

"We're pals now, me and old Phil." Wyvette led them into a wide room.

Three metal tables lined up before them. An array of instruments and equipment filled other tables. Large movable lamps were positioned overhead in addition to lights embedded in the ceiling. A tall man with reddish-blond hair stood at a mobile computer desk on wheels. His long fingers typed on a silicon keypad. Two other staff members worked with brisk movements on other tasks. They aimed curious glances at the newcomers. One, a young brunette, dropped a tool she held. She flinched at the sound of it hitting the floor.

"We have a job to do despite interruptions. Stay focused, Melania," Dr. Simeon barked without looking away from the computer monitor or keypad.

"Yes, of course, doctor. I'll be more careful," the young woman replied instantly. Her tone was deferential. The brief curl of her lip held more contempt than respect.

"He's a real joy to work for, right?" Wyvette whispered to Zen.

"I assume you're the famous Dr. Zenobia Batiste. I'll be with you in a moment." Dr. Simeon didn't stop typing.

"Of course, Dr. Simeon," Zen replied in an even tone. She smothered a laugh when Wyvette rolled her eyes.

Dr. Simeon turned to them after another two or three minutes. His expression eased a bit when he saw Peter. "Ah, Agent Navarro. How are you?"

"Fine, thanks. And you are correct, this is my senior colleague Dr. Batiste. And of course, you have met Agent Young." Peter gave him a respectful nod.

"Yes. Agent Young has hovered around my exam room for hours now." Dr. Simeon squinted at Wyvette. His jaw flinched when she grinned at him.

Zen strode over to him, gazed at the computer, and then faced him. "We have two murders to investigate, Dr. Simeon.

Agent Young is doing her job. I'm afraid we'll be *hovering* here quite often. You have finished reports on both victims."

"Humph." Dr. Simeon scrutinized Zen for a few seconds. His icy blue eyes gave her a head-to-toe gaze. "Which one do you want first?"

"Mikhail Navalny... Please," Zen replied.

Dr. Simeon grunted a second time. "Follow me. My notes are accessible on the server. We can talk in my office."

"Great," Zen replied with a mild expression.

Dr. Simeon shot a glance at her as if looking for signs of sarcasm. Then he turned to his assistants. "I expect the results of those indole and oxidase tests to be written up before you leave. And make them free of typos this time."

"Sir." The young man bobbed his head as if eager to please while Melania made a sour face.

They followed him through a doorway down a short hall lined with three offices. Dr. Simeon's office was the third one. He tapped in the access code and the door clicked open inward. Inside, a desk sat in one corner. Most of the room was decorated with awards, certificates, and licenses. The doctor sat at the desk. He stared at the camera of the monitor. The retina scan opened to his apps. The wallpaper, a photo of him with a group of scientists, vanished. Colorful icons appeared. He used the touchscreen to find what he wanted.

"Mikhail Navalny. Not in the best of shape considering he was approved for space travel. Judging by the state of his liver, he drank too much. He was on his way to serious health issues. But no," Dr. Simeon added before they could ask. "Toxicology results show he wasn't intoxicated. He had small amounts of THC in his system, probably had smoked the night or even two nights before. His associates say he'd last partied on his day off the weekend before."

"Episodic binges," Peter added.

"When he drank, he was all in, according to them. His liver confirms it. Early tissue damage. One of his friends says he had a tough childhood. But he was not drunk when he went off that platform. As I told Agent Navarro, he had defensive bruises on the knuckles of his right hand. At some point he was grabbed around his wrists. See here." Dr. Simeon flipped the monitor around to show photos of Navalny naked on a table. Peter and Zen leaned closer to examine it. Wyvette gazed sideways at the wall.

"He seems strong enough to fight off an attacker." Zen pointed to his arms and legs. "Doesn't look weak at all."

"Mr. Navalny was physically fit enough to perform his duties. Still young enough to pass cursory review. But the years of partying would have eventually taken a toll. He must have gotten into a new designer drink. It's underground. Some enterprising space brewer created The Black Hole. Causes rapid and prolonged intoxication, a giddy all-powerful sensation I'm told," Dr. Simeon said with a shrug.

"Then why do they call it The Black Hole?" Wyvette asked.

"Because the hangover is intense, and many suffer depression for at least a few hours. Which is why it was declared illegal," Dr. Simeon replied.

Peter turned to Zen. "One of the black market products I told you about earlier."

"So far, Crius command and security aren't too concerned. No deaths or major problems associated with it. And as I said, Black Hole was not a factor in Navalny's death. The trajectory measurements confirm he was shoved with force. He did not fall." Dr. Simeon gazed at photos of his deceased patient.

"And Roman Bocci?" Zen looked at Dr. Simeon.

"Your star ship captain's amateur postmortem is correct. Mr. Bocci suffered a powerful application of a sonic stun gun. Someone got close enough to press it directly on his chest." Dr. Simeon looked from Zen to Peter as he spoke.

"He had his shirt on when the flight attendant found him slumped over," Wyvette said as she stepped closer. She winced at the picture of Bocci's corpse but didn't look away.

"Someone was able to get close to him but not attract attention. Does that sound likely?" Peter said to Zen.

"He shared a cabin with the other UN staff but they weren't on top of each other. If they were sleeping or in another section, maybe." Zen frowned as she worked through the logistics of killing someone on the ship.

Wyvette looked at Zen. "Someone he'd let take off his shirt."

"Theodora Riley," Zen murmured.

"His lover, another UN staffer," Peter explained aside to the doctor.

"No sign of recent sexual activity. Your second victim had a drug in his system. Nartrex is a sedative used by veterinarians on small animals. Not used on humans for the most part. Mainly because it's known to cause paralysis that persists for hours, sometimes days."

"Damn," Wyvette whispered.

Dr. Simeon cleared his throat loudly. "Now if that's all, I'd like to get some lunch. Then get back to my regular duties. Thankfully, I haven't been called on to do autopsies before. Let's hope this isn't a trend." He grimaced at them as if they'd brought him troubles.

"Thank you, Dr. Simeon. We'll let you know if we need additional information. Though it's not likely since your work has been so thorough," Peter added quickly.

"Indeed." Dr. Simeon swept out a hand to the door, a less-than-subtle invitation for them to leave.

"Good-bye, and thanks for the meticulous postmortems. You've also given us information that will help when we interview witnesses." Zen nodded at the doctor and extended a hand.

Dr. Simeon's chilled exterior melted somewhat as he shook Zen's hand. "Glad I could help. Our little world has been rocked by wild rumors. A quick resolution will be reassuring."

Moments later they were in the hallway headed for the exit. The security guard waved at them as they left. Pedestrian traffic had picked up once they were outside the medical building. The wide corridor resembled a busy small-town street.

"Speaking of lunch." Wyvette looked around them.

"A few minutes ago, you were grossed out by pictures of dead bodies. Now you're looking for snacks?" Zen quipped. She checked her smartwatch for message alerts as they strolled along.

"I need a full meal, preferably home-cooked style. I'm tired of prefab, freeze-dried crap." Wyvette wrinkled her nose in distaste.

"I didn't think the food was bad. You scarfed down what they served on the ship." Zen swiped past two messages from her father. No doubt he wanted an update on her search for Lexi. He could wait since she didn't have one.

"I hear there are two three-star cafés on Crius. You can't compare freshly cooked meals to what we had," Wyvette asserted.

"I've become friendly with the chef at a third place, a deli that serves salads, soups, and the best Chicago-style pizza on Crius. Let's go there," Peter said.

"Great. I don't want anything heavy. Soup and salad are perfect." Zen tapped a short message to Hadley. The she locked the smartwatch screen. "I'm feeling a bit hungry myself."

With Peter leading the way, they opted for the twenty-minute walk to the deli. By the time they arrived it was two o'clock in the afternoon Earth time. Zen had checked the calendar for the day. It was Tuesday.

Peter glanced at her. "I have a digital clock and calendar in my apartment; the same projected on the wall of my office. It's easy to get turned around in space, but especially on a space station. An artificial world with no day or night can really mess with the body. We're used to Earth cycles, yes?"

Zen nodded. "And going home means I have to reset my system each time. Not such a problem for Wyvette."

"Yes, but I worry that maybe she should visit Earth more often. She seems to have almost cut ties there," Peter said low, his gaze on Wyvette, who walked a few paces behind. She seemed intent on taking in every detail of their surroundings.

"I asked her about that. She went to her father's funeral last year. The grandmother she was closest to died the year before. Her relationship with her mother is... distant." Zen glanced back at Wyvette. "She's built a support circle on the colony and Star Flight. I think she's fine."

"You're the expert so I'll take your word for it," Peter said with a smile.

"Hey guys, I saw a clothing store back there with nice jumpsuits. The latest fabrics for space. I might get one," Wyvette said.

They chattered on about the amenities of Crius, comparing it to Star Flight. Zen and Wyvette had only visited Star Flight. Peter described Oculus, the fourth international space station. He'd visited during a short vacation to tour their research facilities. Over sandwiches and salads, they left behind the puzzle of two murders for a time.

"How are your kids?" Wyvette wiped her mouth with a napkin. She bit into her plant-based pastrami on rye.

"I... I haven't talked to them in a while. But they're doing great." Peter looked at the sandwich in his hand and then put it back on the plate.

Zen cleared her throat and tried to get Wyvette's attention. Fortunately, Wyvette became distracted by her food. She didn't notice the way color drained from Peter's face. The mention of his two daughters, ten and fourteen, seemed to have taken his appetite. Zen knew the reason. His oldest daughter had found news reports about Peter's arrest. She'd read the salacious descriptions of his frequent encounters with sex workers. His ex-wife suggested he give the girls "space." No wonder he went deeper into space on his vacation rather than back to Earth.

"Astra is loving the expat student life," Zen said to switch the subject. "My father managed to get my niece a fellowship, so they're together. Brianne is like a big sister."

"And keeping an eye on her so she doesn't get in trouble," Wyvette said around munching a potato chip.

"Yes. Daddy knew I would worry, so... he made it happen. Brianne jumped on the idea. She can study with leading UK specialists in oceanography. She's very committed to conservation."

"Sounds wonderful, talking about fish and seaweed all day." Wyvette shrugged. "I hope she doesn't stop Astra from having fun, too."

"Astra is barely seventeen, too young to be partying so far from home. She's there to learn; add value to her academic and future career bio. Not party," Zen replied. "Ugh. I sound like my mother."

"Mysterious spy approaching," Wyvette said.

Imirah strolled up. She waved to the waitress behind the counter. The young woman nodded and grabbed a menu. Dressed in deep purple that was almost black, Imirah wore knit leggings tucked into ankle boots. Her top was a body-hugging sweater. A scarf was looped around her neck.

A black faux suede cropped jacket completed the look. Heads turned to stare at the statuesque woman.

"I'll have a cup of vegetable soup," Imirah said and handed the menu back to the waitress.

"And the usual glass of sorrel?" the waitress said.

"Yes, thanks." Imirah smiled at her.

Wyvette waited until the waitress was gone and then squinted at her. "You following us?"

"Of course. I find you folks endlessly fascinating," Imirah tossed back. She crossed her shapely legs after sitting down. "It's not like I don't have own interests to pursue.

"Which would be?" Peter gazed at her.

"Well, I was supposed to back up Lewis, but it seems he doesn't need me. So, I'll take care of other things." Imirah thanked the waitress for the glass of sorrel and took a sip.

"Other things like..." Zen gestured at her to go on.

Imirah glanced around. The crowd in the deli had thinned as workers returned to their jobs. Still, she lowered her voice as she leaned forward. "Directors Anderson and Batiste have told you the international political situation on Earth is dicey."

"How do you know... Why does she hack into every damn thing?" Wyvette shook her head as she looked to Zen and Peter for answers.

"I'll teach you a few tricks one day, youngster." Imirah grinned when Wyvette gave her a heated scowl. Then she grew serious again. "I'm to look for signs that a trained assassin or government agent is at work. So far, the methods to kill either victim could be their mark. And speaking of

Lewis, let's go. We're meeting him at the scene of Navalny's death."

"Wait, what?" Zen looked up at Imirah, who now stood.

"What about your soup?" Wyvette shoved the last bite of the sandwich in her mouth.

The waitress appeared as if on cue. She handed Imirah a covered to-go paper cup. "Here you are, ma'am."

"I know the way." Imirah beamed at them as she gestured for them to follow.

"These super-secret agents get on my nerves," Wyvette whispered aside to Zen.

"Yeah, but they can be useful," Zen replied. Started to say more when her smartwatch vibrated. She opened the text. A tiny unicorn danced to a Lexi's favorite childhood tune. A location, directions to it, and a time appeared below it.

Chapter 6

Minutes later they walked down a wide corridor. Vehicle and foot traffic reminded Zen of New York City on a busy weekday. They passed a few store fronts for the first few city blocks. The area became more like an industrial sector the longer they walked. Fewer people were around. Most were dressed in corporate uniforms. Security officers appeared from time to time. Imirah had insisted that they go on foot. Using credits to take a cab would be traceable. Commander Gusev messaged to reschedule their meeting, so they had more time.

"They already got eyes on us. We could have saved time and steps," Wyvette said but followed Imirah anyway.

"The average crook doesn't have access to advanced tech, not even here." Imirah kept up a conversational tone as they walked.

"We don't have a tail," Zen replied.

"My trusty app detects and blocks tracking. You're correct. Common criminals have a difficult time getting their hands on advanced tech. Believe it or not, security from Black Rock and Space Command is pretty good. Even out in the wild space frontier."

Imirah went on describing what she'd learned since arriving on Crius. Wyvette peppered her with questions. Some Imirah answered. Most she sidestepped with vague replies, to Wyvette's annoyance. Still, the young agent pressed Imirah for details. Their banter wasn't hostile but a good-natured rivalry. A game matching wits.

"Was that message another disturbing update from Clive?" Peter spoke to low and close to Zen's ear as they trailed after Imirah and Wyvette.

"Hadley sent over more information on Bocci and Navalny. We can go over it later," Zen replied without returning his gaze. She picked up her pace to get closer to Imirah and Wyvette. "Hey, are we almost there?"

Imirah pointed to a digital sign overhead with "Quadrant 8" on it and a sign pointing the way. The entrance spanned seventy-five feet at least. Enough space for large vehicles to pass through. A truck rumbled past them, boxes and equipment piled in back. They continued on the pedestrian walkway for another quarter of a mile. They arrived at a door. Imirah typed a code on a keypad next to it. Then she pressed her left thumb on another pad. Finally, she stepped close for a retina scan.

"Damn, three-factor authentication," Wyvette murmured.

"Like I said, security is tight. Changes have been made since Navalny's death." Imirah led the way once the door clicked and slid open. It closed behind them automatically when all four had cleared the threshold.

"I hope Lewis has something useful for us," Peter said.

"And he gets to the point," Zen muttered.

Peter looked at her. "You have someplace you need to be soon?"

"Clive did say we need to move fast," Zen replied. "Wow, this place is…"

"Bigger than anything I've seen in space. Like the huge lunar cavern under Marius Hills." Wyvette let out a whistle as she turned in a circle while gazing up.

Multilevel platforms were set in the circular walls. The lowest was accessible by a flight of stairs. To their right was a wide service elevator. Another one was at the other end of the huge facility. Lights blinked on three giant panels. A steady hum filled the air. Creaks and bumps rang out every few minutes.

"Welcome!"

Ewan Lewis stood three stories up on a platform. He held a digital clipboard in one hand. His dark tan work clothes and the bright orange hardhat with an LED light in the center made him fit right in. A company logo on his jacket completed the cover. He bounded down the stairs nearest him, jumping to the floor over the last two steps.

"You look quite official. I thought they would have fired," Wyvette said as he strolled over to them.

"Why do you say that?" Ewan tucked the clipboard under his left arm.

"Imirah says you were outed." Wyvette glanced at Imirah and back to him.

"You dare to question my skills?" Ewan lifted one dark blond eyebrow at her.

"It's okay if you're not the superhuman super spy everybody says. We won't tell." Wyvette put a forefinger to her lips and made a shushing sound.

"Oh, but I am. The issue of my identity has been resolved. Sadly, my accuser had an accident. He's unconscious and on his way back to the lunar colony for treatment. Space stations can be dangerous places." Ewan pulled the tablet from the crook of his arm again.

Zen bristled at his casual attitude. "You used violence against a civilian? I don't know who the hell you work for, Ewan, but—"

"To be clear," Ewan said sharply, his expression hard as stone. "The man threatened what has become a Level Red operation. He had contacts in the UK who could ID me. And he tried to kill me first."

"Let's not waste time debating the ethics of taking out a thug who threatened an agent," Imirah said.

"My superhuman reputation is intact," Ewan quipped with a wink at Wyvette.

Zen huffed in agitation, mainly because she knew Imirah was right. Still, Ewan and Imirah had an easy approach to taking out anyone in their way, and it was unnerving to say the least.

"We're not out-of-control killing machines, if that's what you're thinking," Ewan said as if reading her thoughts. He studied Zen as tense seconds ticked by.

Wyvette cleared her throat loudly. She walked between them and made a circle as she looked around. "So, this is where Navalny fell."

Ewan followed. He pointed to their right to markings on the floor. "Just there. From the fifth level."

Imirah joined them. She looked up and then at the markings again. "Somebody wanted to make sure he didn't walk out of here."

"My confidential source says Navalny was dissatisfied with his work recently. She made friends with his co-workers," Peter put in.

"A research analyst for a Chinese conglomerate with investments in three African nations," Lewis said.

"How did you... Never mind. We have to be very careful about mentioning her. She's taking a big risk." Peter squinted at Lewis.

"I always protect sources," Ewan replied. "Obviously, Navalny wasn't alone. Someone was waiting for him. Or followed him."

"Navalny rotated between three girlfriends, but there was no drama. They knew about each other," Peter said.

"Someone wasn't happy with the man." Ewan tapped the screen of his clipboard. He projected video on a portion of one wall. "Here is what was recorded on the day he died."

They watched ten minutes of Navalny reading digital data and walking up the levels. At the 11:15 mark he looked up. Sound from the equipment made it hard to make out what he said. Then he walked up the stairs. At each flight he would stop for a few seconds and point as if arguing with someone.

"Switch to the camera up there," Peter said.

"There is no camera up that high. Only on the first and second levels. Security is about who gets in. An alert will bring officers here in minutes since they have a checkpoint station not far," Lewis said and paused the video.

"Hmm," was all Wyvette replied in response.

"I have a degree in civil engineering, in case you're wondering." Lewis winked at Wyvette. He grinned when she made a rude noise in response.

"Let's see the rest then." Imirah pointed at the projected video. "What the hell?"

The video continued showing the first level, with no sign of Navalny. Then after a few seconds, Navalny walked down the last flight of stairs. He continued to tap his digital clipboard, presumably entering data. Ewan watched as the other four walked closer to the wall. They stared as if that would make more appear. Then all of them turned to Ewan with baffled expressions.

"A Deepfake. Very good one, too. This was no amateur job." Ewan stopped the video on the section that showed Navalny supposedly leaving.

"This was on the day he died?" Wyvette blinked hard at the image and then turned to Ewan.

Ewan pointed to the time and date display in one corner. "Also matches the time of death established by Dr. Simeon."

"Gave the killer plenty of time to get out. Also, delayed the body being discovered. Station security monitors the video feed. They would have seen a routine inspection." Zen frowned at the images.

Before anyone could reply, two employees entered the vast chamber. The video image vanished when Lewis tapped his clipboard. They stopped short, startled to find a crowd inside. Lewis strode over to them and had a brief exchange.

"Sorry, sir. We were told the area was clear for normal operation," a woman with pinned-up braids said.

"No problem. I was showing the investigators from Earth around. Carry on." Ewan waved at them to proceed. They gawked at Zen and the others as they walked by. Then he turned to Zen. "Follow me. My office isn't far."

Ewan led them through a smaller door and down a narrow hallway. They emerged some one hundred yards along to a locked exit. He pressed his thumb to a screen and the door unlocked.

"Secure exit and entrance," Imirah said.

"Someone cloned access codes and thumbprints maybe?" Peter brought up the rear as they left. The door clicked in place behind them.

"Next to impossible. I'll explain later." Ewan pointed to a UTV. "It will be tight, but you'll all fit."

A short drive brought them to the Goddard Facility Management headquarters. Zen shook her head at the company logo. "They've got the contract and you work for Robert Goddard. Makes perfect sense."

Ewan had been undercover at the global company before. Zen met him during her investigation that uncovered the Lodestone Project. Wyvette let out a low whistle as she jumped out of the UTV to stand beside Zen. Peter had not been an OSI agent, but he was familiar with the case. The three exchanged a glance but said nothing. Ewan cleared them through security. An elevator took them to his second-floor office. Once the door clicked shut, he docked his digital clipboard and leaned against the desk.

"As I was saying, I convinced the boss that I should personally handle the risk management assessment report after Navalny's *accident*."

"Which most on Crius now have heard wasn't one," Peter said.

"We prevented word of his death being released for as long as we could," Ewan replied. "Can't keep that kind of news contained indefinitely. Crius is a small town. Complete with a rumor mill. We might find it instructive to attend his services Thursday morning."

"His what?" Imirah and Wyvette blurted at the same time.

"There's a non-denominational chapel in Quadrant Three. All faiths use it. His family will have a livestream available. Three members of the clergy are here. Roman Catholic, an imam, an orthodox Ethiopian Christian priest," Ewan said.

"Then we can record the funeral and study who shows up later," Zen said.

"Yes. Of course, I'll attend along with other officials from the Crius command offices." Ewan squared his shoulders, getting in character as a member of station management.

"Was Navalny religious? If he was, I missed it in his profile," Wyvette said.

"His family is Russian Orthodox. Both Christian priests are familiar with their funeral customs," Ewan replied. He looked at Zen. "I have a staff member who is an expert at digital media. He thinks maybe he can break down the Deepfake video. You and I could go see him now."

"Wyvette, you go with Peter to interview Navalny's closest friend again. Find out what he was unhappy about," Zen said.

Peter turned to Wyvette. "Two people. One German guy he used to work with, a drinking buddy. The other is the lover he spent the most time with."

"Ewan can follow up on the video, but don't expect too much. Deepfakes are so effective because the editing or alterations are next to impossible to trace." Zen heaved a sigh and looked at her watch. The text message icon blinked at her with a tiny number 2 in one corner.

"We can't totally rule out Theodora Riley for Bocci's death," Wyvette added. "She had motive, opportunity, and means. We should talk to her again while we're tackling witnesses."

"You mean Dr. Simeon's report. Do you really think she planned his death so well, down to having a drug to incapacitate him?" Imirah gave a snort of skepticism. "I've met the girl. She's not that devious."

"Dr. Navarro is a whiz at getting witnesses to relax and talk, especially the ladies." Wyvette grinned when Peter blushed pink.

"You give me too much credit, Agent Young." Peter cleared his throat.

Zen shook her head. "According to Theodora, she found out Bocci was cheating on her just before they boarded. Devious or not, she didn't have time to work out an elaborate payback killing."

"Excellent observation. Unless you believe she just happened to be carrying a designer drug and a sonic stun gun," Peter put in.

"See if she can give you clues to Bocci's personal life we might not have in a report," Zen said.

Wyvette nodded and swiped the screen of her smartwatch. "Will do."

"And you?" Peter glanced at Zen's wrist as she looked at the alerts again.

"I'll check in with Hadley. See if she has new information. And call Astra," Zen said. "I'll check in with you all via direct message later."

"Is she okay?" Peter continued to gaze at Zen.

"What?" Zen blinked at him.

"Your daughter, I mean. I hope everything is alright," Peter said.

"Astra is fine. Just a regular mother-daughter check-in. Always good to keep in touch even at her age. And she's farther from home than she's ever been." Zen blew out a breath to steady her nerves and her voice.

Peter turned to Wyvette. "Ready, partner?"

"Theodora answered my message. She'll come to the Space Command offices in three hours. Think we can finish by then?" Wyvette replied.

"Sure. If not, I'll let you go meet her." Peter went to the door and opened it. He glanced at Zen one last time before he followed Wyvette out.

Ewan tapped the screen of his docked digital clipboard and stood straight. "Okay, logged my site check and off to my tech expert. Ladies..."

Zen and Imirah walked out ahead of him. In the hallway, Ewen greeted two employees, waved good-bye to them, and strode off. Zen's mind worked overtime. She didn't notice her surroundings until they were out of the building. Not many people were about since it was still early on a workday. Imirah matched Zen's steps for the equivalent of two city blocks. Then Zen stopped at a corner.

"See you later." Zen smiled at the statuesque woman.

Imirah smiled back. She managed to look like a cross between cop and a supermodel most of the time. At that moment, the cop in her came through. She leaned down, though Zen wasn't that much shorter than her. "You're going off grid to do something you don't want your colleagues to know about."

"I don't know what—"

"Hey, I get it. Sometimes independent action is necessary. And we know you're prone to... take initiative during cases." Imirah cocked her head to one side.

"You're letting those spy instincts run wild. Nothing shadowy. Boring work stuff and listening to my kid tell me about her day."

"I'm not asking for details. Do your thing. Holler if you need backup." Imirah winked, patted Zen's shoulder, and strode off. "I'm going to check in with Ambassador Abramov about the international situation."

"Yeah, you do that," Zen called after her and then muttered, "And stay out of my business."

After watching Imirah disappear into a taxi, Zen checked her smartwatch again. Then she studied the wide corridor around her. No one seemed to be taking a particular interest in her. Still, Zen remained alert to being followed. She followed the direction sent to her. Twenty-five minutes later she arrived at a Goddard Space Corporation research building. She scanned her ID badge and the door clicked open. The lobby was elegantly furnished. Muted lighting even gave it a cozy feel. Brown and dark reds softened the usual stark cold of space structures.

"May I assist you? I have noted your authorization to access all areas of Crius. Welcome, Special Agent Batiste," a sincere and hospitable female AI voice intoned.

Muted footfalls sounded behind Zen. A woman stood in an opening that had appeared to be a solid wall a few moments before. Her auburn waist-length braids were pulled into a ponytail with a pink and green scrunchie. Full lips and dark brown eyes behind eyeglasses gave no hint as to her mood.

"Thank you, GiGi. I'll take it from here. This way, Dr. Batiste."

When Zen followed the wall slid shut behind them without making a sound. The silence unnerved Zen, as if she was stepping into a point of no return. She stared at the woman's back as they walked. Nothing about her looked familiar. They arrived at another portion of a wall that slid open seconds after the woman stopped in front of it. Only then did Zen notice the soft green light to one side. An access panel with a keypad was almost invisible. Yet the woman hadn't touched it. Biometric code scan? Zen took care to scrutinize her surroundings as she walked into the room. The woman's voice broke into her thoughts. She hadn't followed Zen inside, but instead stood in the hall.

"Dr. Xavier will be with you in a moment. She's just ending a clinical staffing." The woman executed a crisp nod, pivoted, and left.

"Wait, I—" Zen rushed forward, afraid the door would zip shut. She suddenly felt out of control, and not entirely safe.

"Don't worry. I'll scrub the AI record so no one will know you were here."

Zen spun around to follow the voice. Another opening in the opposite wall was open. A group of young people wearing light blue lab coats chattered away as they mingled in another corridor beyond.

"Lexi?" Zen blurted when she could catch her breath.

"Alex. Dr. Alexandra Xavier."

They faced each other in silence for a full five minutes. Lexi. Alex. The woman who stood before her was a stranger. Not only in appearance. Zen searched for a spark of recognition, an instinctive physical reaction that this woman was her sister. Yet Zen felt nothing. No chills down her spine. No hairs standing up on the back of her neck. Lexi's voice... No, Alex's voice didn't sound familiar. Her body language gave no hint that they shared DNA or even that they'd known each other in the past.

"You... changed your hair," Zen finally stammered.

Alex brushed a hand over her cropped blonde cap of natural hair. Even, perfect teeth flashed when she grinned, an open expression with no hint of artifice. She crossed the room, walked past Zen, and sat in a swivel chair. She waved at another seat for Zen. Still dazed by the unexpected, Zen sat down.

"GiGi, secure the room," Alex said.

"Already done, Dr. Xavier," the AI voice replied.

"She knows me so well. Do you want to interrogate before or after I make us tea?" Alex raised both expertly shaped eyebrows at Zen.

"Tea? You... Girl, I didn't come here for freaking tea! I attended your funeral. Mourned you for years. Hunted down clues to catch your murderer. And you in here talking about tea?"

Zen jumped to her feet. She paced in circles to work out the explosion of emotional energy coursing through her. Alex watched Zen without making a move. The young woman who'd led Zen to Alex returned with a rolling cart. She stopped short to gawk at Zen. Alex gestured at her to leave the cart. Zen noted some signal pass between them before the assistant vanished again.

"I assured Nelda that you weren't a threat to me. Otherwise, she would have restrained you. Calm down or GiGi will ignore anything I say and call security." Alex's voice remained steady, like a therapist talking to an agitated patient.

Zen balled both hands into fists as anger flared once more. Then she realized Lexi was right. The last thing Zen needed was to cause a scene. "Fine. Fix the damn tea. Serve up some answers right along with it."

Alex's expression hardened into a cold glare for a half second. Then it vanished. "You think you're entitled to interrogate me? Wrong. By the way, how are the investigations going? Suspects?"

"I can't discuss ongoing cases. We're following leads." Zen watched Alex pour hot water over tea bags. The scent rose on the steam coming from two ceramic cups with lovely vines and flowers painted on them.

"Lavender and honey. I figured it would settle us both." Alex smiled and extended a cup to Zen.

Zen exhaled and accepted it. Indeed, the smell did take the edge off of her taut nerves. She sat down and took a sip. The tea was sweetened just the way she liked it. "How did you remember—"

"Your food preferences were programmed into systems for your flight here. They transfer to the space station to your living quarters databank when you arrive. Standard for VIP travelers. GiGi knew you were coming," Alex replied. "No, I didn't remember. In fact, I don't have much of a memory of life before space."

"You sound so distant. Almost..."

"Alien is the word you're searching for, Zen. What did our father tell you about me? No wait, let me guess. He shoved me into a psychiatric hospital for my own good. Then he used his relationship with a billionaire to get me out here. Far away from Earth and the risk that I'd screw up his luxe life. And his career. Not to mention the professional prospects of his other wonderful children."

Zen studied her sister over the rim of the cup, sipping as Alex talked. Animosity lay just beneath the surface of Alex's even tone. She willed herself not to match anger for anger.

"Sounds like you need a shot of this stuff." Zen gestured at the second cup still sitting on the tray. "Guess we both do for this reunion."

Alex's eyes narrowed to slits. Then she sighed and picked up the cup. "Well, ask away."

"I..." Zen clamped her lips together. The words formed in her brain but wouldn't travel to her mouth. Her throat seemed to close up. Why did she think it would be easy to ask her baby sister if she'd killed two people?

Alex took a long drink and set down the cup. "I'll help you out. Deep magnetic brain stimulation rearranged my memories. I have gaps but not a complete loss of my past. I can tell you I don't feel guilt they're dead. I remember those girls treating me like shit, taking credit for my accomplishments. James Batiste might have influence, but those girls came from even greater money and power. Legacy kids at our elite university. Is it my fault they underestimated me?"

"You did it then?" Zen pushed out the question as though it was a heavy load.

"What does it matter? I have a new life and important work. Criminal reform has finally caught up to the twenty-second century soon to come. We're about to build the first colony on Titan. And we've found an exoplanet that is like Earth. At least from the data analyzed so far. And it's not Kepler 452b either. My colleagues and I might even be instrumental in finding intelligent alien life. We're going to not just discover new worlds, but *build them*." Alex paced in a circle as she talked. Her eyes gleamed with the excitement of discovery.

"What does it..." Zen's hand shook from the urge to hurl the cup against a wall. Instead, she set it down on the nearby desk with care. "Two people are dead. It matters to their families. The same way it fucking *mattered* to me when I thought you were the victim."

Alex shuddered and tea splashed on her slacks. She didn't seem to notice. "I... I don't know what you want me to say."

"Shit. I don't know either." Zen jumped to her feet and paced again.

"The only family member I remember clearly is Brian. He was always there, giving me advice. Which I rarely took."

"You didn't listen to anyone," Zen said after a few moments. Brian had been more like a father figure to Lexi. Their eldest brother was fourteen when Lexi was born.

"Not true. I studied hard because he said school had value. He told me to ignore snobs at the fancy private school. Even gave me the best comebacks when they made racist comments. Some of my wisecracks at Georgetown Prep were legend."

"I remember the calls from school administrators. Mama couldn't deal," Zen chuckled and shook her head.

"Hmm, yeah. Enola Chatelain Batiste and her precious reputation. You know James stored letters from each of them for me to read. After the treatment, I mean. The doctors weren't sure what I'd remember. Or what the side-effects might be." Alex grimaced as she put her cup back on the cart. "She mentioned the family name six times. My memories might have been spotty, but the hypocrisy rang true. James sounded businesslike, mapping out my future."

"Lexi—" Zen winced when her sister looked at her sharply. "Alex, they both grieved hard after you were gone. Those days were rough on all of us."

"I don't want Brian to know. I feel warm and protected when I think of him. But even those memories are few and sketchy. I don't want him to think of me as a monster. Alexis Batiste is dead. Let her stay in that grave on Earth."

"Do you care anything about what happened to those two women?" Zen couldn't let it go.

"Three."

Zen gasped and took a step to Alex. "Three."

"There were three dead female students during my time there. I wasn't a natural suspect since I was fifteen, a prodigy. Young and innocent."

Alex wore an impassive expression. Zen examined her face as if she was studying a lineup of suspects. The curve of Lexi's jaw was the same now that she looked closer. Her full mouth reminded her of their mother and maternal aunts, too. Yet surgery and advanced cosmetics had given her sister a new face. Her body had no trace of the baby fat of adolescence. Alexandra Xavier worked out. Her toned muscles accented soft curves. Three diamond studs trailed up her earlobes. Seconds stretched to minutes as Zen let reality sink in.

"I understand," Zen murmured. She sat down hard.

"I doubt it, but at least you're not giving me a morality lecture. If it helps, I was defending myself. Now, the subject is closed." Alex stared at Zen with a tough-as-stone set to her chin.

"Are you happy? I mean, with your work here and... Are you married?" Zen looked at her.

Alex sat across from Zen and crossed her legs. "I'm not chained to any one person. And no, I don't have a child. I definitely had more on my mind than a wedding and swollen breasts."

"Right. I don't know what I expected. Actually, I didn't have the imagination to think far beyond—"

"Traveling millions of miles to demand that I explain myself. Correction, redeem your image of me. Because make no mistake, this is about *you*. Not Alexis. Accept that she's gone and you'll be better off." Alex smiled. "Listen to me, giving you advice. Therapy is your field. And catching criminals. In space no less."

Zen rubbed her forehead with one hand. Tension she hadn't noticed tightened in her temples. She would no doubt have a headache later. "I don't chase fugitives."

"Lucky for me then. But I'm not a fugitive, strictly speaking."

"I'm not looking to punish you, Lex—" Zen stopped and cleared her throat. "Alex."

"Good thing because I'm a pretty big deal here at Goddard. I head up the research on establishing viable colonies on planets. Or on moons with a viable atmosphere. Of course, for companies like Goddard it's about the money." Alex shrugged and went to the cart. "Cookie? We have a baker who is the best. Butter pecan. Delicious."

Zen felt a chill. "That was your favorite as a kid. We'd go to Louisiana and our grandmother would take us to pick pecans. She had three trees on her property."

"If you say so." Alex ate the whole small cookie in one bite. She washed it down with a gulp of tea. "To answer your question, yes. I'm happy. With my work and my personal life."

"Good. I—" Zen sighed and nodded. "Good."

Alex's full lips tugged up at one corner in a rueful smile. "I'm sorry for being kind of an asshole. You've had a shock; your baby sister being painted as a serial killer no less. Naturally you wanted answers. But you must realize I'm in a new world. In many ways Earth isn't home to me anymore."

"I see." Zen had to admit that Lexi—Alex—was right. In a way, Zen had found out what she needed to know.

"You're thinking James was right to bundle me into the great unknown. Zapping my brain and banishment were the only viable solutions," Alex murmured. She tilted her head to one side.

"You weren't banished but given a chance to have a life. Something other than being locked way in a forensic prison hospital." Zen gazed at Alex with clinical interest.

"Almost thirty-six months. That's how long before I recovered the ability to handle complex equations." Alex grimaced as if remembering the struggle. "At least the doctors here helped me recover."

"Daddy did it because—"

"Stop. Seriously. Light years away and you're still making excuses for them." Alex heaved a sigh and shook her head. "Sorry again. Of course, he was right in a way. I've come to terms with his decisions. Having him believe my side would have been nice though."

Zen let a few seconds of silence pass before she spoke. "But you don't have memories, you said."

"I wrote it all down in a digital journal. I wanted to preserve my story. I was told the side effects might include amnesia. I didn't want other people telling me who I was and what I'd done. Allegedly," Alex added.

"I see."

"The answer is no. You can't read it. Legislation is in place governing criminal rehabilitation using advanced medical procedures. Our 'sentences' are the deep brain stimulation, therapy, and relocation. In my case"—Alex waved a hand at her surroundings—"part of the agreement is that the past isn't constantly flung in our faces. Not very healing, I'm sure you'll agree as a therapist."

Zen stood. "Thanks for seeing me. You didn't have to, and you're right. You don't owe me a damn thing."

"I figured you didn't need to waste time looking for me. You've got murders to solve. James sent me articles about your career. Famous sleuth gathering suspects in a room and beating the truth out of them." Alex laughed at Zen's pained frown.

"Hardly. You've been reading those sensational tabloid stories. Don't believe everything they say about me."

"Deal. Do the same for me," Alex said in a soft voice.

"Right. Anyway, I'll let you get back to... you know. Your life."

Alex stood, picked up a napkin from the cart, and brushed crumbs from her fingers. "Crius is steeped in secrecy. We're more cut off than any other space settlement. Or at least we were until now. Camouflage is the norm here."

"Being cut off is over now. The UN is probably going to worked overtime to forge a compromise, which means more visits from Earth," Zen replied.

"More meddling that will do more harm than good." Alex shook her head.

"Have you heard any rumors of organized criminal activity? Zen glanced around at the room they were in. She focused on details for the first time.

"You're kidding. Everywhere we humans go a black market springs up. We haven't mastered a truly egalitarian society. Some have more than others as usual. People will get what they need or want no matter what."

"I don't mean the latest gadgets or chocolates from Earth. I'm talking serious stuff," Zen said.

"Oh, you mean the gangs."

Zen faced Alex again. "Plural?"

"Two major, a couple of little ones that are into petty stuff. Chocolates and gadgets like you said. The big gang split when five or six members decided to go off on their own. All of it happened before my time. Now they mostly stay out of each other's way. But I hear they might combine and become one gang again."

"Any violence break out?" Zen asked.

"Not for a while. Until Mikhail, poor guy." Alex let out a sigh.

"You knew one of the victims?" Zen felt a stab of apprehension in her chest.

"Hey, this is a small town. People with expertise in machinery and tech get shared between facilities, especially the ones that last. We respect space longevity. Mikhail had worked his way up to a supervisory position. He helped solve a few power glitches we had. Nice enough guy." Alex heaved out a deeper sigh.

"You didn't reach out to help me focus on my cases or help me get closure about my little sister. There's more." Zen walked close to Alex and stared hard into her eyes.

"Mikhail and I had a thing," Alex said after a few beats. She returned Zen's gaze with an blank face.

"A *thing*. I'm guessing you mean a love affair," Zen said.

Alex snorted. "Love had nothing to do with it. Don't get me wrong, I liked Mikhail well enough. But ditch the image of hearts and flowers. We had a few nights of satisfying sex and moved on. Of course, there was that one little incident."

"Alex." Zen squinted at her.

"This woman he was seeing got a little possessive. She showed up at my apartment to warn me off. I don't respond well to threats. Girl should have learned to fight before she started something." Alex chuckled.

"You beat her up? Shit, Alex." Zen winced at the complication of her sister being part of the case.

"She left herself wide open. I gave her a couple of pops and girlfriend came to her senses. My neighbor called security. It's all in the police report. I was attacked and defended myself. Old news. Happened almost two years ago." Alex crossed her arms.

"You knew I'd find out you had a connection to Navalny. You weren't interested in getting to know me, learning about your family. Almost twenty years have passed. I told my daughter about you. Brian has two kids. You haven't asked me about them. Any of them. And now this shit!" Zen paced once again as she ranted.

Alex started to speak but Zen's smartwatch went off. The ringtone for an urgent work message trilled. Then again after three seconds. Alex pointed to her wrist. Zen let out a short string of expletives as she swiped the crystal screen.

"Trouble?" Alex wore a frown of concern as she gazed at Zen.

"I have to go. We'll finish this another time. I guess. I don't know. Maybe not." Zen blew out a noisy breath. Then she concentrated her thoughts on priorities.

"Crius is a fun place. Exciting scientific advances are happening here. Things that will change life on Earth. And that's not hype." Alex walked up to Zen until they were inches apart. "It can also be dangerous. Especially when people think their turf is being threatened. Stay alert."

"Don't get it wrong. I can take care of myself," Zen clipped.

"Carry on, Special Agent Batiste." Alex grinned and backed up, both palms raised. She gave a command and a door panel slid open. When Zen was in the hallway several feet away Alex's voice stopped her. "I didn't kill the third victim on Earth, by the way."

Zen whirled around but the panel whisked shut without making a sound. The urgent ringtone went off, forcing Zen to keep going. "Damn it, Lexi. Alex. Whoever the hell you are."

Chapter 7

Zen arrived back at Peter's office in the Space Command headquarters thirty minutes later. Traffic in the space station had been surprisingly heavy. She'd taken a taxi, but it seemed the entire population of Crius had decided to get on the road as well. The driver had explained that shifts at the big companies were changing. Maintenance staffs mixed with shop workers, scientists, and more. Some going home. Others going to work for the evening. Zen let the bustle and the driver's stream of chatter muffle her troubled thoughts. The clamor acted as a broom, sweeping away clutter. By the time she swiped credits to pay the taxi and walked to Peter's office, her mind had cleared.

Wyvette stood in the hall waiting for her. She waved for Zen to follow her. "So, I didn't get all that much from Theodora at first but I got to thinking. Bocci worked as a prosecutor. What if he was chosen for this mission because he's dealt with gangs before?"

Imirah sat on a low, backless sofa along one wall, legs tucked under her. Eyes closed, she took in and let out breaths in a rhythmic fashion. Without looking at the other two women, she spoke. "Centering."

When Zen looked at Wyvette, the young agent shrugged. "Says it helps her mentally order details."

Zen grunted. She could use some meditation after talking to Alex. Instead, she pushed the problem of her sister into a corner of her mind. "The UN is here about international diplomacy. They make it a point to keep a hands-off approach to crime. Anything they find is handed over to law enforcement, local or international," Zen said.

"Yeah, but what if the local thugs don't know that? Or..." Wyvette said with animation. "Or they know he could have helped us finger them."

"So, you're checking into his past work before the UN." Zen glanced at Imirah again and sighed. "I hope you're about to crack both cases. Sure would be nice to get off this tin bucket."

"But your sister..." Wyvette let the sentence trail off into nothing. She blinked at her scowling boss. "Hmm, Ms. Hadley says she'll check into a list of cases he worked on. Might take a while. She'll have to contact the authorities in Italy and Nice. Get permission to review their records."

"Okay. Anything else?" Zen looked from Wyvette to Imirah and back again. "The urgent message signal?"

"I had to leave Dr. Navarro to interview Theodora. He talked to Navalny's friend first on a job site; the guy said he couldn't take off. The girlfriend got cold feet and didn't show up. Dr. Navarro got to her home, heard bumping, and interrupted a woman slapping her around."

Imirah stretched out her long legs and stood. "Meanwhile, the guy he talked to has disappeared. I tried to locate him as soon as I heard."

"Wait, wait. Circle back to the girlfriend being beat up," Zen blurted.

Wyvette blew out a breath. "Okay. Dr. Navarro used his access override to get inside. A woman was shouting in a language he couldn't understand, knocking her around all the while. Dr. Navarro subdued the suspect and she's locked up."

"And the girlfriend?" Zen asked.

"She's in the hospital. Cracked rib, contusions," Wyvette replied.

"And she's unwilling to talk to Peter again. Memory is fuzzy," Imirah put in.

"Getting your ass beat will do that for ya," Wyvette retorted.

"Wow, I leave you people alone for a minute and hell breaks loose." Zen turned when Peter walked in, looking harried. "Ah, our superhero returns."

"It's been a day for sure," Peter said, his Spanish accent coming through from the stress. He raked fingers through his dark blond hair.

Zen watched him march over to the water carafe and pour himself a cup of water. "Anything from the attacker?"

"Nothing but mean glares and grunts as she was being booked. A nurse is checking her for injuries. I thought you'd want to be there when I interview her."

"Which is why I sent you the '911' text," Wyvette said. She clapped her hands together. "I can't wait for this! Off to find out about our perp."

Imirah grinned as they all watched Wyvette rush off on a mission. "The girl lives for this kind of action."

"I could do without it. I'll go check in with the booking officers, see what the search of her person reveals. Then I'll talk to the nurse to make sure she's okay for questioning. I'll get coffee for me, hot chocolate for you. Right?" Peter went to a panel and typed in the orders. The Space Command full-service café would deliver it.

"Perfect. I could use a shot of something sweet and hot before tackling another unruly female," Zen murmured.

"I'll direct message you. Until then, might as well relax. Thank your lucky stars you missed all the excitement." Peter brushed his shoulders and tugged his clothes into place. Then he strode from the office.

Imirah alone seemed unruffled by the latest developments. She said nothing for ten minutes as Zen looked at her tablet. Then she walked over to Zen, both hands on her hips. "So, how is little sister?"

Zen flinched but didn't look up from the screen. She moved away to put space between them. As if proximity might give something away. "Don't know what you're talking about."

"You've been hanging out on the moon for over a year. Back and forth. Back and forth. Always trying to get authorization for a flight to Crius." Imirah nodded when Zen's head shot up. "We knew about this station."

"We?"

"Interpol. My bosses sat on it for a few months, debating on what to do. I mean, building a space station isn't a crime. Finally, because we work closely with the UN the decision was made to approach the White House. Let them break the news," Imirah said.

"Giving the US time to develop a spin strategy, some way to minimize damage." Zen thought about her father in the thick of those discussions.

Imirah grunted. "Yeah, and look how well *that* worked out."

"To be fair, telling your allies they've been bamboozled is kind of hard to dress up," Zen wisecracked.

"It was stupid to let Crius develop for so many years. They should have told their closest allies much sooner, cut them in on the benefits." Imirah waved a hand. "Well, the cat is out of the barn now."

"The saying is the cat's out of the bag, Imirah. The barn thing is a whole other—" Zen sniffed when Imirah gave her a bored look. "Anyway, I had duties in space. Nothing to do with Crius."

"I let you in on a little secret. The UN intelligence division has known about Crius for some time. The Global Space section has access to telescopes. They thought it was an asteroid at first, then one of Saturn's many moons. But their astronomers and astrophysicists ruled that out very fast. They told us and we figured it out quickly." Imirah nodded as her words sank in with Zen.

"Then why didn't the UN confront the countries involved?" Zen frowned at this new piece of the puzzle.

"Because—"

Imirah broke off when a bell tinkled that someone requested entry. A delivery person arrived with a takeout tray. He placed the cups and a bag of food on a table. Zen thanked him and he left. Imirah looked in the bag and gave a cry of delight. She pulled out a pastry with minced dates and nuts in a clear package. Zen grabbed the bag and pastry out of Imirah's hands.

"You were saying." Zen dropped the bag and pastry on the table again.

"The decision to simply monitor the situation was strategic. International relations at the time were tense. Also, it gave the UN a chance to monitor activity related to Crius. Nothing suggested warlike or imperialistic intent. Mostly the aim seemed to be scientific. If Crius succeeded, the UN could pressure the countries to share all information. None of those nations could operate Crius without collaboration from the US and Europe indefinitely anyway." Imirah's gaze kept straying to the bag of treats.

"And the UN could also prove they weren't part of building Crius. Politics." Zen grimaced at the gamesmanship at play.

"Have a heart. There are four cups and plenty of pastries for all. I've been working for twelve hours straight with no food." Imirah managed to put on a sad face.

"You're a super human, remember?"

"Hybrid. I eat just like you." Imirah retrieved the pastry, bit into it, and hummed with pleasure. "You must admit that this place is well run."

"You're saying that based on Danish? Girl, please." Zen shook her head as she watched the lithe spy devour the treat.

Peter returned. "Our suspect has bruises but she's fine. In shape to be interrogated, for sure."

"Good." Zen got the cup of hot chocolate and handed him his coffee. "I'm afraid we won't have time to snack. We should hit her ASAP."

"Yes, indeed. Exactly what I would do." Imirah patted her mouth with a napkin.

"I don't mean literally, Imirah," Zen said.

"Too bad. While she's shaken up and cut off from her handlers—"

"Remind me not to delegate any suspect interviews to her," Zen said aside to Peter.

"Noted." Peter wore an amused expression as he glanced at Imirah.

"Fine. Take the long way around. I'm off to check on somethings." Imirah used a moist towelette to wipe her fingers with their manicured nails.

"I'll catch up to you in a minute," Zen said quietly. "I need to talk to Imirah."

Peter looked from Zen to Imirah and back. Then he nodded and left. Imirah picked up a cup of tea and stirred in two packets of sugar. She gazed at Zen over the rim of the cup. Imirah assumed a relaxed waiting posture.

"You have questions for me."

"How did you know about my sister?" Zen said, her voice soft. Saying aloud that Lexi was alive rattled her. Especially telling Imirah Suri with her murky objectives.

"Electronic access to the Lodestone Project server. The age, sex, and race of Patient X-12 couldn't have been a coincidence. Her treatment coincided with your sister's funeral services. Which made me wonder. Why take the extraordinary step of sending her to a secret location near another planet?" Imirah drank the last of her tea and put down the empty paper cup.

"How many know?" Zen tensed for the answer.

"Only me," Imirah said.

The vise around Zen's chest loosened a bit. She blew out a long breath. "Why did you look into Lodestone?"

"I heard talk about a confrontation between you and Peter on Star Flight. You've never trusted him because of Lodestone. I became curious about the treatment and the use of it in your country."

"What do you plan to do about what you know?" Zen frowned at her.

Imirah gazed back at Zen for a few seconds before answering. "If your sister has no link to Vlast or the threat to international peace... nothing."

"She's doing research on establishing colonies," Zen said in a defensive tone.

"Yes, and cutting-edge work on modifying the atmosphere of planets to make them habitable for humans. She's become a leading space bio-engineer."

"But you're trying to figure out if she's working for someone other than Goddard Corp." Zen voiced the same question nagging her.

"Dr. Xavier has an impressive bank account. Of course, that could be because she's a well-paid scientist. Her work for Goddard is very valuable to them. She helped create superior xenobots that extract minerals in substantial amounts."

Zen let the question of Lexi's source of riches hang in the air between them. "I don't want Lexi, Alex, harmed."

"Understood," was Imirah's inscrutable reply. She nodded at the door when Zen's smartwatch chimed. "I think Peter is anxious to start getting answers."

"Aren't we all." Zen waved for Imirah to leave. Then she locked Peter's office. "You want to observe, I guess."

"I have other lines of inquiry to follow. And I need to check in with Ambassador Abramov." Imirah walked away without further explanation.

"Damn it." Zen hurried to follow Peter's directions. She sent Wyvette instructions via text as she walked.

Three minutes later she arrived at the entrance to three small rooms set aside for interrogations. Peter stood in the hallway talking to a Space Command security officer. The woman nodded as if taking instructions, then she went into one room. Peter gestured for Zen to follow him. He led her to an anteroom. A bank of monitors sat on a long desk. Only one was on. The small screen had the livestream of their suspect sitting at a table. The female officer Peter had been talking to entered with a cup of water and pill package.

"She's offering her pain medication. She refused it from the nurse," Peter explained.

They watched as the woman shook her head with a scowl. Peter tapped an icon on a control pad and the audio came through. The suspect spat a colorful array of insults at her guard. The officer put both containers on the table within the woman's reach. Then she took up a position against one wall. The suspect muttered more curse words as the officer assumed a bored expression.

"Let's go," Zen said after watching the woman for a few seconds.

Seconds later the entered the room. Their suspect had tousled red hair with purple on the ends. Her hair color choices accentuated violet eyes and pale skin. She raised one purple eyebrow at them when they entered.

Zen sat down first, then Peter carrying his tablet. They both gazed at her as if in expectation for a few seconds in silence. The woman made a great show of yawning. She slouched in her chair with one arm slung over the back.

"Begin recording. Agents Zenobia Batiste and Peter Navarro present. It is April twenty-eighth, twenty-three hundred hours, Earth time. Also present..." He glanced at the officer.

"Officer Jalisa O'Bannon with Space Command Military Police, Sector Three."

"I want my lawyer. I know my rights," the suspect said.

"What's your name, please?" Peter spoke in a muted and polite tone.

The woman wore a fierce grin. "Ви можете піти в пекло."

Peter held up a palm when the security officer pushed away from the wall where she stood. He glanced at the screen of his tablet. "Ah, Ukrainian. Another clue to your identity. And no thanks. I won't go to hell. The long trip into space is enough for me."

"You'll be charged with assault at the very least. A freighter leaves in four days. You'll be on it headed to jail. On Earth."

Zen spoke in a matter-of-fact manner, her face impassive. She assumed a relaxed posture but stayed alert since the woman wasn't handcuffed. A slight twitch in the woman's facial muscles signaled Zen's words had hit home. To her credit, though, she gave no other sign. The door clicked and Wyvette entered. She gestured that Officer O'Bannon could wait outside.

"Ma'am, sir. Check your inboxes," Wyvette said. She stood against the wall where the officer had been moments before.

Zen glanced at the suspect and then at her smartwatch. She read a text and then tapped the screen. After a few minutes, she looked up at the woman. "Hello, Manya Clarke. You grew up in the Lambeth district of London. Lots of gang activity. Seems you were an early recruit. Your commitment to crime continued on visits to your Russian grandmother in Samara."

"Impressive. The little errand girl knows how to use a search engine app."

"You're fluent in four languages. Not the typical low-level criminal," Peter added, looking up from his tablet.

Manya transferred her hostile gaze to him and affected a tight smile. "Humph."

"Yet here you are doing muck work for Vlast, acting as mindless muscle to rough up people. Maybe we're overestimating her talent." Zen shrugged as she gazed at Manya.

"Or maybe the folks in charge don't think much of her potential. Who's the real 'errand girl' in here?" Wyvette smirked at Manya.

"You know nothing," Manya snapped. Her eyes flashed but she made no threatening moves.

"I think you're right. They don't have much confidence in her handling the big stuff. I mean, she's been with them for six years. She should have risen higher in the gang by now." Zen studied Manya for a few moments and then smiled. "Thank you for cooperating."

Manya's eyes narrowed to slits. "What are you talking about? I haven't told you anything."

"You know it. *I* know it. But your buddies? Meanwhile you'll sit here as the hours tick by," Zen said.

"And we won't correct them. Not that they'd believe us anyway. Wonder if they know she's been arrested?" Wyvette switched her gaze from Manya to Zen.

"News travels fast on Crius I hear," Zen replied. "We'll find out more. With or without you."

"He knows me better than—" Manya flinched at the grin on Wyvette's face.

Peter sat forward with a gentle yet firm look on his face. "The sooner you tell us what we want to know, the faster we can get you off Crius. The ship that brought us here will leave in another twenty-six hours. Being on it will be a more comfortable ride than a freighter."

"You'll still be locked up but at least not in a section with space waste," Wyvette clipped.

"You wouldn't... I have rights." Manya's protest came out with less confidence than before.

"We'll observe your rights. Absolutely, Ms. Clarke. In a holding cell with two well-trained security officers." Zen assumed an air of nonchalance.

Manya pounded the table and stood. "Let me out of here. I can make bond and—"

Zen stood as Wyvette took a step closer. "You have interfered in a major murder investigation. With ties to a criminal organization that could smuggle you back to Earth.

We consulted with the local court here on Crius. There will be no bond," Zen said. "Sit down."

"My lawyer—"

"Is on the way. We contacted one of the general counsels on Crius. Unless you have your own attorney?" Peter continued in "good cop" mode. His reasonable tone even hinted he was trying to help Manya.

"Someone paid by Vlast perhaps." Zen pointed to the chair.

"You cops! Just as crooked as any gang. At least we don't pretend to be saints defending the weak." Manya breathed hard. The effort not to explode into violence seemed hard on her.

"We can debate our differences and similarities later—after we have a nice talk." Zen's fierce tone and expression had the desired result.

"Damn police the same everywhere." Manya muttered expletive-laced insults but sat again after a few seconds.

Zen let Peter take the lead. She gestured for Wyvette to leave since her presence only increased the woman's hostility. For three hours he led Manya through a series of questions with care. Manya seemed to forget Zen's presence after a while. Peter extracted information while appearing considerate toward Manya. He kept the woman's focus on him. Neither seemed to notice that Zen quietly left the room. Officer O'Bannon stood ready to intervene in case Manya became aggressive. Zen joined Wyvette in the observation room.

"Well, what do you think?" Wyvette kept her gaze on the monitor showing Peter and Manya.

"She's confirming the gang is involved in the usual crimes. Drug manufacturing, a bit of organized sex work, theft rings—which is good news." Zen crossed her arms as she studied Manya.

"Define good. Vlast has gotten its scummy hooks in a major space installation. Some of the tech developed here could be used to wipe out police officers on Earth. Hell, armies. They could be talking about taking over entire countries."

"I know, but she hasn't mentioned anything close to those ambitions." Zen pointed to the screen.

"Like you said, she's not high up in Vlast. They're not telling her the big plans."

"Could be, but Peter has massaged her ego. Manya wants to prove she's not just a flunky." Zen shook her head. "The guy knows how to get in the head of a woman."

"His good looks help. And he knows how to use that Spanish accent. Notice he let it get deeper the longer they talked." Wyvette smiled at Peter's image.

"Yeah, reinforcing that they're both from Europe. Not like us uncouth Americans," Zen said with a laugh.

"I ain't mad. Long as he gets the goods." Wyvette's grin faded after a moment. "What are we going to do about Vlast, boss?"

"We're here to solve two murders. Ewan and Imirah are here to deal with international crime and espionage. Let's focus on tracking down who sent her to rough up the witness," Zen said.

"Okay, I'm on it." Wyvette's words trailed off into a deep yawn. She rolled her shoulders and rubbed the back of her neck.

Zen caught the bug, yawning as well. Her entire body felt drained at the same time. "We all need to get some sleep, including Peter. We have enough to follow up on for now."

As if he was on the same wavelength, Peter stood and left the room. Officer O'Bannon entered and led Manya out. The officer firmly grasped one of the woman's arms. Manya glared at her but didn't physically resist. Five minutes later Peter joined Zen and Wyvette in the observation room. He also looked tired.

"Ms. Clarke hasn't had an easy life," Peter said. "So, now we can review her statement."

"We should eat and get rested, then talk about our next move. Or we'll be zombies unable to think straight." Zen let out another reflex yawn as if to underline her declaration.

"Yeah. Guess I got caught up in the thrill of following leads. Crius doesn't simulate a day-to-night cycle. My body clock is thrown off," Wyvette said.

"Residential units are equipped with tech that creates a nighttime effect. Complete with the sound of rain, insects, or wind. The higher-end apartments have more amenities. Some bedrooms have ceilings that transform into night skies with stars, or blue skies with sunlight. But maybe Crius will be retrofitted later," Peter said. "It was created some time ago."

"Too bad we don't have that fancy stuff." Wyvette reached up high with both arms in a stretch.

"OSI and Space Command are not footing the bill for us to have luxury accommodations," Zen said.

"Before we go, here's more on Manya Clarke." Wynette pulled her seven-inch table from the inside pocket of her jacket. "Clarke worked as a translator for a little while, but apparently the legit life wasn't for her. Two of her brothers and an uncle are members of a London gang. Her grandfather was notorious in Russian crime circles. He was killed in 2068; a rival took him out on the streets of Moscow."

"So, she is likely a member of Vlast or least one of their operatives. Too bad." Peter frowned.

"Don't tell me you feel sorry for her," Wyvette said.

"She's a product of her environment. Yes, she's made bad choices, but still... I see something in her," Peter replied.

"I see a criminal willing to follow orders. She might have killed that woman," Wyvette clipped.

"I know." Peter seemed unconvinced Manya had no redeeming qualities.

"Hey, take a break from trying to rescue bad girls," Zen said quietly to him.

"I tracked her associates using the station's CCTV system. Cross-referenced facial recognition with registered residents. I also got ahold of those who came over undocumented. It's hard to stay under the radar on a closed world like Crius, but not impossible." Wyvette looked at her tablet again.

"Plenty of places to hide," Zen said.

"Exactly, and apparently plenty of security personnel willing to look the other way. Most are people escaping for a chance at a better life. A unit of security deals with immigration issues. But they're very lenient, especially since those folks are exploited a lot. Low pay, the most dangerous and unpleasant jobs," Wyvette explained.

"But there is a criminal element as well," Peter put in.

"Yep. There is a cottage legal industry helping people obtain authorization to stay. One officer said they can tell who has gang ties. They have money to hire a lawyer and get their documents faster. But hanging out with crooks isn't illegal," Wyvette said.

"Immigration policy on Earth limits entry to anyone with convictions or even an arrest history." Zen looked at her colleagues.

"What about second chances, rehabilitation? You can't hold a person's past against them forever. Besides, such a law would keep out people with the skills needed in space," Peter said.

An awkward silence fell. Wyvette cleared her throat and gazed off as if fascinated with something on the wall. Before, they would have been talking about Peter. Now, she knew both of them were thinking about her sister.

"Balancing public safety and justice for victims against rehabilitation is a paradox," Zen replied. She tried to push away her emotional connection to the subject.

"Programs like Lodestone did provide a way to address competing needs." Peter studied Zen as if concerned about her.

"Yeah, that and shooting folks into outer space." When they both looked at her, Wyvette shrugged. "Facts. Anyway, I think this guy is her boss. Frank Jurgen."

"Bring him in, see what he knows. Trace his movements before and around the time Navalny died."

Zen and Peter discussed next moves as they walked out. The three separated outside Space Command headquarters. Wyvette went off to a nearby café for dinner. Zen headed back to her apartment. All she wanted was sleep. Peter waved goodbye to them and strode off. Once back in her temporary home, Zen enjoyed a warm shower. She ate a light snack of a bagel and fruit juice. Then she climbed into bed and pulled the covers up to her chin. She had to admit the fabrics developed for space were so relaxing. The bedding was designed to provide warmth or cooling depending on normal human body temperature. The pajamas she'd bought for the trip were the same. Zen drifted into half-sleep with no problem.

Persistent buzzing made Zen turn over. She snuggled deeper into the fluffy pillow beneath her head. She'd dreamed of a summer day visiting her grandmother in Louisiana. A field of grass and wildflowers stretched ahead of her. Her three favorite cousins bounced around. One flying a kite. The other two playing a game they made up, which the four did often. Dragonflies drifted along in the air; their translucent multicolored wings glittering in the sunlight. So serene. Insect buzzing increased. Angry bees flying straight for her. Zen batted them away and then she was awake. Her smartwatch seemed to be fussing at her to get up.

"Alright, alright," Zen muttered.

An AI voice announced the time. She was surprised to find six hours had passed. It was the next day. Zen decided breakfast was a great idea. Or rather her growling stomach did. A bowl of oatmeal with dried apple chunks worked wonders. Her mind cleared, ready for the tasks ahead. All they'd learned filled her thoughts. She mentally arranged facts into categories of confirmed and unconfirmed. She was getting dressed when the entry request bell chimed. She pulled the shirt over her head and fluffed her braids back into place. Still wearing slippers, she went to the door.

"I knew you'd be here early, ready to track down—" Zen tapped the panel to unlock the door.

Alex stood holding two tall paper cups with a local coffee shop's logo. "Good morning. I brought you a gift. I'm sure government coffee can't compare to a caramel mocha latte with vanilla whipped cream."

Zen stood aside, too stunned to react as Alex strolled into the living area. "Uh, how did you—"

"Find you? Civil servants are always put in basic accommodations. Quick process of elimination. Besides, you people didn't exactly hide your arrival. Wanted to put the local rabble on notice." Alex took a tour of the apartment without asking Zen's permission. She disappeared into the bedroom for a few moments and then returned. "Not too bad. I could upgrade you."

"Upgrade." Zen blinked at her.

"I have a two-bedroom, two-bath apartment in Quadrant Five. One of the better neighborhoods." Alex chuckled when she faced Zen. She held out one cup. "Drink your latte. It will help."

"Thanks." Still off balance, Zen accepted it and took a drink. "Hmm, I usually have café au lait or hot chocolate but this is good."

"I'll remember next time," Alex said as she continued to examine the room. "I'm guessing your house back home is way better. I did ask. Not a lot of questions though. Daddy says you've all done well. He sent pictures of my nieces and nephews, by the way. Seemed... pointless."

"I didn't mean to call you uncaring, cold."

"A sociopath who only thinks of my own best interests? Yeah, you kinda did." Alex laughed again at Zen's grimace. "Relax. I didn't come to fight."

Zen's investigator instincts clicked on like a light switch. This was no warm reunion, and Zen hadn't expected it to be. She and Lexi had gotten along as kids, but they weren't especially close. Zen would have to examine those memories closely. For now, she didn't have much time to explore family dynamics.

"Why are you here?" Zen waved at her to have a seat.

Alex sat on one of two barstools at the peninsula of Zen's compact kitchen. "You want to know more about Vlast. Yes, I know the tag they use on Earth. Not here though."

"For someone cut off from Earth you know a helluva lot." Zen remained standing with her arms crossed.

"Knowing who's who and keeping your eyes open is key out here," Alex replied in a mild tone.

"Who was Navalny to *you*? He was quite popular with women, I hear."

"His charm was overrated. Didn't age well, which is why a few nights were enough."

"I have no clue about your taste in men. Tell me," Zen retorted.

Alex sipped from her cup. She looked at Zen with a bored expression. "Do you want the info or not? Tick-tock on your investigation."

Zen pushed against the urge to pursue Alex's motives. "You still have a gift for being aggravating as hell. Go on."

"Mikhail wasn't crime boss material. He didn't have the brains for it. Not that he was dumb. But his ability stopped at a certain... level, let's say. Anyway, he was in over his head, trying to be a big player. He didn't realize the stakes were higher than some black-market goods or designer drugs." As Alex warmed to her subject her eyes gleamed with excitement. "I think he stumbled and it got him killed."

"What stakes?" Zen sat down on the barstool next to her.

"Control of Crius and everything we produce. World domination. Which includes advanced weapons," Alex replied in a grim tone.

"Weapons, but..." Zen flinched at the dominoes that fell as she realized the implications.

"Ah, you get it. Buried beneath the seemingly benign scientific projects is another program. The kind of weapon that could wipe out entire countries. With no residual toxic fallout. No contaminated soil or air. But we have a way to stop them." Alex put the cup down and leaned toward Zen.

Zen stared back at her sister's eager expression. "What's this we stuff?"

"I narrowed down the location of their lab to Quadrant Eight. There's a huge warehouse type of space. But mostly it's not needed. Four years ago, the construction division built a satellite station."

"Wait, what? That's can't be. NASA, ESA, or one of the other space programs would have detected—"

"Not with the cloaking capabilities developed here. It's close enough to another moon that it won't show up. Anyway, Vlast isn't interested in Mawu. Research on seeding atmospheres and water generation has moved there."

"A second unknown space station will…" Zen felt the weight of what she was learning. "We can't let this news reach Earth."

"Dear sister, you're not thinking straight. A common enemy could unite those bickering countries." Alex snapped her fingers at Zen's nose as if to wake her from a daze. "Think."

Zen blinked at her and frowned. Then one word in bold red letters seemed to flash in the air between them. "Weapon."

Chapter 8

Imirah, dressed in a different dark purple outfit, paced in Ewan's office. She made a circle in the middle of the floor while the others sat. Seated at a table, Zen and Peter watched her. Ewan sat at his desk, his fingers moving fast over a silicone keypad. The wide screen of his computer flashed images. He stopped to swipe the touch screen several times.

"So, we can conclude that you didn't know about Mawu," Peter said mildly. His bland mask didn't falter when Ewan shot a heated look his way.

"I've been focused on finding out intel on Vlast, thank you very much," Ewan growled. "Not to mention information that helps you two find a killer."

"The second space station isn't seen as a big deal here. The gang seems to have no interest in it either," Zen said.

"And how did you find out about it?" Imirah strode over to where Zen sat, both hands on her narrow waist.

"A scientist let it slip. The most important issue is this weapon getting in the hands of a powerful criminal gang," Zen added.

"People with aspirations of establishing a global dictatorship. Well, that would settle the debates on which country has the most power." Peter gave a laugh that held no true humor.

"I'm glad you can joke about it, Navarro. Meanwhile, we'll go down in history as the people who fumbled and allowed it to happen," Ewan snapped. His attention didn't waver from the screen.

"He's worried about his reputation. At a time like this." Peter rose and walked over to stand behind Ewan. "Don't worry. No one will blame you for not finding out about Mawu or the weapon."

Ewan stood with growl. "Thanks. I feel so much better."

"You were on Crius less than three weeks before we arrived. And the picture here is complex. A lot of moving parts to track for us as a team, let alone one person," Zen put in.

"Yeah, well." Ewan blew out a harsh breath. He turned back to glare at the computer screen. "The weapon disrupts entire systems of infrastructure. Most of what runs countries are connected to servers. Entire power grids. Water systems. Communications. From one control panel an operator could launch malware to shut down the works."

Imirah looked at them, her full mouth curled up at one end. "Mass panic would soon follow. We all know how humans react when basic services fail. Amazing how you revert to uncivilized and venal so quickly."

"You're part human. And don't forget, I've seen you in action," Ewan said with a smirk. "Government systems are operated wirelessly. They have the ability to block radio waves on multiple frequencies. Vlast is working on a hack."

"Vlast has definitely leveled up over the past fifty years. Contraband rare minerals, designer drugs, and brothels are no longer enough," Zen muttered. "Some of the leaders are former government officials. They want to be heads of state."

"How did you come by such details?" Imirah stared hard at Zen.

"We've all been following leads."

"Leads like... your sister," Imirah shot back.

Peter faced her with a scowl. "Imirah, I don't think we have to—"

Imirah held up a palm at him, her gaze still on Zen. "Yes, we most certainly do need to know about Alexis Batiste. She was a prodigy in astrophysics; went to university at fifteen. She expanded her studies to aerology and then dabbled in astrobiology. If mastering the subject in record time could be called dabbling."

"None of which implicates her in building a weapon of mass destruction," Zen clipped.

"We know she has a propensity for violence, law breaking. That is a strong indication that she would be drawn to Vlast. These people are smart and ruthless," Imirah said, driving home her point. "Did she bring you the information?"

Zen winced at the bull's eye hit from the statuesque woman. Imirah's supermodel façade masked a brilliant intelligence operative. "I've spoken to her twice. She... reached out to me."

"The first time she gave you a bit of information. Her big reveal came in the second meeting. Correct?" Imirah pressed on.

"Yes." Zen had a glimmer of where Imirah was going.

"You're getting too close. Revealing the existence of this weapon is to pull you away from the murders," Imirah declared.

Ewan strode back to the touch screen and swiped too rapidly. "They, whoever *they* are, don't know about us, Imirah. We can concentrate on the global implications. While OSI investigates the murders. I have an idea or several on sabotaging this weapon system."

Imirah turned to Ewan. "And breaking the news about Mawu?"

"Handled through the right channels, the existence of Mawu will be barely a blip. I'll tell them about the weapon system and that it's destroyed at the same time." Ewan continued to work.

"Where does the name Mawu come from, by the way?" Peter asked.

"An African moon spirit deity, the creator of worlds," Imirah said aside, her focus on what Ewan was doing.

Peter's face lit up. "Ah, makes sense. Titan is a moon. The space station mimics a moon as camouflage. Scientists enjoy naming new discoveries or creations."

"I'm going to need help with the mechanics of this thing. I know of only one person already on Crius. She has the skills, and I can trust her." Ewan stood and faced them.

"Your informant?" Zen asked.

"Sela Hahn," Imirah said. She didn't flinch when Ewan glared at her.

"We all need to know the players in this game."

"Let's hope you're as good at getting intel on our suspects. Maybe spend less time surveilling your own team," Ewan snapped.

"Emotional attachments can trip up the best agent," Imirah said in a flat tone. "So far, I'm the only one with zero. Wyvette is sexing up that reporter."

"Crude way to put it," Zen mumbled.

"But accurate. Ewan has grown close to his informant, though I wouldn't call it an affair. Your sister has an undetermined involvement. And Peter, well, let's just say he can be empathetic to a fault. Especially when it comes to underdogs." Imirah made each point with the cold logic of a seasoned operative. A tense silence followed her speech for a minute or two.

Peter spoke first. "I'd hardly call Vlast underdogs."

"I'm not talking about them. A group of humanoids and hybrids have formed a community of sorts here, as on the moon," Imirah continued. She looked around at them.

"You mean like the lunar colony they established," Zen said, referring to her previous case at the lunar colonies.

Peter's eyes sparkled. "They could be developing technology or making discoveries that can change life on Earth!"

"I'm glad you're excited. However, sentient humanoids don't give a shit about you people," Imirah said bluntly.

"Have they joined forces with Vlast? And not because they care about them either, but it furthers their goals," Zen added before Imirah could respond.

"Three hybrid humanoids helped them build AI being used for the weapon system. The good news is they didn't know it was a weapon. Not at first," Imirah said.

"Then they can help kill the damn thing," Ewan replied with energy. "If you make the contact, I'll take it from there."

"Like I said, they don't care how humans go about destroying each other." Imirah looked just as disinterested.

"Yeah. They're interested in keeping the status quo here. Let life on Crius tick along as usual. Except the murder of two humans has brought unwanted attention. Not to mention the international turmoil on Earth," Zen said.

Imirah looked at Zen with interest. "Go on."

"Point out to them solving our cases, getting the diplomatic issues settled and Vlast neutralized benefits them. Crius is a huge asset, not to mention the second space station. Lexi and her team are developing methods to make planets or moons habitable. No way will any government demand be dismantled." Zen looked at the others and nodded.

"Do we care what the humanoids might be working on?" Peter looked at each of them in turn.

"They don't have a history of making moves against humans," Imirah murmured, more to herself than to Peter.

"Except for Emme Gaida." Ewan avoided looking at Peter, who'd been infatuated with the lovely humanoid.

"She was an anomaly. We checked." Imirah waved away Ewan's point. Then she faced Zen. "Agreed. I'm sure they'll see the logic in stopping the weapon. I doubt they have information that will help your murder investigations."

"They may know more than they realize though," Zen argued.

"I'll ask. You should get more answers from your sister."

Zen felt a stab of guilt, which didn't make sense. She didn't share responsibility for what Lexi had done on Earth. Nor should she feel bad about questioning her. Much as she hated to admit it, Imirah was right. Her feelings about Lexi—Alex—were all mixed up, like a boiling pot about to spill over any minute. Yet Zen was determined not to prove Clive right. Zen wouldn't let finding Lexi derail her investigations.

"Of course," Zen said with a sharp nod. The tension that grabbed at her shoulders made her neck ache.

Peter studied Zen. "I should question Alexis."

"Alex. Her name is Dr. Alexandra Xavier. She earned a double doctorate in two fields." Zen spoke with a trace of pride she probably shouldn't feel.

"Lived up to her potential professionally at least," Imirah mumbled.

"Your relationship precludes you being present during a follow-up interview," Ewan said.

"She won't be shocked when Peter calls her in. She knows you follow the rules, the good girl of the family," Imirah added.

"Got us all figured out, huh?" Zen chafed being scrutinized by three sets of eyes, all seasoned in sizing up subjects.

Imirah's expression softened. "You knew coming on this mission would be tricky. You never once thought she might become a suspect given her... history?"

"Nothing about Navalny's murder looked like... I mean, based on what my father told me about her life." Zen huffed out a breath and stared at the ceiling for a few seconds. The other gave her space to grapple with muddled thoughts. "You're right. I can't be in the room."

"I'll set up the interview," Peter said.

"Don't mention anything about a weapon or Vlast to Sela Hahn," Imirah said to Ewan.

"I'm pretty sure my informant can't help with more details about Navalny or his activities," Peter said.

Zen turned to him. "Right. The woman with the shady boyfriend."

Peter nodded. "I don't want to put her at risk any more than I have already. I've arranged for her to find new living quarters. Space Command will keep an eye on her."

"I suggest you have security pay the ex-boyfriend a visit, warn him off. It won't arouse suspicion. There have been instances of domestic disturbances where they intervened," Ewan said.

"The last thing we need is a third killing." Imirah looked at Zen. "Are we good here?"

"Yes," Zen clipped.

"I have problematic family members but that's a story for another time," Imirah quipped. "I'm going to a humanoid social event in the community later. I'll report back on their response."

"You're going to bring up mobsters and a scary weapon at the party? I don't think that will go over well," Zen said with a wry laugh.

"More of a networking event among those with similar experiences." Imirah pulled Zen aside while Peter and Ewan debated next moves. "I wonder why your sister chose to give you information. How would she benefit?"

"Less attention on her if we settle things? Or maybe two murder investigations and a criminal gang threaten her scientific work. Not sure it matters. She gave us what we need," Zen replied.

Imirah shook her head. "Dr. Xavier is like a ghost. I can't seem to find anyone willing to talk about her. I mean, nothing more than she puts in long hours. Likes caramel mocha lattes."

"So? She's been staying out of the mess, concentrating on her work. She seems genuinely committed to it." Zen thought back to how Alex's eyes sparkled as she talked about her team.

"I'm missing something. I feel it in my circuits." Imirah's lovely face twisted into a frown.

Zen blinked at her. "Did you just say..."

"My parents taught me that joke. I was in the hospital a lot. They tried to help me feel less like a freak because of added parts. I was born with a lot of medical complications, but thanks to modern science..." Imirah shrugged.

"I thought all hybrids were—"

"Created in a lab like one of those ancient horror movies?" Imirah gave Zen a pointed gaze.

"Sorry. That bit of humanoid bias slipped right out, didn't it?" Zen searched for a way to make amends.

Imirah waved a hand. "I know what you meant, Zen. The 'anti-robot' crazies even get worked up about lives being saved. I better get going. I want to check a few leads before the mixer."

"Does that include more digging on my sister?" Zen tried to keep her tone neutral. "Like I said, so far I don't know any reason to mistrust her information."

"She's good at covering her tracks. Learned from the best. Your father." Imirah raised both shapely eyebrows. Then she strode off without another word.

"Damn. I hate when she's right and then makes a dramatic exit," Zen muttered.

"I'm going to meet Sela. She could be invaluable in getting a worm or malware in the Vlast system. In case Imirah's pals won't help." Ewan stood and stuffed mobile tech into every available pocket. His black jacket seemed to have plenty.

"I'm going with you. Don't waste time trying to talk me out of it. The murders might be related to your mission," Zen added, pointing at his broad chest.

"I was only going to say grab a jacket. The sector she's in is purposely kept cold for the tech," Ewan drawled. "I know better than to argue once your mind is made up, Special Agent Batiste."

"I've got loose ends to tie up with our witness and the suspect. Forms to complete, reports to file. You'd think we could ditch bureaucracy at the dawn of the twenty-second century." Peter checked his smartwatch for messages as he complained.

"But you're so good with the details," Ewan joked.

"Humph." Peter shot an annoyed glance at him and turned to Zen. "I'll check in with you later."

"Okay." Zen watched him leave. "Why are you two bickering?"

"You try being shut up with him nitpicking for days. He's like a fussy elderly aunt." Ewan allowed Zen to leave first and then locked his office.

"You mean he called you on taking unnecessary risks. Stopped you from doing anything that might jeopardize our investigations." Zen grinned at the sour look Ewan gave her.

"Open to interpretation," he grumbled.

Twenty minutes later they were on a service elevator to the third tier of Crius. Special access authorization was required for entry to Quadrant Four. Ewan's undercover position allowed him to go anywhere within Crius. Zen tried not to look down as the eleven-by-eleven-foot elevator car rose higher. It moved smoothly for the most part. A few creaks and squeals made Zen flinch.

Ewan, observant as ever, eyed Zen after a few seconds. "You good? We're only halfway up. The ride down is truly thrilling."

"I'm fine. I'd feel better if I could see cables or bars holding this thing up." Zen gazed through high-performance glass. Multiple levels flashed by showing foot and vehicle traffic yards beyond them.

"Don't worry. The maglev coils and liquid helium are quite reliable. Until they aren't." Ewan's blue-gray eyes twinkled with mischief.

Zen squinted at him and swatted his muscular arm. "Funny guy. They teach you jokes at spy school?"

"You've faced down killers, rode across the galaxy to get here, and a little ride on an elevator has you spooked," Ewan said with a laugh.

"It's not exactly *a little ride*," Zen said. Still, his teasing had eased her nerves. She laughed with him.

"Ah, we have arrived. Sela's section is just a short walk from here. No more harrowing rides." Ewan took the lead as they headed down a long corridor.

Moments later a pale woman with freckles and red hair met them in a hallway. "Come with me. My supervisor is on the prowl. It seems as if everyone is on edge with everything going on."

Ewan and Zen exchanged a quick glance before following her. She led them through a maze of smaller hallways to a compact room. Zen looked around at blinking lights. Metal cabinets lined the other walls. She studied the woman with suspicion and then looked at Ewan. He seemed alert but not alarmed.

"The equipment will interfere with electronic listening devices and our voices won't carry beyond the walls," the woman said as if she could read Zen's questioning expression.

"Sela, this is Special Agent Batiste with the Office of Special Investigations."

"Why is she here?" Sela Hahn cut through his speech before Ewan could continue.

Ewan blinked at her abruptness. "You must know about two deaths—"

"Of course I know," Sela snapped. "I mean, why did you bring her to my section. If we're seen together my co-workers will talk. They still think of you as just another useless Crius administrator. Everyone knows she is police."

Zen studied the woman closely. She was about an inch shorter than Zen, maybe five feet six inches tall. Her red hair was pulled into a tight bun. She wore the typical comfortable knit clothing, a shirt and matching pants. Her clothes were dark gray. Zen was sure she'd have been looking out the window nervously if there were any. Her anxiety was expressed as simmering anger.

"And everyone should know that Crius administration must cooperate with my investigations. Mikhail Navalny visited this quadrant often. I need to examine everywhere he went," Zen said, her tone calm. "That's what we'll explain once we go. Stay here until we're well away and then leave. After we talk."

Sela's taut expression didn't ease as she examined Zen head to toe. Then she faced Ewan. "I've told you everything I could find out. Navalny did minor errands that allowed for black market selling of tech. That's it, that's all I know."

"We're onto something more serious. Maybe Navalny found out something too dangerous to the gang. A weapon," Ewan said in a low voice despite Sela's precautions.

"I know nothing about a weapon, and I don't want to know." Sela's Scandinavian accent deepened as her agitation increased. She scowled at Ewan. "You said I would not be placed in danger. And yet you bring her to my doorstep."

Zen stayed calm in the face of her anger. "My investigation—"

"I don't care," Sela snapped. "I have work to do. My director will be looking for me any moment now. Go to the

Goddard Corporation sector. They're more involved with the kind of tech Vlast is interested in. Navalny spent more time there than here."

"How do you know?" Zen shot back before Ewan could speak.

"He said so. You're the investigators. Haven't you talked to his lover? Alexandra Xavier. She knows more, or don't you want to implicate a fellow American?" Sela glared at Zen.

Ewan shot a quick glance at Zen and back to Sela. "We're following multiple leads, Sela. Calm down."

"Don't patronize me. Wait for my text assuring you the hallway is clear. Then leave. And don't contact me again." Sela punched in a code. The door slid open and she was gone.

"I hope Imirah convinces the humanoids to help," Zen said.

He glanced at the alert on his smartwatch. "Let's go."

They followed through with their plan. Ewan took Zen to the main office complex on the second level of the building. He introduced her to the director and his assistant. She made the usual speeches about the investigations and covering all areas of Crius. Ewan and Zen looked for signs that Sela's bosses were suspicious. Satisfied they'd accepted the explanation for their presence, they left. Ewan said nothing during the walk back to the elevator. They took a self-driven taxi to Space Command Headquarters. He punched in the destination and settled back in the seat beside Zen. The electric golf cart-type vehicle smoothly blended into traffic.

"How reliable is she?" Zen asked.

"I was about to ask you the same thing, only about your sister. Did you know about her affair with Navalny?" Ewan stared at Zen.

Zen huffed out a long breath. "She told me it was a fling. We already knew Navalny had multiple lovers over the year he was here."

"She knows the weapon exists and that Vlast is interested in it," Ewan replied.

"Yeah, but... wait a minute. Vlast is into crime, but I don't see them diverting resources from making money to build that kind of tech. Not for years." Zen reviewed what she knew and saw glaring holes in the story. She twisted in her seat to stare back at Ewan. "That would take the kind of money governments have at their disposal."

"We've arrived," Ewan announced unnecessarily. Space Command Headquarters was hard to miss. "We'll discuss more inside."

The vehicle bumped to a stop. He led the way to Peter's office without speaking more. Zen shot furtive glances at his strong profile as they walked. A few officers greeted him as the undercover role he'd assumed. They made joking remarks about keeping the trains running on time. Ewan gave good-natured replies, but his smile seemed forced. Once they got to Peter's office, they found Wyvette had returned.

"We have a problem," Peter said instead of a greeting.

"We have multiple problems, and they keep having babies." Zen sat down hard in a chair.

"Yeah, well. This one involves your... Dr. Xavier. She's didn't answer Dr. Navarro's calls. Her office says she's taken a vacation. I checked, and she did arrange it before we got here," Wyvette said.

"You think she's avoiding you." Zen shot to her feet again and faced him.

"The short answer is yes. At some point she had to know we'd connect her to our case," Peter said.

"So, she planned ahead. Not a good one though. I mean, Crius is big but we can still easily find her," Zen said.

"Um... not exactly." Wyvette glanced at Peter.

"Very unexpected," Peter murmured.

"Hey, like I said it was planned. If Dr. Xavier isn't involved in any way and feels like she's helped us as much possible..." Wyvette shrugged.

Peter nodded and finished her thought. "Then she'd see no reason to cancel her excursion."

"One of you spit it out before we're all old and have grandchildren," Zen snapped.

"She's gone to Titan," Wyvette said.

"What?" Zen and Ewan blurted out at the same time.

"Yeah. Goddard and two other companies pulled that one out of the magician's hat like a rabbit. It's all over the news. At least Jacques will be distracted from us for a while. He's thrilled to have a scoop for Earth," Wyvette replied.

"But.. but Titan's atmosphere—" Ewan broke off and waved a hand at the OLED TV screen on Peter's office wall. The moon's image floated there.

"They've developed suits that allow for long-range trips, generating breathable air. The compact units are far better than any O2 device built on Earth so far. Also, look at this. Two dome structures on the surface. She's going to kayak on one of Titan's methane lakes, a small one. I mean, isn't that incredible?" Peter became animated as he used the remote to show them new images. The screen flashed to show the surface of Titan and the two buildings in question.

Wyvette stared at Titan wistfully. "And maybe hang glide in Titan's skies. Her trip is more of a working vacation. She's going to send back data. Damn, I would kill to go with her. Earth's moon is okay but there's not a whole lot to see. I mean outside of the caverns, and even those are—"

"You can get excited about the science of it all later," Ewan broke in.

"But the science is relevant to each case. Processes and technology developed on Crius has pushed space exploration forward by a hundred years. And your sister has played a crucial part here," Peter said.

"Like you said, boss. Dr. Xavier has to come back. We can make headway in the meantime," Wyvette put in.

Ewan faced the three of them with a frown. "Her trip could be a distraction. We know she and Navalny were lovers. If his murder is connected to Bocci, and she knew he was on board the *Phoenix* bringing us here."

"All of which is speculation," Zen put in quickly.

"I call them new leads to follow," Ewan replied. "We need the connection between Navalny and Bocci. I'm sure there is one now more than ever."

Wyvette took out her tablet computer. "Roman Bocci worked as a prosecutor. We knew that already. He worked with prosecutors in Nice, Rome, and Finland on fighting organized crime. That includes people with ties to Vlast."

"You're suggesting a revenge killing?" Ewan said.

"Nah, that wouldn't make much sense. They could have zapped him on Earth a long time ago if that was the case. But I stumbled on something that might explain his murder."

Wyvette synced with Peter's television. A news article from 2084, a little over one year before, appeared. The others said nothing as they read. More silence as all three turned to Wyvette with different versions of puzzled expression.

"What does Bocci being on a local game show have to do with anything?" Zen said.

"It's the *reason* he was on. I found two other articles after he won big." Wyvette swiped again.

"He snatched prize money from a gang leader and they wanted him dead?" Ewan said with a dry chuckle.

"Roman Bocci is, well he *was*, a super facial recognizer. He won because of his memory. A reporter interviewed him later and that fact came out. Which resulted in the other articles. He was even studied by medical researchers working on brain mapping." He can remember faces better than 99.9% of us. Well, us humans. Which means..." Wyvette waved a hand like a schoolteacher prompting her students.

"He could have spotted someone or multiple people on Crius who don't want to be recognized," Zen said and looked at Ewan.

"Only the top officials knew we were coming to Crius in sufficient time for a plan to kill him," Ewan said.

"Someone high up is corrupt," Peter added.

"Or even members of Vlast." Wyvette nodded when the three older agents looked at her in surprise. "They've had time to get embedded and rise through the ranks."

"How many people have we looked into here?" Zen glanced at Peter and then at Ewan.

"I ran profile information we had through several of our filters. Search parameters should have flagged anything connected to Vlast. Multiple keywords like Russia, arrests, gangs, and so on." Ewan shook his head.

"We missed something?" Wyvette looked around at the others.

"But Navalny had connections to felons," Wyvette countered.

"I can't imagine they could eliminate everyone with a record," Peter replied.

"The gang picked people with clean backgrounds. Then when the timing is right, put them to work," Zen said.

"A time-tested technique in spying. Recruit someone few would suspect, a sleeper. Then only activate them when needed or when they're finally in a position to be an asset." Ewan pointed to Peter's computer. "May I?"

Peter nodded. "Sure, but I don't think—"

"We've accessed most encrypted servers and the Crius cloud," Ewan said in an offhand way as he sat in Peter's chair.

"How efficient." Peter shot a side-eye at Zen.

"You do know we're all from *democratic* governments, at least on paper," Zen clipped.

"Not to mention the UN has rules, or I thought so." Wyvette strode over and stood looking over his shoulder. "Damn, I need training on cybersecurity."

"We only employ digital access strategies on critical assignments. I think preventing global destruction might qualify." Ewan ignored the silicon keyboard and used the touch screen.

Zen joined Wyvette in looking at the screen. "I have an idea. Cross-check the financial records of top three levels of Crius officials, including private companies. See who paid their bills. I'm talking education, technical training, all of that back to their teen years."

Ewan looked up at Zen. "You sure you never worked as a CIA or NSA field agent?"

"My father taught me to follow the money," Zen said with a dry laugh.

While Ewan and Wyvette continued to search, Peter gestured to Zen to follow him. When she joined him away from his desk, he lowered his voice. "What do we do about Dr. Xavier? She hasn't been open with us."

"She lied to me. Which means she's up to her neck in something shady. But we don't know what that something is. So far there's no connection to Lexi, I mean Alex, and the weapon system," Zen said.

"True. But still..." Peter glanced at the image of Titan still on the large TV screen.

"Yeah. If she lied once, who knows what she's doing down there." Zen followed his gaze with a frown. Before she could say more Ewan let out a grunt.

"Bloody hell," Ewan blurted, his British accent sharpening as he muttered more curses.

"More bad news," Zen mumbled aside to Peter.

"Doesn't sound like he's found a reason to celebrate." Peter followed her to stand in front of his desk.

"So, my tech team came through. The weapons system isn't simply software. It's Mawu." Ewan looked up from the computer monitor at them with a tight expression.

"An entire space station is a weapon?" Peter's face drained of color. "But the UN Global Space Agreement of 2046..."

"Prohibits the deployment of WMDs within seventy million miles of Earth. I know." Ewan blew out a low whistle.

"We're way beyond that. So technically Mawu isn't a violation," Wyvette said.

"Mawu could be moved in position fairly quickly if a government felt it necessary," Zen said.

"Not confirmed. We don't know—" Ewan stopped at Zen's frown.

"Why would such a tool be created if they couldn't move it when needed? One of the projects out here is creating more mobile space objects." Zen turned to Peter, the physicist.

"A two in one. Mawu is capable of functioning as both a space station and a ship."

"Goddard Corporation got the contract to build it. Sorry, Zen." Ewan wore a look of genuine sympathy.

"Get me a shuttle and a suit. I'm going to Titan," Zen said. "Screw family sentimentality."

Chapter 9

Wyvette followed Zen to her apartment. For a time, Wyvette watched in silence as Zen packed a small space travel kit. They'd left Peter and Ewan at Space Command Headquarters. Zen ignored the two men as they tried talking her out of going. Her authorization as the lead OSI special agent meant Space Command's top general would follow instructions. There were few safety reasons why she would be denied. As it turned out, trips to Titan from Crius had become routine over the previous two years or so.

"I'm not impulsive or just plain crazy," Zen said. She dropped supplies provided by the medical unit into her backpack. Then she tested its weight. "Perfect. It's under at three point seven ounces." The guys at Space Command's space travel unit says it shouldn't be more than five pounds."

"I think we need to discuss this a bit more. Dr. Xavier has to come back to Crius. Her job is here."

"Wyvette, you heard what Commander Gusev said. The Titan outpost can sustain human habitation indefinitely. We don't know how many camps are there." Zen faced Wyvette. "Lexi is smart. She knows my priority is solving the murders. She's dropped breadcrumbs for us to follow."

"She figures you'll put doing your job ahead of chasing after her. I know, boss."

"Stop calling me boss, Wy. Makes me feel old," Zen quipped to lighten the mood.

Wyvette's stern expression didn't soften. "Your sister is *right*. You should stay on Crius. We've got solid leads on both murders. And you said yourself that Imirah and Ewan are here to handle the international intelligence."

"You think I'm losing focus because Alex Xavier is my sister. The sister I believed for years was a murder victim. Instead, she's a killer."

"An emotional shock would throw anybody for one hell of a loop, boss. I mean, Dr. Batiste," Wyvette replied.

"It's possible she helped create a weapon that could wipe out millions on Earth. She was Navalny's lover, and she works for Goddard Corporation." Zen used three fingers to tick off each point.

"Look, we have no evidence Dr. Xavier knew Roman Bocci was a threat. Someone on Earth messaged Crius he was on the way. Or maybe somebody already here saw the passenger list and knew Bocci had to go. Imirah sent me her update. Navalny had a spike in income, possibly blackmail money. If he used your sister to get information and then tried to use it—"

"Alex, Lexi... Shit! I keep getting twisted up on what the hell to call her. My own sister. I have no idea what else she's done or what she's capable of." Zen picked up a cup and threw it. It bounced off the wall instead of breaking.

Wyvette crossed the room and picked it up. "Good thing this stuff is shatterproof."

"Sorry. It's just… I've been wanting to break something for the last thirty-six hours." Zen huffed out a long breath and dropped onto the sofa.

"I think it's safe to say you should call her Alex. She's not the same kid you knew. For a lot of reasons. Listen, I don't know much about this Lodestone treatment thing for criminals, but Dr. Navarro says it changes who you used to be." Wyvette put the cup on the peninsula that separated the living area from the galley kitchen. She sat next to Zen.

"Yeah." Zen massaged her temples to ease the tension pulsing into a headache. "Okay, okay. You're right."

"You'll have a chance to call Dr. Xavier on her bullshit later." Wyvette placed a hand on Zen's shoulder. "I checked with her team. They just made another breakthrough on some of their work. She's definitely coming back."

Zen gave her a wan smile. "I see you've been busy."

"I learned from the best." Wyvette grinned. "Save that travel kit for me. I might take a side trip to Titan before we head back."

"Deal." Zen's expression turned sober again. "Here's something else. Ewan knows that the weapon was a government project. They've lost control of it to Vlast."

"Holy shit!"

"I say we meet up with Peter, Ewan, and Imirah. Time for everybody to come clean on what the hell we're up against." Zen broke off when her smartwatch trilled a ringtone for an incoming call. "Hey, Peter, I was about to call—"

"There's a big disturbance in Quadrant One, the docking terminal. Sounds like we have a gang fight on our hands.

Space Command and Black Rock Security are on the way. I sent a junior officer to pick you up." Peter spoke to someone else, a second and third muffled voice in the background. "See you there."

"Okay, I..." Zen blinked at the display of her watch. Peter had already ended the call before she could reply. When she glanced up, Wyvette was gone. Zen's front door was still open.

Wyvette came back seconds later. "Good thing I picked up a sidearm from the local cops. I'm ready. I think our ride is here." She pointed to Zen's watch.

"Yeah, right." Zen looked at the notification blinking on the tiny digital screen. "Officer Janine Turner, ID verified. Let's go."

The fifteen-minute ride felt like torture. Officer Turner looked no older than twenty with her blond hair in a ponytail beneath her Space Command cap. She did an expert job of maneuvering through the traffic in open areas of the large space station. Jumbo screens broadcast the warning for Crius residents to avoid Quadrant One. The male announcer's voice was firm, yet calm, as he explained law enforcement was handling a disturbance. He went on to say that there was no threat to the general population. Knots of people stood staring at the screens, talking to each other. No doubt rumors would be flying.

"Officer Turner, how much do residents know about crime here?" Zen turned to the young woman driving.

"People with less money buy stuff on the black market all the time. Most still think Mikhail Navalny's death was an accident. Command and the civilian leadership did a pretty good job of squelching rumors." Officer Turner wore a half-grin at Zen's look of surprise. "Dr. Navarro, with Space Command approval, used me to get intel by mingling with crowds. Picking up on gossip as it were."

"You obviously knew what you were doing. I'm impressed," Zen replied.

"Thank you, ma'am." Officer Turner's cheeks flushed pink, a pleased smile on her young face.

"Something feels off about this." Zen looked around at the people they passed in various uniforms and everyday wear.

"Gang warfare is always wrong time, wrong place, boss. Special Agent Batiste," Wyvette added when Zen squinted at her.

"I mean, it feels wrong... I know, I know. Gang fights are always wrong." Zen shook her head.

"Here we go."

Officer Turner pulled up to a staging area outside the corridor to Quadrant One. Space Command and Black Rock Security officers talked into two-way headsets. Others grabbed rifles and sped off in UTVs toward the action. Peter broke away from one group as he waved and jogged over to them.

"Two factions of a gang are fighting over an unauthorized shuttle. It's full of contraband. A Black Rock Security officer stumbled on one faction trying to unload it. Before he could call it in or try to stop them, they shot him. He's expected to survive. Only because the second gang showed up. They got word their delivery was being hijacked." Peter spoke in a rapid-fire fashion as he glanced over his shoulder at officers. "Look. Commander Gusev gave me access to livestream. Officers here all have bodycam. Security UTVs all have onboard cams as well."

"Damn," Wyvette mumbled as they watched the display on Peter's tablet.

"Both groups have taken cover and refuse to surrender."

"It's not like they can go anywhere." Wyvette frowned at the scene playing out in miniature on the small screen.

"My guess is at least one group thinks they can hop on the shuttle and escape," Zen said.

"If that's a long-haul shuttle it could easily make it to one of the other space stations before getting to the moon. Then be smuggled to Earth. This is good." Wyvette nodded.

Peter frowned at her with an expression of confusion. "Explain how."

"With a little work, we can trace the route of that shuttle. Those guys won't get far, which means suspects will be arrested. Someone will talk, you can bet on that. Space Command and the Lunar Police will crack open the black-market supply line." Wyvette looked on as officers exchanged information and command instructions.

"These guys either bungled their operations or the gang leaders didn't know about somebody's side hustle," Zen said.

"A bit of side profit is something most criminal organizations tolerate. But only if it doesn't involve stealing from *them*," Peter replied. "If that contraband is full of high value items that Vlast deals in, then this dust-up shows they have a weak point."

"And that they've lost some control. Real bad news for the thugs," Wyvette said.

"Unless… this is not bad news at all for them." Zen frowned as she stared from the screen to the buzz of activity around them.

Before Wyvette or Peter could ask what she meant, a loud explosion and shouts echoed down the corridor from Quadrant One. Every officer set off at a dead run toward the trouble. Commanding officers yelled instructions despite the headsets everyone wore. An armored vehicle rolled forward on smooth treads with only a loud hum to announce it.

Officer Turner ran to them. "Lt. Honoré says to hang tight. The CIRT Team set off percussive RCA grenades. We're about to get this mess under control. Be back in a sec." The young woman raced back to her commanders, presumably for more updates and instructions.

Wyvette grinned when Zen and Peter looked to her with matching puzzled expressions. "Critical Incident Response Tactical. RCA means riot control agent. On Earth most folks still call it tear gas, but that's not exactly accurate anymore. Out here, we have a different kind. It first causes extreme pain to the eyes and skin. That brings targets to their knees until the mild nerve agent makes them temporarily paralyzed. Officers have helmets that protect them."

Commander Gusev strode over to them as Wyvette spoke. Her short brunette hair was brushed back, giving her a decided military look. "We have the scumbags in hand. Four of them tried to board the shuttle and fire it up. So, I gave the order to gas 'em. You think this free-for-all has some bearing on your investigation I take it. Otherwise, you wouldn't be here."

"Don't know yet, but it sure offers an opportunity to ask your suspects what they know about Navalny and Bocci," Zen said.

The commander studied Zen for a few beats as if sizing her up. Then she gave crisp nod. "Fine. Our probable cause is crystal clear. They'll be headed to jail either on the moon or Earth. You can have access to them. It'll take days for the prisoner transport ship to arrive."

"Thanks, Commander," Zen said.

"I'll contact you when the arrangements are made. As you can imagine, we've got to sort out quite a bit before then. Secure the contraband, get the suspects locked up. Reassure the public."

"Of course. We'll wait to hear from you." Zen dipped her head in appreciation, which also acknowledged Commander Gusev's authority.

"Excellent." Commander Gusev pivoted and walked back to her troops.

"Like she had a choice," Wyvette said with a snort.

"Best to be diplomatic, Wy," Zen murmured. "We need to regroup."

"My office?" Peter glanced around. "It will take some time for them to process the scene and the suspects."

Zen nodded instead of trying to make herself heard over the burst of noise from the officers. Peter led the way to his UTV with the Space Command seal on both doors. On the way, Zen messaged Ewan and Imirah with a short update and a request to meet them there. Foot and vehicle traffic at Crius seemed lighter.

"Folks kinda cleared off the streets," Wyvette said, echoing Zen's thoughts.

"Yeah. I'm guessing those PSAs were taken with a big grain of salt." Zen noted the number of gazes turning to stare as they drove by.

They arrived at Space Command Headquarters to find it just as full of activity as the crime scene. Peter parked the small electric vehicle, and they went inside. Officers and civilian employees alike moved quickly but with assurance. When the finally shut themselves in Peter's office, he immediately ordered food and drinks.

"I take it we have hours of work ahead of us. While I was dealing with our latest witnesses, I saw Hadley sent results of her research." Peter took off his jacket and hung it on a rack.

"Let's divide them up between us," Zen said. She used the kickstand on her tablet to set it on the table before her.

"Agreed. I have an extra monitor in case one of you wants to link you tablet to it. It'll make reading easier on the eyes." Peter swiped his desk monitor as he spoke.

"That would be great. My eyes ain't as young as they used to be," Wyvette quipped. She giggled with the two older agents made sarcastic noises at her.

In the end, he sent for a third monitor. All three spent three hours reading Hadley's background research on twenty key players on Crius. Then they turned to the passengers from their flight to the space station. Peter was the first to fall against the back of his chair with a sigh. He stood, stretched, and cleared away the remains of empty paper cups. All three had taken breaks at various times to eat sandwiches.

Wyvette looked up from her monitor. "Hey, where's Lewis and Imirah?"

Zen checked her messages. "Ewan says he's been helping interrogate the prisoners from the Q1 riot. Imirah is getting a briefing from her bosses."

Wyvette had split her screen. One half had reports. The other had a table with notes by each name. "Okay. I've finished going through eleven reports. Two people of interest. Fallon Blanc, the UN envoy assigned here on Crius, and Theodora Riley. Both had state department internships. Blanc at the UN Embassy in Paris, Riley in New York City. Both worked as translators for various agencies. Blanc for an international corporation that has subcontracts with NASA. All either while they were in college or grad school."

"Sounds normal," Peter said.

"They both had working class parents. Riley's family actually hit hard times because her parents were alcoholics. Blanc didn't have it as tough, but he's no trust fund kid. Though his family seems to have been pretty stable. His mentors and references all talk about his ambition. So..." Wyvette tapped her screen. "I looked into how they went to school and got those sweet job opportunities. No direct link to Vlast."

"Why couldn't they make it easy and put the gang on their resumes?" Zen joked.

Wyvette laughed. "Yeah, right. Anyway, I messaged Hadley to check their mentors and anyone who gave them references, or made a call to get them plum assignments. This man and woman have shady backgrounds. No arrests, but their names were mentioned in several probes."

"More digging is in order on them," Peter said.

"Hadley hit a wall." Wyvette looked from Peter to Zen and back.

"Which is information in itself," Zen said.

"No charges. Only mentioned in probes where a couple of employees below them were fired and/or charged," Wyvette replied.

"What charges?"

"Insider trading. Stealing business trade secrets, and money laundering. Nothing mentions Vlast but I smell organized crime," Wyvette said.

"Well done." Zen stood and rubbed the small of her back. "We've got not one, but two intelligence agents right here. I'll bet they can punch a hole in that wall."

"Already thought of it. I sent Imirah the deets. Um, maybe I should have checked with one of you first?" Wyvette glanced between them. She blew out a sigh when both shook their heads.

"You were right to take initiative," Peter said with a brief smile. Then he put his reading glasses on again. "I'll look closer at the profiles I examined."

"Me, too. Wyvette has drilled down in a way I hadn't considered." Zen did a series of stretches before she sat again.

Almost an hour later they came up for air again. Just as they started to discuss their findings, the door chimed. Peter checked the video. Imirah waved at him from the hallway. He tapped the code and the door whisked open. She strode in carrying takeout bags.

"Ah, I see you've eaten." Imirah dropped the bags on a side table along one wall.

Wyvette popped out of her seat and sniffed the air. "Sandwiches hours ago. What ya got?"

"Chinese mixed veggies, wonton soup, shrimp fried rice, and crab rangoon. I figured you needed something substantial. And better than what the dining hall here could provide." Imirah wrinkled her nose at the mention of Space Command's cafeteria.

Peter crossed the room and peered into a bag. "I hope you have at least one eggroll in there. I—" He broke off and looked at his smartwatch. "The suspects have been booked. I'll sit in on the interviews." He waved at them and left.

Zen eyed the bags with suspicion. "Shrimp and crab way out here?"

"Not genetically modified but cloned from cells. They're grown in the Crius acquaculture farm. Don't worry. The local chefs gave them the seal of approval. So do I." Imirah waved a hand at the cardboard cartons. "Dig in."

"You're my new best buddy." Wyvette scurried over to find paper plates in a separate bag.

Zen turned to Imirah. "Have you found out anything to help us?"

Imirah sat in the chair across from Zen. "The youngster—"

"Hey, don't damage our new friendship with that 'youngster' crap," Wyvette said around a mouthful of shrimp fried rice.

"Sorry. *Special Agent Young* was right," Imirah peered over her shoulder at Wyvette. "I traced a maze of connections. Riley's mentors both have ties to criminals.

Who in turn have ties to Vlast. It's complicated. No evidence Riley is aware of the it though."

"She works at the UN with a diplomat who handles international treaties. Then she's on the same ship as Roman Bocci. if you believe it's all coincidence, I got some beachfront property on the moon for sale cheap." Wyvette snorted and dug into the food again.

Sometimes the straightforward answer is the right one. She was our first suspect," Zen added.

"Granted," Imirah conceded. Her arched eyebrows pulled together as she frowned. "But you didn't find the weapon. Why didn't Abramov notice something off about their interactions?"

"The ambassador had other things on her mind. Like the escalating hostility between nations. She spent her time reading dispatches every time we passed a communications relay satellite," Zen said.

"There are all kinds of ways Riley could have ditched the murder weapon. My guess? It's pulverized in a hunk of recycled junk. On the way to being part of a building or something," Wyvette said.

"We need to corner Theodora Riley. Wyvette and I will handle her. Peter will have to stay here interviewing witnesses." Zen went to her tablet to message him.

"I'm going to hit the streets, or what passes for streets around here. I don't trust Sela Hahn. I think she's holding back," Imirah said.

"Me, too," Zen replied.

"Wyvette wiped her hands on a large wet wipe and returned to her monitor. "Sela Persson Hahn. No ties to crooks or espionage. Parents and grandparents paid for her education. Jobs with legitimate outfits. Well, what passed for legitimate with big corporations. None of them have clean hands. But nothing related to garden variety crooks."

Something pricked at the back of Zen's mind. "Persson?"

"Yeah, her maiden name. Divorced from David Hahn, a biologist on Earth, a year before she came to space. It was ugly, according to the public court records. And before you ask, he's clean as a whistle. Not even traffic violations." Wyvette leaned back in the chair.

Zen turned to Imirah. "What don't you trust about her?"

"I don't know, just a feeling in my gut. That bothers me even more. I almost always stick to logic."

"Guess it's the circuits," Wyvette quipped. She ducked when Imirah aimed a playful swat at her head.

"That feeling must be contagious. Something about her seems off to me, too. Wyvette, send Hadley a message to widen her search on Sela Hahn, including her family," Zen said.

"Her father was a successful businessman. Mother spent her time on philanthropy funded by the family fortune. When she wasn't attending fancy parties. Grandparents on both sides the same." Wyvette shrugged but turned to send a message.

"Look at the great-grandparents if you have to. Siblings, cousins. There's always more to find if you look hard. Successful business people rarely get fortunes by following all of the rules," Zen said.

"You have a cynical view. I like it." Imirah glanced at her own smartwatch. "I'm off then. Places to go, humanoids to see."

"Keep in mind they're just as corruptible," Wyvette said.

"But for right now it's the humans causing all the problems. As usual." Imirah left with that quip hanging in the air.

"Well, I can't disagree with her this time." Wyvette looked at the door as it whisked close behind Imirah.

"I'm sure you'll find a way later," Zen teased. "Okay. Theodora Riley is in the UN offices, according to the ambassador."

"She might try to disappear, at least temporarily, if she knows we're coming." Wyvette stood and grabbed her jacket. She placed the sidearm in a slim waist holster. The jacket came down long enough to conceal the compact pistol.

"I told Abramov we needed to wrap up loose ends on Bocci's background. Theodora will think we're looking at him, not *her*." Zen shrugged into her own jacket as well. "Sure you need a gun?"

"Non-lethal load, boss. Rubber bullets with a small electrical dart at the point. Enough to bring down a charging bull or a really big guy. With everything happening, I'm gonna make sure I'm prepared." Wyvette patted her hip like a gunslinger from the old American West.

"How reassuring," Zen murmured but didn't object. The battle-ready young agent had a point.

Wyvette surprised Zen by leading the way to a UTV. She'd managed to arrange access from a Space Command officer she'd befriended. With an onboard map, Wyvette drove them to the sector with a new UN center. The building had been constructed quickly once it was clear Crius was no longer a secret. The UN Secretary had insisted and the White House had acceded to the request. Quadrant Two housed most of the space station's administrative offices, including quarters for the leadership. Zen was surprised to see parents with young children.

"Guess people need the comfort of family even out here. Nature takes its course, huh?" Wyvette remarked as she gazed at them as well.

"Posted out here for years? Yeah. Guess I shouldn't be all that shocked." Zen looked around.

The administrative sector had wide corridors for streets lined with trees. Artificial sunlight came from large LED lights hidden overhead. The ceiling simulated a blue sky with puffy clouds. A digital screen flashed the time as three o'clock in the afternoon. Obviously, the leadership had put more effort into making this sector more like home. Wyvette found a parking spot a few yards from the UN office's entrance. A long digital screen displayed member nation flags above it.

"I've been itching to get behind the wheel." Wyvette sighed with satisfaction as she climbed from the driver's seat.

"And you finally got your chance." Zen left the passenger seat to join her on the pedestrian path.

"J, Officer Turner I mean, introduced me to the guy over the vehicle pool. Being taxied around is okay, but there's nothing like being in control. Nice, huh?" Wyvette looked up at two- and three-story modular structures around them.

"I think the US has more control of this space station than we've been told," Zen said quietly as people walked past.

"What makes you say so?" Wyvette continued in wonder at their surroundings.

"Look at the size of the UN building. They obviously cleared space for it to placate the UN. I think all of the international personnel in residence is a ploy. Thanks to our so-called leaders making unwise decisions, we've got gangs and two murders on our hands." Zen tugged her jacket into place. "I'm fed up with their crap to be honest. But the politicians aren't going anywhere. We'll have to keep cleaning up after them."

Wyvette grinned with the optimism and go-getter energy of youth. "On the bright side we have job security."

They went through routine security protocols in the lobby that took about five minutes. After another five-minute wait, a grey-haired man escorted them to a large second-floor office. Ambassador Abramov's office had floors that looked like polished marble. An impressive wooden desk sat in the center of a gorgeous carpet. The ambassador didn't look up from the monitor on her desk. She swiped through screens and typed on a virtual keypad. Theodora stood to her left, twisting her hands together.

"Is this Moroccan wool?" Wyvette bent down and brushed a hand over the fabric. She stood to find several sets of eyes gazing at her in puzzlement. "An academy classmate grew up in Rabat. Her dad was an importer and... Ahem, never mind."

"Synthetic from a company on Crius, but the pattern is Moroccan. You have a good eye," a man they hadn't met said. He smiled at Wyvette and then turned to Zen. "Fallon Blanc, UN Security General. I understand you have more questions for Ms. Riley."

"I don't know why. I've answered all your questions," Theodora said in a shaky voice. "I've told the ambassador and General Blanc everything. I was a fool to fall for Roman."

Ambassador Abramov pressed a button. The computer folded flat on her desk. "A poor choice of lovers is the least of my concerns right now. The Russians and the African Union are both furious with the United States. Your White House seems determined to make things worse. We haven't been this close to a major conflict between multiple nations in..."

"Since the last time a country acted in their own interest? Which would be maybe two years ago?" General Blanc waved a hand at the ambassador, who puffed up in outrage. "Sorry, Katrina. I don't mean to minimize the seriousness of what is happening on Earth. The ambassador is quite right. Ms. Riley has been reprimanded and will be dealt with once she returns."

"I accept full responsibility for my lack of judgement." Theodora dabbed at the corner of one eye and then stood straight.

"Now that you've been caught," Ambassador Abramov retorted. Her glare made Theodora go pale. Then she faced Zen. "As you Americans say, we have bigger fish to fry."

"Nobody says that anymore—" Wyvette stopped at a look from Zen. "Sorry."

Ambassador Abramov ignored the comment. "May I remind you both that we're millions of miles from Earth. Ms. Riley knows the details of all negotiations. Her input is needed. I can't simply replace her with someone else. We've spent countless hours preparing for this mission. Not to mention the long meetings with Crius leadership since we arrived."

"What the Ambassador means is we have reached a delicate stage that could turn things around. Interruptions could mean the difference between détente or shots fired," Blanc put in.

"At least six nations have weapons that could wipe out entire cities. None of them would be dumb enough to start a world war nobody could win," Wyvette said. "Which means we have time. Sorry again."

General Blanc beamed at Wyvette. "You impress me again, young lady. You're correct. But smaller actions could be taken. Actions that can disrupt multiple economies, including your own. We're more interconnected than ever, a major improvement in my opinion. But there are still those who would like to see us return to the antiquated policies of isolationism and xenophobia."

"Like the nationalists in America," Zen replied.

"Who are using Crius as a prime example of why they're right. Three US congress members are arguing their case as we speak," General Blanc said.

"Even going so far as to propose your government cut off UN funding and withdraw from space treaties in place since the nineteen seventies." Ambassador Abramov rose from her desk and came around to stand in front of Zen. "So, we need to wrap up any lingering minute details you want to question Ms. Riley about. I understand you have urgent issues at hand as well."

"The violence in Q1. And I have just gotten notice two other disturbances have broken out," General Blanc tapped his smartwatch.

"Damn it," Wyvette whispered and shot a side-eye at Zen.

"Local law enforcement is responding. I came here to investigate one murder. Now I have two," Zen replied in cool tone.

"Yes. The second one happened right under *your* noses," Ambassador Abramov clipped.

"And *your* vetted employee confessed to it. The motive? An affair *you* knew nothing about." Zen returned the ambassador's formidable gaze with one of her own.

General Blanc glanced from the ambassador to Zen. "I take it you have new information."

"I do. We will speak to Ms. Riley in another room you make available. That way you both can get on with pressing tasks," Zen said.

"I don't have anything to hide. We can talk right here." Theodora looked at her brooding boss. Then she turned to General Blanc for more sympathetic support.

"I can do without more sordid details of your love life, Theodora," the ambassador said before the general could reply. "But proceed."

"The information may be relevant to your mission," General Blanc said.

"Let's get this over with so we can focus on our priorities." Ambassador Abramov marched back to her executive chair and sat down. She gave Zen a regal wave of one hand.

Zen pushed down another tart comment for Abramov. Instead, she turned to Theodora. "Who is David Elizondo, Ms. Riley?"

"I don't... The name doesn't immediately ring a bell." Theodora's eyes narrowed for a second. Then she recovered and adopted a blank face.

"He works for a company with ties to organized crime. We found coded messages in your IP history between you. What exactly is it you do for him, or his *associates*?" Zen pressed on.

"My employment record before I was hired at the UN is spotless, as is my time here. Aside from falling in love with the wrong man, I've done nothing wrong," Theodora said, and lifted her chin to stare down Zen. Gone was the weepy jilted woman. Her stone façade dared Zen to prove her accusations.

"You rose through the ranks at the UN. That way when needed you could be called on and never be a suspect. Security checks would eliminate you. No obvious ties." Zen watched Theodora but her expression didn't change.

"This is a waste of time. You said yourself Roman died from a sonic stun device. No such thing was found in my belongings. And no, I didn't have a chance to toss it away. Your people dogged my footsteps on that ship. I admitted we argued—"

"A smooth move, confess and be ruled out," Wyvette put in. She moved closer to Theodora.

"What about the space marshal? She's trained to kill. Check into her background. She could have organized crime connections, too." Theodora's icy gaze aimed at Wyvette could have formed icicles.

"So, you admit knowing that two people who helped you get important jobs have criminal ties?" Zen said. "We have advanced tech here on Crius. We can scan your clothing for changes in the microfiber. Turns out those new devices emit tiny mineral deposits. Not from the electrical current. From the gun's metal."

"Yeah." Wyvette gave Theodora a wicked grin.

"You had motive and opportunity. Not because he was cheating on you, but because Bocci was a threat to Vlast on Crius. He was going to recognize one or more people here from his days as a prosecutor," Zen went on.

"Don't be stupid. I wouldn't risk my career, my life for a group of crooks like Vlast. You have no proof," Theodora snapped.

"An officer is scanning your living quarters right now. Maybe they'll find the device. Broken down into pieces to look like something harmless. Like a woman's shaver." Zen crossed her arms. "You're right. You didn't have a chance to dispose of the murder weapon. The flight attendant discovered Bocci dead faster than you intended. You had the cover story that he was ill, would sleep mostly on the last leg of the flight. You were counting on him being discovered once we prepared for docking."

"Which means you got your instructions at the space port before we took off," Wyvette added.

"Check the video at the space port. You'll see Roman slobbering all over some bitch with long black hair," Theodora snapped.

"Which gave you the perfect setup. Play the lovesick betrayed lover who mistakenly thinks she killed him." Zen stopped when a soft chime on her smartwatch announced a notification. "The results of our search and—"

Theodora shoved her way past General Blanc and rushed the door. Thrown off balance, the short yet compact man tumbled over a chair. He hit the floor but was on his feet seconds later. Wyvette raced after Theodora but the electronic door whisked shut, just missing her nose. Ambassador Abramov shrieked in shock. She crouched behind her desk as if expecting gunfire.

"What the hell just happened?" General Blanc shouted.

"I'll get her." Wyvette tapped the access panel next to the door, but it didn't budge. "Damn, she managed to type in a lock code on her way out."

General Blanc spun around. "Katrina, override the lock."

"Wha..." Ambassador Abramov's dyed blond curls were just visible.

"Get up, woman. The emergency security code to secure this room has been used. She's getting away."

Blanc rounded the desk and yanked Abramov to her feet. He hit the key that opened her computer. She blurted out a series of numbers and symbols. Blanc entered them on the touch screen. Wyvette shot through the door the moment it opened wide enough to get through.

"Aren't you going to follow your agent?" General Blanc pointed to the now-open door as he spoke to Zen.

"Wyvette has studied every meter of Crius. She'll know where to look. Also," Zen glanced at her smartwatch. "Ms. Riley's options are limited. It's not like she can hop on a shuttle to leave."

Before Zen could continue, a series of pops made them all jump. Ambassador Abramov went under the desk again. The general crouched but scurried to stand beside Zen. Wyvette came back huffing, her eyes bright from the chase. "Wyvette held her gun up in the classic position of cop, pointed to the ceiling.

"She's down."

Chapter 10

Three hours later Zen and Wyvette returned to the ambassador's office. Peter joined them in person, not content to listen in via video conference. General Blanc had spent the time ordering his security detail to secure every device in Theodora's office. They would scan all secure and non-secure messages she'd sent.

"I had no idea what she was up to," Ambassador Abramov asserted for the fifth time. "How could I? I don't personally do background inspections on every staff member I hire. I rely on others to do their jobs properly."

"Like the boss said, she was a carefully positioned sleeper. They didn't use her for years," Wyvette said.

Ambassador Abramov squinted at Wyvette. "Discharging a weapon inside a diplomatic building is a serious offense. I thought you people were trained to use alternative, less lethal methods."

"She's not *dead*. I just stunned her with a rubber bullet. The digital distance meter calculated she wasn't close enough for it to kill her. I mean, probably not. See—" Wyvette took out her gun to show the ambassador, who drew back from her in alarm.

"Not now, Agent Young," Peter said in a quiet aside to Wyvette. He took care to guide her hand holding the weapon back to the holster.

"No worries. The safety is on." Wyvette had the eager look of a kid with a new toy.

"We all feel much better." General Blanc gave her a quick smile and grew somber again. "Ms. Riley was close to delicate negotiations—a serious concern. To put it mildly."

"I didn't know!" Abramov slapped a hand on the smooth surface of the desk.

"Yes, Katrina," General Blanc replied. He didn't flinch when she glared at him.

"Don't patronize me, Fallon. I'm not going to be replaced with someone you prefer, so get that damn smirk off your face," the ambassador hissed. It was the first hint they weren't on good terms.

"Let's focus on the implications of Ms. Riley's infiltration, shall we?" Peter put in, his tone a smooth injection of diplomacy.

"Apart from killing Bocci, I don't think she's done much damage," General Blanc said. Then he blushed, his olive complexion tinged with pink. "That sounded more callous than I intended."

"What did she say about me?" Ambassador Abramov blurted.

Zen exchanged a glance with Peter before she turned to Abramov. "If there's something you need to tell us now is the time."

"Wha... are you implying I—" Ambassador Abramov sputtered for a few seconds before she pulled it together. She raised her chin as she looked at Zen. "I have—had—nothing to do with whatever illegal acts Theodora Riley committed."

Wyvette eyed the ambassador. "But you just asked—"

"Related to our work," Ambassador Abramov snapped with a hostile side glance at Wyvette. She faced Zen again. "I wanted to know if she confessed to revealing confidential or even classified details of my meetings."

Zen looked from the ambassador to the general. "Keep your communications strictly about negotiations related to the future of Crius."

"We don't yet know her contacts here, or who at the UN might be her backup," Peter put in.

Ambassador Abramov's face paled. "You're saying... Oh my god. They'll think I lost control of my office completely." She grabbed the edge of her desk as she walked to her chair and sat down hard. "I have to reassure them my communications are secure."

"I notified my security colleagues on Earth. They've scoured her office at UN headquarters in New York. Everyone has been cleared. Including any connections from their past," General Blanc said with a crisp nod.

"Then it seems she was a lone wolf," Peter replied.

"I would imagine getting her embedded at the UN was deemed too important to risk. The more people involved, the greater the chance for a slip." General Blanc replied. "My guess is her contact communicated with her anonymously. She doesn't know who he or she is."

"Yes. The reason a sleeper agent is effective is that you don't use her or him until absolutely needed. And maybe only once. We're still looking to find how she connected to her contact," Peter said.

Ambassador Abramov roused from her fretting silence to glare at Zen. "Agent Batiste, you said your people had found her messages or texts."

Zen gazed back at her, unbothered. "A bluff, one that worked better than expected. She was agitated, off balance because she didn't know how much we'd found out."

"Good play though, boss. She had a VPN routed through servers with links to the Darknet," Wyvette said.

"It wasn't a stretch to assume her digital tracks would be there. Most criminal activity takes place on the Darknet or Black web. Whatever they're calling it these days," Zen explained to General Blanc and Ambassador Abramov.

"You lied!" Ambassador Abramov became the picture of an outraged matron.

"Bluff, lie. Tomato, too-maa-toe." Wyvette grinned and winked.

"And the weapon she used to kill Bocci?" General Blanc asked.

"Newer weapons can be switched to look like or even be common objects. Another guess," Zen said.

The ambassador stood and strode around the desk to confront Zen. "My point, *Special Agent Batiste,* is that you don't have solid evidence that Ms. Riley has done anything wrong. You intimidated an already devastated and grieving young woman. Isolated her in a bleak room somewhere and—"

"She confessed, ambassador," Zen snapped.

Peter wore a softer "good cop" expression as he turned to Ambassador Abramov. "Two officers found the device in her apartment. She'd reassembled it as an electric toothbrush, but she had two. That was the tip-off."

"Yeah. Why would you travel with *two* toothbrushes? Nobody is that into dental hygiene," Wyvette said with a snort.

"The extra components that made it lethal were concealed in the lining of a carry-on bag," Peter continued. "Faced with knowing we'd found it and that we were tracking her on the Darknet, she talked. A little at first, but then she seemed relieved to finally tell her story. Operating in secret is immensely stressful and lonely."

"Ms. Riley actually fell in love with Bocci. Their affair was real, which definitely wasn't part of the plan. Six hours before departure, the message came through to kill him. The mob discovered Bocci was going to Crius. Too late for an experienced hitman to get to him. She was slipped the weapon at the moon spaceport. But she wasn't going to go through with it," Zen said.

"Roman Bocci must have had some kind of magic. The effect he had on women." Wyvette gave a low whistle and shook her head.

"She blurted out the truth to Bocci right before the 'other woman' showed up to see him off. Even so, she planned to forgive him. She still dreamed of a life with the man," Zen went on.

"Mr. Bocci didn't really understand what she'd told him at first. He was distracted by the rush of boarding a long space flight and intense last-minute discussions about the mission. When they did get a chance to talk alone, he was appalled. He had no intention of going along with her betrayal. In fact, he made the fatal mistake of admitting his feelings for her were less romantic... and more carnal." Peter cleared his throat and blushed.

Zen looked at the ambassador. "He was going to tell you and us about Ms. Riley's admission. She had the weapon on her. Bocci didn't get a chance to even leave his seat."

"Give the guy credit. He might have been an unfaithful serial cheater, but he was dedicated to his job and the assignment. RIP." Wyvette made a gesture as if saluting his memory.

Ambassador Abramov slumped against the desk once more. "How could she? After all I did to advance her career. I don't understand."

Wyvette shrugged. "That was kinda the point, ma'am. Get in good with those at the top and then—"

"I think she gets it," Peter broke in with a whisper.

"Oh, yeah. Right." Wyvette glanced at the Ambassador's expression of pain. "Sorry."

General Blanc gave the ambassador a less-than-sympathetic glance before he turned to Zen. "Where do we go from here?"

"Ms. Riley will remain in custody, naturally, and be sent to Earth with other suspects. A prisoner transport ship was scheduled already," Peter replied.

"We need to find out who these criminals were trying to protect on Crius. He or she could be sabotaging negotiations as we speak." General Blanc frowned as he glanced from Peter to Zen and back.

"Intelligence personnel have been informed. We can't say more right now," Zen spoke up before Peter or Wyvette replied.

General Blanc's face flushed with anger. "Are you saying agents are on Crius without my knowledge? I'm head of UN Security in space."

"Sir, you know very well that intelligence operations depend on a strict need-to-know basis to be effective. Without knowing who is involved, they needed to keep their presence under the radar. For their safety and to not further complicate the crisis." Peter delivered his speech in an even, composed voice. As he spoke the tension eased from General Blanc's face.

"I hope they get results," the general clipped, implying he'd raise hell if they didn't.

"I'm told they plan to liaison with you the moment their investigation warrants it." Peter nodded in reassurance.

"I'm well aware that covert operations are a necessary tool. I will cooperate fully, of course." General Blanc appeared mollified. He glanced at his UN colleague once more. "Cheer up, Katrina. These fine agents have rooted out the rot in your patch. That's a reason to celebrate."

"Surely you must be joking," Ambassador Abramov barked. "Or delusional."

"We can proceed without worrying about leaks. And you worked hand in hand with the OSI special agents to deal with the Riley situation," General Blanc asserted.

Abramov's scowl at him relaxed a bit as his meaning sunk in. She grabbed the bone he'd thrown her. Standing straight again, she regained some of her self-possession. "Yes indeed. In fact, it took a concerted effort to uncover a deeply concealed plot."

"Cooperation is always key from top officials," Peter added in a quiet, authoritative tone.

Wyvette turned her back away from them to face Zen. "The bullshit is getting so deep my eyes are stinging," she whispered.

"Shush." Zen put a hand over her mouth to smothered the guffaw threatening to erupt. Instead, she cleared her throat. "The important thing is we caught a killer. Now we need to figure out who's responsible for murdering Navalny."

"Yes." Peter lifted his chin and gave Zen a brief nod toward the door. "Thank you both."

"Right. We should be going. If we have any updates that affect your negotiations, I'll be in touch. Otherwise, local security is handling any criminal activities." Zen spoke in the bureaucratic tone typical of government types, one she knew would reassure Abramov at least.

General Blanc's thin lips twitched with mirth but he struck a serious pose. "Thank you, Special Agents Batiste and Navarro. And to you, young lady."

The ambassador spouted a few more face-saving ramblings as they left. Once they were outside, busy corridors prevented Peter from saying anything. Yet Zen could tell he had something on his mind. They walked to where Wyvette had parked their UTV. Peter folded his long legs to get in the small back seat. Wyvette didn't start the electric engine. Zen twisted around to face Peter.

"Okay, spit it out," Zen said.

"I didn't want to share too much in front of Abramov or Blanc. I think we have a strong lead on who killed Navalny and why," Peter said with uncharacteristic excitement in his hazel eyes. "We found his cell phone. It was concealed in a panel near his living unit. Officer Turner went into the service corridor behind the apartments and got the signal. Just in time, as it happens. The battery was only on six percent."

"Thank goodness for long-lasting charges," Wyvette said.

"Please tell me he was Theodora Riley's contact. That would tie things up nicely," Zen said.

Peter shook his head, dashing her hope. "No, but he was trying to 'negotiate' getting more lucrative cuts of black-market deals on Crius. Plus, he was trying to convince the gang leaders he should be in charge of an offshoot on a future Titan colony. The potential profit on Earth for rare minerals and more developments could be huge."

"But why would he want to stay on Titan? That's going to be a hard frontier life for a long time," Wyvette said.

"My sist—" Zen stopped and heaved a sigh. "Alex Xavier says her team has made great advancements to aid human colonization. Water production, breathable air being just two. And think about it. She's on vacation on Titan. That tells me they established a viable outpost already, with recreational opportunities."

"Yeah, this place is full of surprises. Goddard and the other big companies could have a city there already for all we know," Wyvette replied.

"Entirely in the realm of possibility. In fact, based on articles by colleagues and other professionals, I'd say in the realm of probability," Peter said with a nod.

"So, Navalny wanted to be a big wheel in his own little growing business." Zen faced forward again and gazed ahead as her thoughts spun.

"He was anticipating a growing community. Or maybe he knew about a colony on Titan," Peter said.

"No need to fight for scraps on Crius—or Earth, for that matter. Not when he could be the king of his castle on Titan. But if Goddard didn't want anyone to know…" Wyvette's voice trailed away.

"Then someone there could have killed him to keep the secret. Dr. Xavier is the head of the project," Zen murmured.

She didn't need to voice what her colleagues were thinking. Not only did Lexi, or Alex, have a huge stake in the Titan project, but she had a known propensity for violence. Heavy silence stretched for several moments. Peter and Wyvette seemed willing to let Zen process the direction the case could turn.

"Of course, Vlast leaders are known to strongly dislike having someone encroach on their territory," Peter said finally. "He played a dangerous game."

"I think he may have leveraged the situation," Zen said after a few seconds.

"How?" Peter leaned forward until he was between Zen and Wyvette.

"Once word got out about Crius, the station command knew UN control would come. I'm betting so did the gang's leadership," Zen replied.

"More eyes and ears on everything that moves on Crius," Peter added with a nod.

"Exactly. They'd scuffle to consolidate their setups, conceal and save as much as possible. Navalny used the urgency of keeping secrets to press his chance to make it big. What better place to move more operations to Titan?" Zen continued to stare at the foot traffic moving along beside them on the pedestrian walkway. But her thoughts were on Saturn's largest moon.

"Actually, quite ingenious and forward-thinking of him. He must have gotten the idea from—" Peter stopped the thought and glanced at Zen.

"My sister over pillow talk. I'm going to have a very intense talk with Dr. Xavier when she gets back." Zen turned to Peter. "Do we know when? And don't tell me you haven't thought about her as a suspect."

"Dr. Xavier has extended her stay another week at least, with approval from Goddard's Crius CEO. She can work remotely from there. A decision made in view of violence from criminals," Peter said. He shrugged when both women snorted their skepticism.

"I'll bet more of Goddard's scientific and tech R&D is on Titan than their competition knows. Wyvette, check with Space Command on shuttle traffic to the moon." Zen tapped Wyvette's arm as she spoke.

"No problem. Janine can help me get the info." Wyvette flipped her wrist and typed a text on her smartwatch.

"Goddard is the richest company on Crius. I'm guessing they're way ahead of the other two or three. In terms of development, I mean," Peter put in. He slid back from between to the two front bucket seats of the UTV.

"Goddard built the first private shuttles and long-haul space ships decades ago. How much you want to bet they've got a secret fleet of shuttles somewhere?" Zen turned to Peter again.

"If their project leaders can vacation on Titan? Yes, indeed," Peter answered. "I'm parked down the street a bit. Meet you at my office?"

"Yes. By the way, have you heard from Ewan and Imirah?" Zen frowned at the notion of the two shadowy spies on the loose.

"Ewan had to play his part at the facility maintenance department. Damages from the fight in Quadrant One and Quadrant Three. Their employees had to replace entrance panels and security passcodes on suspects' living quarters. He's been busy, but also his duties gave him an excuse to do his own searches." Peter checked messages on his smartwatch as he spoke.

"And Suri?" Zen peeked as Peter swiped.

"No idea. Space Command has the gang members ready for transport. We've gotten as much from them as is useful. See you shortly. Clive and your father want a full update." Peter patted Zen's shoulder. "Don't worry. So far, I haven't seen a direct line to Alexis."

"Yes, but signs keep pointing to her. Too many to be coincidences," Zen said quietly.

"Janine, Officer Turner is on it about private shuttle flights. Not that there's anything like traffic control," Wyvette said.

"See you in a little while." Peter left at a brisk walk.

Zen's heart thumped at the thought of Lexi. In her mind, Dr. Alexandra Xavier was still the sixteen-year-old sister she'd last seen on Earth. She could close her eyes at any given moment and see her smiling face, hear her laugh. The girl who loved playing pranks. Lexi Batiste, master of sarcasm from the time she learned to talk in sentences. The teenager who drifted closer to the edge, a line no one saw her crossing. Zen definitely didn't. Or maybe she hadn't looked close enough.

"Promise me something."

"Anything, boss," Wyvette replied promptly.

"Do your job, follow the evidence no matter what." Zen stared off into the distance. "Set me straight if I even look like I'm trying to protect her."

"Always have, always will," Wyvette said without hesitation.

"You said that fast enough. Like you've already been thinking I might choke in a pinch." Zen turned to her with a half-smile.

Wyvette met Zen's gaze without a flinch. "I can imagine how tough it is when clues keep leading to somebody you care about. Like body blows knocking the wind out of you."

Zen studied Wyvette's sober expression for a few seconds and nodded. "The truth bites hard sometimes."

"A good cop knows that the law balances evidence against circumstances. And motive. We don't know what Dr. Xavier has had to face on Crius. The rules are a hell of a lot different in space," Wyvette added.

"And you're a damn good cop, Special Agent Young." Zen's voice cracked with emotion. She squeezed Wyvette's hand and let go. "Okay. Let's see what fresh shit has hit the fan."

Twenty minutes later they arrived at Space Command headquarters. When they got to Peter's office, they found three uniformed officers with him. Officer Janine Turner was one of them. Peter spoke into his headset. From what Zen could gather, he was speaking to the colonel in command. Wyvette got into a whispered side conversation with Officer Turner. Zen divided her attention between watching Peter and Wyvette.

"Yes, sir. I should have an update for you by twenty-three hundred hours." Peter tapped the earpiece to end the call.

"Sure. We don't have to sleep," Zen murmured.

"You're right. We all need a break. But first, a briefing on what I've learned so far." Peter looked at the Space Command uniforms. "Thank you, officers. You've done excellent work."

"Sir," the two male officers aid at the same time. They took their cue to leave and strode out.

"Thank you, sir." Officer Turner stood at attention. Then she shot a side glance at Wyvette. "See ya later."

"Done." Wyvette nodded to her new pal. Then she faced Peter and Zen at attention as if waiting for marching orders.

"We should get Clive on a live satlink video call so he can get the update," Zen said.

Peter waited until the door to his office clicked shut completely. He rose from his desk and sat in the chair next to Zen. He gestured for Wyvette to join them. When she'd sank onto the nearest chair, Peter sighed.

Wyvette grimaced at his expression. "Uh-oh. Bad news coming."

"Navalny played a dangerous game. He tried to sell access to the weapon's control system to the highest bidder. He used a trojan virus to hack the mainframe," Peter said.

"He had the balls to go up against Vlast out here by himself. I'm impressed," Wyvette said. Then she blinked. "Except he's dead. So, maybe not all that impressed."

"Big risks carry a high price," Peter said with a grim smile. "He wasn't alone. Which is why that group of people was trying to get off Crius. They wanted to take the contraband, a way to finance their escape, and get away from Vlast."

"The others, still loyal to Vlast, were trying to stop them. It wasn't just a fight over smuggled goods. I knew there was more to it," Zen said.

"Scientists at Goddard and another big tech company developed a new internet dubbed the Outernet. Using space satellites. I don't know the details but—" Peter broke off when the access panel beeped. He went to his desk and unlocked the door.

Ewan strode in. His usual self-possessed façade had been replaced with a harassed scowl. "Every time I turn around another damn obstacle pops up and smacks me in the face."

"I just told them about one new wrinkle." Peter got up and poured liquid into a glass. He handed it to him. "Drink this juice. Electrolytes and protein will help."

"Thanks." Ewan gulped from the cup and marched to Peter's desk. "I need your computer with access to the system."

"Yes, sure," Peter murmured with a side-eye at Zen.

"Like we could stop him," Wyvette joked but in a whisper.

"The whole new internet, the Outernet as Peter has told you, was created inadvertently for Vlast. The Goddard and New Gen corporations thought it would be for new colonies. Vlast was using it because police and intelligence agencies now have entry to the Darkweb networks." Ewan spoke in his crisp British accent as if addressing a larger audience. His gaze and fingers never left the touch screen.

"Clive and my father need to know all this information." Zen looked at Peter. "Why did you hesitate?"

"We're not sure your father should be updated just yet..." Peter broke off. He looked at Ewan as if seeking support.

"You're implying my father isn't trustworthy? And who the hell is 'we'?" Zen snapped.

"I know he's touched a sore spot. First your sister and now Director Batiste." Lewis continued to work.

"Me? You brought it up," Peter shot back at him.

Ewan seemed satisfied with what he saw on the screen. He closed the window came around the desk. "Fine. We need straight talk."

Imirah came through when the door whisked open. "Don't bother getting pissed. I hacked your door's access ages ago."

Peter shot to his feet. "You did what?"

"Calm down. I scrambled the innards again so I'm locked out. Just now. And yes, you can get the tech guys to fix it. Weak security. I put in a report to Commander Gusev already. You're welcome." Imirah poured her own cup of water. "I take it you've told them about the Outernet, the weapon, Navalny?"

"Yes." Ewan crossed his arms and leaned against Peter's desk.

"And that you suspect my father is a traitor," Zen snapped with a scowl for everyone except Wyvette.

"Peter to introduce the topic accurately," Ewan said.

"We mean Director Batiste has his own... agenda, shall we say. On behalf of the White House. You see, the weapon and even the Outernet were part of the American government's efforts to stay ahead of Russia, China, and North Korea," Imirah put in.

"And a few other countries," Ewan said.

Imirah nodded and went on. "Our job is to keep their bumbling efforts from setting off a massive shitstorm."

Ewan stood straight, paced, and talked. "How the bloody hell did they let an international criminal organization get their hands on them..."

"Hell, they didn't even know Vlast had their tentacles in Crius," Imirah put in.

"We've kicked the biggest hornets' nest in the galaxy." Zen got up and went to the carafe. "You got any wine?"

"We all need clear heads. I'm saving the best 2056 vintage for our victory celebration." Peter looked at them all. "And no, my friends. I'm not going to tell you where I keep it."

Wyvette let out a skeptical grunt. "You definitely think the wine glass is half full."

"I have confidence in the people in this room. I've seen you all in action." Peter smiled at Wyvette.

Ewan turned to Zen. "May I speak frankly about Director Batiste without you hitting me?"

"You've been loyal and done his bidding for years. So, yeah. I'm eager to hear it."

"I respect him. However, I'm loyal to preventing bloodshed and stopping totalitarianism above all." Ewan's suave, wry-humored Brit façade had vanished.

"Sounds like Superman," Wyvette murmured.

"James sincerely believes he's doing the right thing with Crius, the weapon system, and the Outernet. He's straddling a tightrope between maintaining America's status as a power player and promoting more global collaboration. He's convinced we're at least one generation away from global governance. Until then we have to prevent any of the authoritarian governments from becoming dominant," Ewan said.

Zen rubbed her temples as a tension headache started to build. "Good God, Daddy."

Ewan shrugged. "Your father is convinced he's advancing the principles of a united Earth, one with a global governing body. As he says—"

"You have to crack eggs to make an omelet," Zen finished. "I know all his favorite archaic sayings."

"I don't think we should tell Mr. Batiste about our present situation just yet," Peter said.

"We need to secure both for UN control to make sure no one superpower has them. Then we check in." Imirah looked around at them all. Dressed head-to-toe in dark green, her stylish sweater had a hoodie. The stance made her like a comic book hero, too.

"That's how we prevent a world war," Ewan added. "Are you in?"

"You three work for the American government." Imirah tilted her head to one side.

"Not tell two powerful men, one of them our boss, what we're doing." Wyvette blew out a slow whistle.

"You've made progress on both murders, that should satisfy Clive and take some of the pressure off in terms of the international situation," Ewan put in.

"Actually, we know who killed Bocci. It was Theodora Riley after all. She's the sleeper. The plot twist is she actually fell for the guy. But I'm guessing you know already because you track us." Wyvette raised both eyebrows at Ewan and Imirah.

"I've been busy with the weapon and getting control of it," Ewan said.

"Me too. Occupied with other things," Imirah clipped. Her tone made it clear she wouldn't go into more detail.

"I take it she's been secured." Ewan looked from Peter to Zen.

"Yes," Zen said.

"We're close on Navalny, too. Manya Clarke gave me a lead. The hitwoman who took out Navalny. She botched the job because it didn't look enough like an accident. Space

Command officers are on their way to get her before Vlast can shut her up. Permanently," Peter said.

"Of course," Imirah said. "She's a liability. You don't think they can get to Ms. Clarke?"

"I doubt they care about her in the short-term. Ewan's team is keeping them busy trying to hold onto the weapon system." Peter nodded to Ewan.

"Correct. Peter told about his interrogation of Manya Clarke. She knows Vlast will get around to her eventually," Ewan said.

"Staying silent was no longer in her best interest." Peter spoke like a hard-edged intelligence interrogator.

"You made sure she knew it." Zen nodded.

"Ms. Clarke is smart. She didn't need me to spell it out or much convincing. She mostly got there on her own." Peter checked his smartwatch. "The officers have pinpointed the killer's location to Quadrant Eight."

"We can get the minor cases out of the way," Imirah said. When Zen scowled at her, Imirah blinked. "What?"

"I'm sure the victims' families wouldn't consider their deaths *minor*, Imirah," Zen replied.

"Compared to a war that could devastate major nations and push us into a dystopian nightmare. But I get your point. Now you know why I'm not a social worker." Imirah waved a hand at Zen and then turned to Ewan. "Where are we off to next?"

"We should talk to—" Ewan's next words were drowned when the intercom system went live.

The colonel's voice boomed from speakers embedded in the wall. "Officers down Quadrant Eight. All available security, move out. Special Agent Navarro, contact me ASAP."

Wyvette stood. "I want to go. I hope J. isn't hurt."

Zen placed a hand on her arm. "Let's get more information before we rush in."

Peter connected to the colonel directly via video link. The officers cornered the suspected assassin. She was armed with heavy artillery. While the colonel was talking, Peter's smartwatch ringtone sounded. A breathless voice came over the compact speaker.

"Sirs," Officer Turner said. "Two officers wounded, one fatally. Suspect cornered in a maintenance corridor. Three more suspects came at us, I guess her backup." Loud pops sounded. "Gotta go. Will report later."

Wyvette spun to face Zen. "They need all hands over there, ma'am."

"I'll go with her." Imirah pulled out a weapon from an invisible pocket.

Zen gave Imirah a nod of gratitude. She looked at Wyvette. "Call when you get onsite and give regular updates."

"Done, boss."

Wyvette hurried through the door that Peter had already opened. Imirah gave Zen a thumbs up gesture for additional reassurance and strode after her. The door whisked closed but not before they saw four uniformed officers race by. Ewan looked at his smartwatch. He read in silence for a few seconds. Then he tapped messages. Peter spoke to the colonel again. Zen watched them both, the urge for action pushing her from the chair. Before she could race off, Peter's voice stopped her.

"I have a vehicle waiting for us. Let's approach with caution. We don't need to get in the way of officers already on the scene." Peter spoke in a level tone as if he knew Zen needed a steady influence.

"Imirah knows back ways to get there, but she'll make sure they're safe." Ewan went back to Peter's computer as he spoke. "I need to continue on the weapons. Vlast is cleaning up loose ends, trying to hijack the systems, securing their control on their black-market operation."

Zen yanked the sleeve of Peter's jacket. "Let's go."

Traffic had largely been cleared by Black Rock Security. The private firm's officers stepped up to provide routine policing while Space Command handled Quadrant Eight. Though they hadn't needed to work hard. Most of the Crius residents cleared the corridors. A shelter-in-place signal had sounded moments earlier. Zen clenched her jaws for the entire ten-minute ride. She hopped from the passenger side the minute Peter stopped the UTV. Three officers with rifles stood at the wide entrance to Quadrant Eight. They nodded to Peter as he marched toward them.

"Sir, proceed to Sector A, to the left. It's cleared," the young officer said with a sharp gesture of his head.

"Thanks," Peter replied and led the way.

They had to stop and step aside as a medical team pushed a wheeled bed with deliberate speed. A female officer lay under a sheet, blood staining the shoulder of her uniform. The fabric had been cut away and a bandage applied. An IV was inserted in the back of one of her hands. Once the medics had passed, Zen outpaced Peter to get closer. Just as they entered the incident area, another man pushed a second stretcher. This one had a body bag. Peter made the sign of the cross and whispered something Zen couldn't hear. She tried not to think of having to make a next-of-kin visit to Wyvette's family on Earth. The young agent had become more than her junior colleague. Zen's heart beat hard as she searched the crowd for her. Another series of percussive pops caused the floor to vibrate beneath their feet. Zen started to race into the crowd, but Peter grabbed. He pulled her back by both shoulders. She shuddered as more shouts came from the officers beyond.

A gruff male voice came through the two-way radio of the team commander nearby.

"We got 'em, ma'am. Suspects secured. Send EMTs in."

"Acknowledged. Initiate crime scene protocols for the forensic team," the incident commander replied. She waved an okay signal at Zen and Peter.

"But where is Special Agent Young?" Zen yelled.

Before the commander could reply, Officer Turner appeared. Wyvette held onto her friend with her left arm wrapped around Officer Turner's shoulders. Officer Turner walked slowly as Wyvette limped along beside her.

Zen gasped as she watched her nightmare come true. "Oh God."

"I'm okay, boss. You should see the other guys." Wyvette laughed when Janine rolled her eyes. Then she flinched in pain, one hand on her midsection.

"I can't wait to get off of this orbiting ball of confusion." Zen held onto Peter's arm. He rubbed her shoulder to comfort her as his only response.

Chapter 11

The next five hours, Zen and Peter were content to let Space Command, Ewan, and Imirah handle things. They got reports on the scene from the team commander but would get full briefings later. The local crime scene analysis team, CSA for short, had moved in quickly to gather evidence. Wyvette went to the hospital to get checked out. Zen and Peter, both dead on their feet from going hours without sleep, retreated to their respective apartments. Zen didn't so much fall asleep as pass out on the sofa. The only item of clothing she took off were her shoes and socks. She felt like a toy with a dead battery once her body hit the soft cushions. She woke up in the middle of the night. Her digital clock glowed red numbers showing it was just after midnight, US Eastern Standard Time.

Zen showered and sank back onto the sofa. A brief text to check on Wyvette reassured her, and she went out again. Her alarm tinkled like a gentle cascade of musical notes. Slowly rousing, she sat up and rested against the cushions. An AI voice announced the time as six o'clock in the morning. Zen checked in with Wyvette once again before washing up. She was eating breakfast when her doorbell chimed. Peter's face appeared on the screen from the doorbell camera. She tapped the controls to let him in.

"Good morning. I stopped to get you a treat." Peter held up a bag. "But I see you've prepared something already."

"Instant oatmeal. Quick and filling, but not very satisfying." Zen pushed aside the half-full bowl and grimaced.

"With your permission?"

"Be my guest. I didn't even have the energy to put on coffee yet." Zen waved approval to him.

Peter smiled at her and entered the kitchen as Zen sat at the kitchen peninsula. He found the egg substitute. In minutes he'd scrambled them, toasted thick slices of French bread, and brewed café au lait. He worked as soft music played on the sound system. A news update came from the Crius radio station. Both paused at the serious male voice. He gave a summary of headlines, including the "disturbance" in Quadrant Eight.

"Jacques Clairmont with the Global Associated Press is here with us with more insight on the spike of crime."

Peter and Zen exchanged frowns as Jacques starting talking. He went into a series of theories about gang activity and why violence had occurred. All of them had to do with opposing factions being in conflict. Then he talked about criminals finding a safe haven on Crius.

"Nothing about Lexi—Dr. Xavier." Zen sighed and drank from her cup. The smooth brew soothed the tension in her throat.

"Clairmont is busy chasing the link between Crius, the murders, and international tensions," Peter replied.

"You sound sure about that."

"I've kept in touch, with help from Wyvette. I may have committed to giving him an exclusive," Peter said and seemed to brace for impact.

"May have, huh? You know damn well you did." Zen chuckled and went back to eating eggs. "Smart move. You can control what story he gets and keep him distracted from the real stuff."

"He hasn't stumbled on the big story. Offering him access to Earth's famous space super cop would be a great way to do it."

What the f—" Zen choked on a mouthful. She coughed a few times as Peter gently tapped her back. She brushed his hand away.

Peter went to the sink, found a glass, and filled it with water. He handed it to Zen. "You're still a prime story, a big 'get' they call it in press circles. Once again, you've solved murders and saved the day."

"*We* did it as a team along with Space Command," Zen protested after sipping water. She put the glass down. "Thanks for throwing me to the media wolves."

"Embrace the fame. Besides, it serves a purpose." Peter sat again and continued his breakfast. "This is tasty. I warmed up beignets, too. Life on Crius can be quite pleasant."

"Yeah, if you look past the mob fights, sex trafficking, and theft," Zen retorted.

"Which you've also played a large part in cleaning up." Peter lifted his mug of steaming coffee as if toasting her.

"You didn't." Zen gaped at him with her eyes wide. "Peter!"

"I led Clairmont where he was already going. You're making his career, Special Agent Batiste." Peter chuckled at the rude noise Zen blurted in response.

"Screw his career."

"He's willing to hold back information in exchange for talking to you and us. That's useful," Peter said. He nibbled toast and said no more.

Zen finished her breakfast. Peter had heated the plates so that the food didn't go cold. Then he served beignets sprinkled with powdered sugar from the nearby café. They ate in silence for another fifteen minutes, listening to more of a local broadcast. Finally, Peter insisted on doing the dishes. He looked at home doing house chores.

After a few minutes Zen laughed as she watched him.

"What is so amusing?" Peter glanced over his shoulder and went back to scrubbing the small skillet he'd used.

"You remind me of that old saying, 'You'll make someone a wonderful husband one day.' So domestic," Zen teased.

Peter wiped the last of the dishes dry. "My former wife would disagree. Vigorously."

"Have you been able to see your children? I'll understand if you don't want to talk about it," Zen added quickly.

"One reason I've been on the moon and touring the space stations. She's fighting visitation. You can imagine her reaction to my petition for shared custody. Why return to

Earth if I can't see my girls?" Peter blinked hard and looked away.

"Sorry to hear it."

"Now she's using my job with OSI against me. I'm in a dangerous profession that would put them at risk."

"That's bullshit. It's not like we bring suspects home with us," Zen said.

"Yes, well, she'll use any leverage now that my past isn't as potent a weapon." Peter took care arranging the dish towel on a hook. Then he sat on the stool next to Zen.

"If you need me or Clive to write a statement, just ask."

"Thanks." Peter gave her a weak smile.

Zen saw the pain beneath it. "No problem."

Peter sat straight and seemed to push aside the subject of his personal troubles. "Speaking of the cases and our boss..."

"Yes, reporting in and 'editing,' as Ewan called it, the details," Zen muttered.

They left, but not before Peter put the finishing touches on tidying up. Zen watched him with amusement. He bustled around, intent on putting things right. Then she thought how odd a working couple they had become. She'd started out despising him, thinking of Peter as a twisted monster. One who had gotten away with murder. Her hostility toward him came from thoughts about Lexi. The murder victim; the sister who turned out not to be a victim at all. Now Zen grappled with the notion of rehabilitation for people who had done the most heinous crimes. She'd recoiled at the idea of Lexi's murderer receiving what seemed a slap on the wrist. Yet Peter, for all his vices, had not killed anyone. And Lexi...

Peter's voice interrupted her musings.

"The hospital is on our way," he said. He allowed Zen to go first as they exited her apartment. "Not really, but we'll both feel better if we see Wyvette for ourselves first."

"Okay," Zen said with a short laugh.

"What?" Peter walked beside her.

"We've been spending too many hours together. We're starting to think alike." Zen shook her head.

"Please keep that view between us. I don't want Major-General Malone coming for me." Peter winced as if the idea caused him pain.

His reaction only made Zen laugh more. He glanced at her as if failing to see the humor. Peter let Zen drive, giving her updates that came on his smartwatch. For her part, Zen enjoyed maneuvering the small electric vehicle through Crius traffic more than she expected. Focusing on the controls and the surroundings served to center Zen. Her mind sorted through next steps. Peter directed her to a side corridor reserved for hospital personnel and deliveries. They arrived outside the hospital's restricted entrance. She parked in a space set aside for official vehicles.

Zen hopped out of the UTV. "Twenty dollars says she's dressed and ready to leave with us."

"That's a sucker bet. We both know Special Agent Young," Peter replied with a grin.

Following directions from the receptionist, they went to a second-floor wing. Peter nodded to the Black Rock security officer stationed near Wyvette's room. Zen and Peter exchanged a glance when they heard familiar voices.

They followed the sound to Wyvette's room. A spirited debate was ongoing.

Officer Janine Turner pointed a forefinger at Wyvette's nose. "You wait for the doctor to clear you, girl."

"I got shit to do." Wyvette winced when she lifted her right arm. She grimaced as Imirah helped her into the jacket.

"She's right. Her tests are clear; just a minor concussion and some bruising on the shoulder. I accessed the hospital system," Imirah said, lowering her voice.

Officer Turner's eyes went wide. "You hacked into confidential medical data!"

"Just Wy's, nobody else's. I'm no black hat." Imirah was impassive in the face of the young officer's outrage.

"I'm glad you're on the side of the law." Officer Turner shook her head at Imirah.

Imirah winked at her. "Most of the time."

"Anyway, a minor concussion is treated with *rest*," Officer Turner continued after a squint aimed at Imirah.

Zen entered the room. "She's right, Wyvette. You've done excellent work. We have two strong suspects. Most of the evidence has been gathered. Officers are searching the home of our new prisoner. You don't have to be at headquarters."

"I feel good except for a few twinges here and there. I heal fast. Always have," Wyvette protested. She sat in the chair with a small groan. "Ignore that."

Imirah chuckled as she put Wyvette's shoes and socks on the floor next to her. "Listen, she's dressed and ready to go. At least she can observe the interviews."

"Thank you," Wyvette mouthed with a grateful look at the spy.

Jacques Clairmont knocked once and entered the room. "Morning all."

"Hello—" Zen moved aside in surprise as he rushed over to Wyvette.

"Should you be up and leaving?" Jacques knelt next to her with a frown.

"I'm okay." Wyvette's voice wavered a bit.

She let the reporter moved closer. He embraced Wyvette gently and she sniffled. The other women moved outside into the hallway to give them privacy. Peter had gone to consult the nurses at the circular medical station for the floor.

"She almost caught a bullet last night. A couple of gang members showed up to help the suspect escape. Wyvette was standing near the service corridor where they came busting through," Officer Turner explained. "She got knocked around but she disarmed one. I took out his buddy."

Zen studied the young woman for a few seconds. "Dead?"

"Hmm." Officer Turner nodded as she looked away.

"Your first time?" Imirah let the rest of the question hang in the air between them.

"Yeah. I've had to subdue prisoners before but never... You know." Officer Turner let out a shuddering sigh.

Zen rubbed the young officer's shoulder. "You and Wyvette have earned a few days of rest."

Officer Turner squared her shoulders. She faced Zen and Imirah with a fierce gleam in her eyes. "I want the trash that caused this shitstorm in cuffs."

A woman in pale green scrubs approached. "I'm Lyla Jacobs, the nurse for this patient. We appreciate your concern for Ms. Young, but—"

"We know. Only three people allowed to visit at a time. But this is law enforcement business," Zen said.

"Keep it brief." Nurse Jacobs shot them a friendly but firm warning glance and went into the room.

They heard her fussing at Wyvette for being out of bed. Peter arrived with Wyvette's treating physician a few moments later. He confirmed what Imirah had already told them. The order for her release had been issued. The nurse hovered around Wyvette, making sure she had all she needed. Jacques insisted on carrying her bag. Her uniform was clean and pressed. Officer Turner had brought a change of clothes for her.

"Now that I know the youngster is okay, I'm off. Tell you about it later," Imirah said when Zen started to ask.

"Yeah, sure you will." Zen eyed the cagey spy. Imirah gave Wyvette a final pep talk before she left.

"Go home first," Zen said when Wyvette emerged from the hospital room with Jacques by her side.

"I'll cook your favorites." Jacques turned to Peter and Zen. "She wouldn't eat the hospital breakfast."

Wyvette scowled at Jacques. "Snitches get stitches."

Peter smiled at Wyvette. "You need a hot meal and a break."

"I slept all night," Wyvette protested. "Hospitals are creepy, but they've got good mattresses."

"Wonderful. A hearty breakfast will only strengthen your recovery." Peter looked at Zen for support.

"You already know that I agree, Wy," Zen said. She hugged Wyvette, careful not to squeeze too hard.

"Yes, ma'am." Wyvette gave a noisy sigh of resignation.

"The colonel at Space Command has set up interviews with our suspects in two hours. You can write up your statement later. There's really nothing you have to do right now. If you come to headquarters, you'll just sit around waiting," Peter said in a kindly uncle tone.

"Yes, sir." Wyvette seemed less petulant as she looked back at him.

"You've done your job. We're proud of you," Peter added.

The nurse bustled up. "I'll just get your wheelchair. We strictly follow procedure, young woman," she said before Wyvette had a chance to argue.

"Everybody ordering me around," Wyvette grumbled. Still, she allowed the nurse to hold her arm and guide her away.

"I'll meet you at the elevator," Jacques called after them. Instead of leaving, he turned to Zen and Peter. "So, who have you arrested? My sources say you have the person who killed Navalny and the perp who killed Bocci right under our noses on the ship. Any details on motives and—"

"We have two suspects in custody but at this point, we can't release any additional details because the investigation isn't complete. I'm sure Commander Gusev will release a statement shortly." Zen rattled off the officialese like a pro. She smirked when Jacques rolled his eyes.

"Seriously, Agent Batiste? You just broke two of the biggest cases ever. On Earth or in space. Don't you want to revel in another feather in your super cop hat?" Jacques held up his smartwatch to record Zen's response.

Zen's tight smile froze. "What I'd like to revel in is kicking—"

"No comment." Peter grabbed Zen's right arm, pushed past Jacques, and marched them to the stairwell. The security officer blocked Jacques from following them.

"You'll have to talk to me eventually. The UN negotiated Global Associated Press access. That's me," Jacques called after them.

"Not to this hospital they didn't. Lower your voice or you'll be removed," Nurse Jacobs clipped.

Zen gave Jacques a jaunty wave. "See ya much later."

Peter took each step beside her down the two flights until they reached the first floor. He held up a palm before opening the exit. After a quick check, he gestured for Zen to follow.

"It was the super cop wisecrack, wasn't it?" Peter said low as they passed several people in the hall.

"Yeah. And I'm tired. I want to call my kid and get solid ground beneath my feet. And I miss Malone."

"You're coming down from the adrenaline that's pushed us since we got here. I spoke to Commander Gusev. The *Phoenix* will be here in two days to take us to the moon. From there, a ship home."

"You just put a song in my heart," Zen said with a tired grin.

Peter drove them to Space Command HQ. Both noticed the curious stares they got as the UTV navigated the wide corridors. Then Peter looked overhead at the jumbo screen. News of the arrest along with a video clip of Zen scrolled by. Zen let fly a string of expletives aimed at Jacques Clairmont in particular and all news reporters in general. By the time they arrived at HQ, the result of the media release was obvious. A crowd of locals hovered around the main entrance. Peter steered the UTV down a back corridor for officers only just in time. Once he parked, they hurried into the staff entrance. Commander Gusev stood waiting for them. She was talking in a low and intense manner with the Space Command colonel as they approached. He saluted her and strode off without glancing at Peter or Zen.

"Commander, we can give you a full update shortly. First, we need to contact OSI on Earth." Zen started to say more but Commander Gusev raised a hand.

"I've spoken to Clive Anderson and Mr. Batiste. They know the pertinent details. The situation on Earth is still touchy. To say the least. Your reporter friend has been doing his job a little too well," Commander Gusev said.

Zen pushed down the tart reply that popped into her head. "Mr. Clairmont is entitled to do his job. The UN assured his press association that he could report the facts."

"Facts, not speculation and sensationalism," Commander Gusev snapped. Then she took in a deep breath and exhaled. "I'm not blaming you. I apologize. It's just..."

"I know, ma'am. Believe me," Zen said.

"And we have more problems. I need to get over to Quadrant Seven to meet with the executives of companies here. Your colleagues will fill you in." Commander Gusev gestured to her top assistant, a young woman with auburn braids and brown skin.

"I'll bring the vehicle around, ma'am." The officer saluted and hurried off.

"My colleagues?" Zen glanced sideways at Peter.

"Mr. Lewis and Ms. Suri. They're waiting in your office, Agent Navarro. I'm off to soothe rattled nerves." Commander Gusev waved to acknowledge her assistant waiting at the exit. "Fix the mess your people created."

"What—" Zen blinked rapidly. The commander was already through the door yards away. She spun to face Peter.

"I think that's our cue to see what *our colleagues* have been up to." Peter started off.

Zen followed him until they were in his office minutes later. "Well, don't mind us. Just walk here whenever," she clipped.

Ewan sat at Peter's desk swiping through screens on the monitor. Imirah was at the table staring at a tablet set up with a kickstand. They both waved without answering.

"We saw Commander Gusev on the way here. She's unhappy." Peter peeled off his jacket and hung it up. He sank into a chair across from Imirah.

"Your penchant for understatement continues to amaze," Ewan said in his best dry British accent.

"I'm going to assume she's calmed down then. We took the blast from her explosive temper for you." Imirah finishing tapping on the virtual keypad and looked up.

"Now what?" Zen heaved a sigh. She sat in the chair next to Peter at the table.

Ewan finished whatever he was doing at the computer. He closed several tabs and joined them. "Just as I was going to gain control of the weapon system *and* the new Outernet thingy, someone snatched it away."

"Oh shit. Vlast." Zen looked from Ewan to Imirah, who shook her head no.

Peter sat straight, no longer looking fatigued. "There's a third player?"

Zen also forgot to be tired. She leaned forward. "What does Sela Hahn say?"

"He can't find her." Imirah raised an arched-to-perfection eyebrow at Ewan.

"It's not that I can't... Look, with everything that's happened she's scared. Sela is probably hiding until she's sure we have Vlast under control," Ewan said.

"But that 'somewhere' is a place you can't find," Zen replied.

"Yes. I mean, for now. I've been a bit busy." Ewan rubbed his forehead. "I hope she's okay. I should have kept in touch with her. You saw how agitated she was when we talked to her."

Imirah frowned at him. "You're not her babysitter, man. She's a big girl who can take care of herself. Meanwhile, we need to follow the digital traces to figure out who we're dealing with here."

"What do her co-workers or boss say?" Zen frowned as she pondered this new development.

"She was overdue for time off, so they're not concerned. Sela sent instructions to her team members and a message to her immediate supervisor. I didn't make a big deal about it because..." Ewan shrugged.

"I don't like it." Zen looked at Imirah.

"You can comfort her later, Ewan. We've got bigger issues. Mr. Batiste and Clive know about our little hiccup. Okay, big hiccup," Imirah added when the others greeted her comment with groans.

"Worse. Somehow the UN and three governments were leaked the information. Damn reporter." Ewan slapped a fist on the solid table.

"Wasn't Clairmont. He's no expert at securing his digital devices. I hacked his smartwatch and his tablet." Imirah grinned. "I thought it would be useful. Did it on the flight over."

Peter winced. "If Clairmont finds out, if the UN—"

"He won't; they won't." Imirah looked unrepentant.

Ewan wore a grim frown. "At this point it doesn't matter. The big issue is how long it will take more nations to find out."

Zen studied him for a few seconds. "Let me guess. They'll demand that heads roll. And my father's will be the first one they want to see on a stick. A very public execution."

"Not public. Even Russia and China know better. They don't want to trigger an even bigger international crisis. Smaller countries with weapons of mass destruction might take this as a chance to leave the UN. If they do their citizens will suffer," Ewan replied.

"Not to mention the whole 'trigger a world war' thing." Imirah looked at the others with a dismal expression.

Zen took out her tablet from a padded jacket pocket. She pulled up reports from Hadley. "What are the chances Sela is behind taking over both systems? She knows about them, right?"

"She knows I was looking for something connected to Navalny. I didn't give her specifics for obvious reasons," Ewan replied.

"She knows who you are though." Zen glanced at him before scrolling through pages again.

"Sela knows that part of my job at Facility Management is securing operating systems. She knows I'm not just a desk jockey engineer. My cover is complete. Me questioning her wouldn't arouse suspicions." Ewan squinted at Zen. "What are you thinking?"

"Something about Sela Hahn..."

Zen's voice trailed off as ideas, hints, or clues slipped through her mental fingers. Shadows that vaporized when she tried to grab onto them. Imirah's practical tone cut through the haze and brought her back to the room.

"We need to find out if these murderers have information about the weapon. Vlast is willing to make the entire Earth unstable because it suits their ends." Imirah stood. "And they'll move on to whatever colonies we have in space next."

Peter stood next to her. "She's right. We have the means to cut off the head of this snake."

"A snake with tentacles. Interpol is coordinating on Earth to disrupt their money flow and black-market supply lines to space," Imirah said. "Shipments headed this way have been confiscated. Black Rock Security and Space Command officers have rounded up Vlast operatives."

"You're doing to them what they did to us. Hitting them multiple places to keep them busy protecting what they've got," Peter said.

"You got it, professor." Imirah grinned at him.

"Sela might have information we could—" Ewan stopped at a scowl from Imirah. "What?"

Imirah leaned on the table, both palms flat on its surface. "Feeling responsible for the safety of an informant is normal. But we have to focus on the bigger picture, Ewan. Think, brother."

Ewan gazed back at her for a few seconds. Then he stood and pushed the chair back with his legs. "Fine. Let's do it. Interrogate the bad guys."

Peter glanced at Zen as the two agents strode toward the door. He gestured with his head for her to hang back. "Imirah is worried Ewan got too… personal with Sela Hahn."

"Hmm. It's possible. Maybe their closeness is what keeps jabbing at me?" Zen frowned.

"What?" Peter gave her a puzzled look.

"Hey!" Imirah had returned to the open doorway, both hands on her waist. "You two must want in on this. Hell, you came millions of miles to catch these guys."

"Yeah, *what* is the trillion-dollar question," Zen muttered aside to Peter. Then she waved to Imirah. "We're right behind you."

For the next four hours they tag-teamed interrogating the suspects. Zen and Peter switched the roles of being good cop/bad cop during their interviews. Imirah had no interest in playing the sympathetic investigator. Peter paired up with Ewan at times. Zen with Imirah. Between them, they were effective at extracting enough bits and pieces to form a picture. They reconvened in the colonel's office. Commander Gusev was also present. She turned to Peter.

"Where are we then?" Commander Gusev looked at everyone around the room and back at Peter.

"They tried to claim ignorance. When we told them what we'd learned from the Outernet, both became more cooperative." Peter looked at Imirah.

"We let them believe their carelessness helped us follow a trail. Also, I may have implied their bosses knew as well." Imirah wore a fierce smile.

"And Space Command is their only way off this station and away from Vlast. Excellent strategy," Colonel Smith said.

"Thanks." Imirah affected a humble shrug that fooled no one.

"Naturally we wouldn't purposely expose them to the wrath of their employers," Peter put in with a raised eyebrow at Imirah.

"Oh, no," Imirah replied. Her denial was just as unconvincing.

Ewan turned to the colonel. "Sir, there is a young woman who was key to my investigation. At great risk to her own safety. If your officers could locate her and provide protection..."

Colonel Smith exchanged a glance with Commander Gusev before speaking. "I see. The problem is we're stretched thin."

"It's not like we can call in reinforcements, Mr. Lewis," Commander Gusev said. "We're guarding prisoners. Putting down outbreaks of violence and then there's the regular patrols. We still get calls from our public."

"I understand." Ewan nodded, but his worried frown remained.

Colonel Smith studied him for a few moments. "Officer Janine Turner took a break, well deserved I might add. I believe she's with Agent Young. I could ask her to search. She's become familiar with your investigations."

"Thank you, yes. That would be much appreciated." Ewan's frown eased a bit.

Imirah pulled Zen aside. She whispered, "I've never seen Ewan so preoccupied."

"Ewan spends a lot of time alone, working. Does he even have a personal life?" Zen whispered back.

"Don't ask *me*. I'm not his housemother." Imirah hissed out a breath. "Fine time to pick a girlfriend."

"Have a heart. I think of him as more human now." Zen shot a glance at Ewan, who did indeed look distracted despite the way he nodded as Commander Gusev talked.

"Shush." Imirah poked Zen in the side when Ewan looked their way.

Zen squinted at her. "You're the one—"

"So," Commander Gusev said and looked around at everyone. "Next steps."

For another two hours they went over plans to secure the two main murder suspects. Navalny's killer was most at risk with Vlast fearing she had the most information to share. Commander Gusev and Colonel Smith laid out their arrangements. They would be transported first. A large shuttle borrowed from Goddard Corporation would take them to Oculus, the nearest space station. From there they would go to the moon for additional interrogation and eventually to Earth. A larger star ship would take the group of rioters in a few days. Colonel Smith outlined how local security was rounding up criminal suspects on Crius.

"I can say with some confidence that we've created a fair amount of chaos for the gang." Colonel Smith broke off when his smartwatch pinged a notification. He stepped away from them. "Excuse me. I need to take this."

"We have to discuss something else," Imirah murmured. She gave the two Crius commanders a side glance.

Peter followed her gaze and turned his back to them. "What?"

Imirah studied Zen for a beat and said, "Dr. Alexandra Xavier."

"You're ignoring the instructions from senior agents to rest." Peter shook a forefinger at Wyvette.

"Instructions, not a command. The doc sent a note that light duties for the next twenty-four to thirty-six hours is okay," Wyvette pointed out.

"Drink your juice." Peter pointed to the glass he'd put before her.

"Yes, Uncle Peter," Wyvette quipped as she complied.

Wyvette and Zen were back in his office at Space Command. Ewan, still a bundle of nervous energy, had hurried back to facility management headquarters. At least that's what he told them. Imirah had worn a skeptical expression at his announcement but said nothing. She'd promised to join them after checking in with her sources. Though she didn't explain what she was checking or why.

"Where the hell is she?" Zen looked at her smartwatch. No message from Imirah. Then she glared at the door as if that would make her appear.

"It's only been thirty minutes," Peter said.

"And I don't like how Ewan is so keyed up. You think he's told us everything?" Zen drummed her fingers on the faux wood surface. Peter and Wyvette wore matching cynical expressions as their answer.

"Boss, Agent Lewis and Imirah don't give up all the facts until they absolutely have to," Wyvette said with a snort.

"Let's go over what we know about Sela Hahn again." Zen tapped the access code to open her tablet.

Peter went back to his desk when the computer chimed notifications of incoming messages. "Colonel Smith says his officers have detained ten people suspected of working with Vlast. Not full-on members, but locals recruited. Two have pretty responsible jobs."

"Okay." Zen frowned in concentration as she opened Hadley's reports.

"I'm hungry," Wyvette complained. She stood and cautiously stretched.

"I've already ordered lunch. Your favorites." Peter continued to swipe through screens of messages. "Should be here in another thirty minutes. You just had breakfast two hours ago."

"I'm still a growing girl." Wyvette went to the television and turned it on.

"No, you're a bottomless pit. You should moderate your intake while you're still young. Trust me, when you hit thirty-five eating like you do will be a problem."

Zen let their chatter about food and the news of security arrests fade into the background. Her unease that something had been missed pricked at her. Sure, they had their two suspects. Solid evidence on both meant there was little doubt of successful prosecutions. She, Peter, and Wyvette had done their jobs. Space Command and Black Rock were in charge of the prisoners. Imirah and Ewan still had their work providing intel to help mitigate the international crisis on Earth. But that wasn't her problem. In theory all Zen and her team had to do was basic paperwork. So, why was she still on edge?

"Sela Hahn briefly did some consulting work for Goddard Corporation on Earth and the Moon. She had glowing reviews. But she got turned down for a full-time position. Tried three times. Goddard HR said they didn't have openings." Zen spoke to no one in particular as she read through the summary.

"Companies always need people. Space living is tough. Even the people who stay need a break. Some folks do job shares." Wyvette found a bag of dried fruit in a cabinet. She grunted dissatisfaction but opened it anyway. Then she sat back down to work.

"Job shares?" Peter asked.

"Yep. Two people have the same job. Split the salary. One works on the moon or even Earth for six to twelve months. The other one does the job in space. Then they switch. The money is very good, especially for scientists or engineers. There's turnover though."

"Then maybe there's a reason Goddard didn't want her. Sometimes the full story is buried or left off records." Zen frowned at the report as though willing it to reveal the full picture.

"Highly paid professionals will sue if their reputations are at stake," Peter said. "When I worked as a physicist and had my... trouble, I sued one university and a private space company. We had quiet settlements. No one wants that kind of news out. Damages business and makes funding partners close up their wallets."

"So, there's a side to Sela Hahn no one wants to talk about. What if she set herself up to be Ewan's confidential informant?" Zen looked at Peter.

"You're as fixated on her as Ewan," Peter replied mildly.

"I'm telling you something is... off about her," Zen insisted.

"Your friend Chloe the hacker sent an update." Wyvette scrolled through tabs on her tablet computer.

"Chloe isn't a hacker, Wy. She's reformed since we were in college. Now she helps me once in a great while with additional research."

"Okay, boss." Wyvette's neutral tone didn't hide her sarcasm. "Anyway, I messaged her a while back like you suggested. You get a copy?"

"Let me download it. I kind of pushed it to the back of my mind. Not like we needed it once we got answers here."

Zen accessed the password-protected document. She read for a few minutes.

"Not much new. I—" Wyvette stopped to stare at Zen. "Boss, what'd you find?"

"I knew there was a detail that should have clicked, one I'd missed."

"Important for our cases." Wyvette leaned over to get a looked at Zen's screen.

Peter glanced at Zen's stunned expression. He left his desk to join them. "What is it, Zen?"

"Sela Hahn's family name." Zen looked from Wyvette to Peter and back at the screen. "She's related to Tuva Persson, one of the girls Lexi... one of the victims."

Peter's office door whisked open and Imirah strode in. "Well, Ewan can rest easy. His cutie pie is safe. "Sela Hahn took a vacay to Titan. Popular place. What did I miss?"

Zen kicked her chair back as she stood. "I'm going to Titan."

Chapter 12

Zen moved around the docking port talking to pilots and flight engineers. She'd explained the situation to Commander Gusev, Goddard's CEO, and the head of their scientific research division. With cooperation from the CEO, Zen managed to avoid revealing Alex's true identity. Both Goddard execs knew her background but not her real name. Commander Gusev and Colonel Smith seemed satisfied with Zen's explanation. Still, they had been reluctant in clearing her flight to Titan.

"You haven't had the extensive space and off-world experience that normally prepares someone. Titan is quite different from Earth's moon," Colonel Smith said.

"Let's just slow down to think about this," Ewan put in.

Peter and Wyvette had followed Zen to Quadrant One. In the past three hours Zen had had met with top Crius leaders to explain the need and urgency of her trip. Ewan, Commander Gusev, and Colonel Smith had shown up as well. Now they were in the departure lobby as the shuttle ship was being prepped. Zen was so keyed up that she didn't want to wait at her apartment.

Peter glanced at Wyvette before he spoke. She gave a slight shrug. "Zen, it will be another two hours before the ship is ready. You have to calm down. Maybe get a light meal. You haven't eaten—"

"I can't put anything on my stomach. Two hours. You know what could happen in that time?" Zen stared through a port window into space.

"Persson is a common name in Sweden. You don't know for sure there's a connection," Ewan said. He drew back when Zen whirled to face him.

"Sela's oldest sibling was almost twenty when she was born. A miracle baby, their fourth child. Sela and Tuva were like sisters because they were close in age. Sela graduated from Dalarna University. On school holidays, she and the victim would go skiing in the Swiss Alps. The family has a chalet there. Is that enough of a connection for you?" Zen snapped.

Zen laid out what she learned in the past few hours. The communications satellites between Crius and the moon were positioned to relay messages with little problem. Chloe worked her magic once she'd been pointed in the right direction.

Sela Persson Hahn had been devastated at the death of her niece. She'd relocated to Maryland after she finished her education. Yet not even Chloe had been able to dig up exactly how Sela knew Lexi was involved.

"Okay, so Sela is related to the victim. But she has no history of violence or breaking the law. Let me talk to her." Ewan rubbed a hand through his hair as he spoke.

"You're in love with her." Zen didn't pose a question. His behavior, the look on his tired face, made it plain.

Ewan glanced over his shoulder. Commander Gusev had left. Colonel Smith spoke to the two-man crew that would accompany Zen. He moved closer to her before answering. Wyvette, sharp-eyed as ever, strode over to stand next to Zen.

"What's up, boss?" Wyvette kept her gaze on Ewan.

"Okay, we have an update. Ms. Hahn hasn't reached Titan yet. She's about thirty minutes ahead of you, Agent Batiste." Colonel Smith called out the update and turned back to the flight personnel. He seemed not to notice the drama unfolding.

"Thanks," Zen replied.

"She'll listen to me," Ewan whispered.

"Good news, agent," the Space Command pilot said as he approached them along with Colonel Smith. "Goddard made its most advanced distance shuttle available. It's fitted up with the EmDrive. *Dragonfly* is a beauty. We leave in two and half hours."

"Thanks, Jeff. Proceed with your departure protocol." Colonel Smith nodded to him.

"Sir." The pilot strode away.

Colonel Smith turned to Zen. "My officer will meet Ms. Hahn's shuttle when it lands and detain her. We've tried to reach her pilot but no luck."

Officer Turner jogged over to the colonel. "Sir, I checked with the flight folks. Ms. Hahn is piloting the shuttle. She's licensed for short hops."

"So, she's ignoring communication," Colonel Smith said with a scowl.

"Not necessarily. Electromagnetic bursts can screw with transmissions," Ewan put in.

"Hmm. Either way, we intend to stop her before Agent Batiste gets there. I'll be at headquarters." Colonel Smith strode off to a UTV and drove away.

"We should stay here, Wy. The port's flight traffic crew have the best space communications on Crius. You can keep in touch with Agent Batiste better here than anywhere," Officer Turner said to Wyvette.

"Guess it'll have to do since I can't go along," Wyvette huffed in frustration.

"Peter needs you to help with our two suspects. Besides, the pilot also has security and police training." Zen rubbed her shoulder. "Next time."

"We've updated Clive. All the digital reports are done. I don't really need Wyvette here." Peter glanced at Wyvette, who beamed at him.

"We have an officer at the landing station on Titan," Zen said.

"But I know the players. You won't have to explain anything to me," Wyvette countered. "C'mon, boss."

Zen felt three sets of eyes aimed at her, waiting expectantly. Logically they were right. Still, the image of Wyvette injured stayed with her. "You're still recovering."

"Cleared medically. See?" Wyvette held up her smartwatch with the ER doctor's discharge note.

"She came prepared, ma'am," Officer Turner put in and grinned at her friend. "Rapid repair treatments work double quick on us."

Peter looked at Zen. "She means the under thirty crowd."

"I know what she means." Zen gave Peter an annoyed squint. "We're not *old*. At least I'm not. You've got a few years on me."

"Ouch." Peter wore the ghost of a smile.

Ewan looked up from checking his smartwatch. "I'm a senior intelligence officer and—"

"Don't even try it, Lewis. Your assignment is in no way linked to my... Dr. Xavier. You can't pull rank on me when it comes to domestic cases," Zen clipped.

"No messages from her?" Peter pointed to Ewan's smartwatch with a look of sympathy.

"You don't know Sela means to hurt Dr. Xavier," Ewan said, a note of desperation in his voice.

"The facts suggest otherwise. She found Lexi and tracked her to Crius. If you were thinking clear, you'd agree. You're too close to this," Zen said.

"My rapport with Sela is *exactly* why I should go."

"Rapport. So, that's what they call it these days," Wyvette muttered aside to Officer Turner.

"Did you cultivate her or was it the other way around?" Zen stared hard at Ewan until he winced.

Imirah walked over to them. She waved at several port employees. "Hey. Word is the action has moved over here. Things have settled down since we rounded up the local scum. What's going on?" She looked from Ewan to Zen.

Ewan's jaw set into a stubborn line. "I could take my own shuttle to Titan."

"Whoa, whoa, whoa." Imirah grabbed one of his muscular arms. "You've seriously gone over the line."

"Protecting informants who have risked themselves to provide us with intel is UN and Interpol policy." Ewan pulled free of Imirah's grip.

"Hahn is on her own revenge agenda that has nothing to do with our mission," Imirah replied.

"You don't know what she—"

"Do I have to remind you there's still a crisis on Earth? I have a positive development. The local humanoid community has agreed to help us secure the weapon system and the Outernet." Imirah grabbed his arm a second time and hissed when he shook her off again.

"Which means your priority is here. On Crius doing your damn job," Zen snapped. When Ewan took a step closer to her Zen didn't move or flinch.

Wyvette pulled out her small handgun but didn't aim it at Ewan. "I wouldn't make that move if I was you."

A port security officer appeared from nearby. She swung the rifle around to her chest as she studied them. "We got a problem?"

Imirah moved close to stand beside him. "Damn it, Lewis."

"I'm going to try talking Sela Hahn out of whatever she has planned. I don't want *anyone* to get hurt," Zen said in a quiet tone.

Ewan blinked a few times and then pulled one large hand over his face. He stepped back. "Just a spirited strategy discussion, officer. All good."

"Sirs." The officer tramped back to her position near the final departure gate.

"Keep me informed. Let's go." Ewan spun around and strode away without waiting for Imirah.

Officer Turner blew out a noisy breath. "Whew. Too real for a minute."

"Yeah." Wyvette secured her gun in its holster again.

"Weapon? Outernet? Why is he so keyed up?" Officer Turner whispered her questions aside to Wyvette

"Help me get ready for the flight. I'll explain later. Some of this stuff is classified, so keep it quiet." Wyvette tugged Officer Turner away by one arm.

"I'll handle Ewan, keep him occupied. We've got a lot to do," Imirah said low, looking around to make sure they were alone.

Peter turned to Imirah. "How did you convince the humanoids to get involved? They typically stick to their directives and leave politics to humans."

"They have their own reasons for jumping in. Stability on Crius is critical to them as well. That's all I can say for now," Imirah replied.

"I get the feeling the humanoids getting involved is about to be a big deal," Peter said.

Imirah maintained a neutral expression. "They have nothing to do with your immediate concern. Dr. Xavier and Sela Hahn. I'm guessing Hahn didn't just take an innocent vacation."

"She's a surviving family member of a murder victim." Peter glanced at Zen and then back to Imirah.

"Ah. The reason for Dr. Xavier's new identity. Everything is so complicated in space."

"Hmm." Peter gave a slight nod.

"Be careful, and don't let the youngster shoot anybody if you can help it." Imirah waved to them and left.

Peter watched Imirah for a few seconds before he turned back to Zen. "How are you feeling?"

"Anxious to leave. Wish I didn't have to. Angry. Frustrated." Zen let out a shout and stamped a foot to release pent-up tension. The security guard glanced their way again but kept her position.

"You'll know what to do, what to say. To both of them." Peter rested a hand on Zen's shoulder.

"I hope so."

"I have confidence you will. I've seen you work."

Zen forced a tight smile when she looked at him. "Imirah has a good point. I'll have my hands full with Wyvette. She's raring to go."

"The energy of youth," Peter replied with a chuckle. "Maybe we should take the gun from her."

"I've fought one battle today. I'm not going to tussle with Wyvette over her favorite toy. Besides, it might come in handy." Zen's expression turned sober again. "We don't know if Sela is armed."

Peter's amusement faded as he nodded. "I'm afraid it's likely that she is. It's also likely she knows we've done a more extensive background check on her."

"Hahn has been here for almost eight months. I wonder why she hasn't tried to get at Lexi before now?" Zen looked out through the port into space.

"She's been studying her, looking for the right time and place. A way to make it look like an accident." Peter followed her gaze at the darkness.

Zen grimaced at the stark yet accurate description of her sister being stalked. "Yeah."

"Let's get you ready. The chef at Space Command has the right balanced meal for a short flight. Nothing too heavy. Interesting enough, calcium-rich foods help the most instead of protein. Even with the new meds to combat bone loss." Peter continued to chatter as he shepherded Zen away from the port.

Zen allowed him to go on, aware he was trying to distract her from grim thoughts. Not that his efforts had a chance of working. They went to a small dining area at the port but Zen ate little. Peter wisely didn't push her to eat more. Instead, he went to the kitchen and returned with the food packed for their trip. Wyvette returned with Officer Turner in tow. They checked their flight suits, helmets, and other gear until it was time for the flight. Zen was happy to keep busy. Their pilot finally appeared.

"Okay, time to go. You can keep your helmets on or off. Whatever makes you comfy. I know you folks mostly keep your feet on the ground. Been out here going on six years, so I'm used to it. The ship has great life support, but hey you never know in space," the pilot said in cheerful tone.

"His pre-flight speech to passengers could use some work," Wyvette quipped.

"Space vets are used to danger." Zen gave Wyvette a good-natured nudge with one elbow. "Like you."

"Yeah, but being this far from Earth is a whole new level. Did you see the size of Saturn? I'm going to be on the surface of my second moon in a few hours." Wyvette shook her head. "Wow."

Zen looked down at the weapon Officer Turner had provided her. "Wow for sure."

Wyvette grew serious. "We're going to get there in time. Your sister will be okay. Anyway, I think she can take care of herself."

"That's what I'm afraid of," Zen whispered more to herself than to Wyvette.

They boarded the *Dragonfly* after another ten minutes of final checks. The pilot had made the trip twice before in other ships. He went through the routine of leaving the docking station with ease. Zen's jitters ramped as they left Crius behind. Captain Jeff, as they called him, turned *Dragonfly* toward Titan.

Saturn's largest moon was the only planetary satellite known to have an atmosphere. Nitrogen made up the majority of air on Titan. With the new methods of generating oxygen in situ, creating breathable environments had become easier. The final challenge was surviving the freezing temperatures. It seemed Goddard had made strides in that as well.

"Boss, we're here. Strap in." Wyvette yawned and stretched.

"Damn. I fell asleep?" Zen blinked and shook her head.

"We've been running on adrenaline for almost three weeks. No wonder with the hours we put in." Wyvette checked her gear and then examined Zen's as well.

"Any contact with Hahn or Lexi? I mean Alex. I have to remember to use her new name." Zen glanced ahead but the pilot was in the flight control cabin, door shut.

"Nah, he can't hear you. I checked in with Agent Navarro and he says no. It's good you got some rest. You okay?" Wyvette studied Zen.

"I'm good. I'm going to check in with the Space Command officer on the ground." Zen switched to cop mode as Wyvette like to call it. She needed to manage her anxiety about Alex to keep a clear head.

They landed a few hundred free from the largest outpost. A small land rover met them. Zen was in awe at the sight before them as it pulled away from the landing station. Only one inflatable pod was left. A series of tall structures rose up ahead. The buildings grew larger as they got closer to them. The airport employee steered the rover into a huge garage. The hangar door shut behind them. Then they went through several air locks. The air was cold but nothing like the minus 200 degrees of Titan's surface.

"What material are these building made of?" Wyvette turned in a circle as she looked up at thirty-foot ceilings.

"Regolith. You know, gravel and rocks on the surface. Pulverized into a kind of concrete. Though I'm no building engineer.

"Amazing." Wyvette walked off. She took off her glove and rub the surface of a wall.

"Ah, a nice cozy seventy-two." Jeff saluted the space command officer that greeted them.

"Captain, Dr. Xavier is at the Ligeia Mare settlement," the officer said.

Jeff turned to Zen and Wyvette. "Ligeia Mare is a large sea about twenty miles west of us. Lovely area, though I won't be building a beach house over there anytime soon. I'm just a poor space soldier. I hear Goddard Corporation has staked a claim out here. This is all with their big bucks."

"What about Sela Hahn?" Zen looked up at him.

"No word yet. Though she did land an hour ago. She took an EmDrive ship as well. Smaller model. Got here fast," Jeff replied and glanced at the officer.

"She'd left in a rover by the time comms cleared up. We had a dust storm that delayed messages from Crius," the officer said. "We get a few shuttles a week from the station now. So, no one would have thought it was unusual."

"Goddard has gotten a jump start on the competition when it comes to settling Titan," Wyvette said.

"Once the scientists did their work, the engineers and builders moved pretty fast," the officer agreed.

"We need to leave for Ligeia Mare," Zen said.

"Lucky for you the surface is pretty calm most of the time. But it's still hazy from the dust," Jeff said.

"Sir, Ms. Hahn signed up to catch the bus to Ligeia Settlement," the officer said to Jeff.

"Thanks. Stand by in case we need you," Jeff replied. He faced Zen again when the officer left them.

"You mean they even got busses out here? Damn!" Wyvette shook her head.

"That's just what they call a multi-passenger rover. But yeah, Goddard is making Titan livable. Not a lot of people here yet though. Mostly scientists and engineers. I'd say no more than two hundred and fifty or maybe three hundred folks between both settlements," Jeff said.

"But Space Command officers are assigned here," Zen said.

"Commander Gusev sent four a few weeks ago. What with the problems on Crius. Three here and one at Utopia, that's the official name of the settlement near Ligeia Mare. Some Goddard executive's lame sense of humor."

"So, how will we get there since the bus has left," Wyvette put in.

"No worries. Six big rovers are available. I checked after we landed."

Twenty-five minutes later they were in the big rover rolling over the bumpy Titan landscape. Zen had to work on being patient. Traveling alien worlds wasn't like an Earth car trip. Leaving the settlement meant double checking mechanical and life support systems. Jumping into a vehicle without preparation wasn't just unwise, it could prove fatal. Wyvette took over checking in with the second officer at Utopia. A female voice came over the two-way radio they'd been provided. Sela Hahn had arrived with five other passengers. She'd had to be checked in as a visitor.

Wyvette leaned close to Zen and lowered her voice. "You think she has an idea someone followed her?"

"I'm not sure. Imirah said Sela didn't give the flight crew or anyone on Crius the impression she was in a hurry. Our investigations on Crius probably pushed her to act faster than planned," Zen replied.

"We've been on Earth's moon for a minute. I mean, it's risky but kinda day to day routine now. But a Titan colony with different conditions? Colonists are beta testers so to speak," Wyvette whispered.

Zen nodded and followed her line of reasoning. "With no one connecting her to Alex, an 'accident' wouldn't arouse suspicion. We might have the element of surprise on our side."

"But if she knows you're Dr. Xavier's sister..." Wyvette looked a Zen with a scowl.

"Yes. We have to move quick but with extra caution." Zen wore a matching frown at the dangers ahead.

"What did we tell Jeff and the local officers?"

"Something close to the truth. That Hahn has a grudge against Alex from a past conflict and it escalated. We said it was related to recent events on Crius."

"Kinda vague. Wonder if they bought it?"

"Doesn't matter. Just as long as they follow orders and provide backup." Zen touched the weapon in her shoulder holster.

Wyvette looked out of the rover's side window. "Yeah. Like most cops they'll do their job. Even if they know there's more to it than they've been told."

"Most important is we told them Hahn could be armed," Zen replied. "Maybe she'll realize her plan is no good. Come quietly."

Wyvette snorted. "Yeah, right. She's crossed the galaxy for payback. Not likely."

Zen jabbed Wyvette in the ribs. "Thanks for the positive vibes."

They grinned at each other and then turned at the same time to watch the passing landscape. The surface of Titan seemed like it had been brushed with neutral watercolor paint. Tans, grays, but mostly dusty reds. Pebbles littered the ground as the rover bumped along. What made them both gasp was Saturn on the horizon. The gas giant with spectacular rings dominated the eastern sky.

"Never gets old." Jeff grinned at them. Then he went back to concentrating on driving.

A few boulders appeared, causing Jeff to steer around them. He explained the dust storms didn't happen often on Titan. That the most recent one was their bad luck. Zen tried not to take it as a sign of things to come.

"There she is. Utopia." Jeff pointed through the wide windshield. "Buckle up for a surprise."

Before they could ask him questions, the comm system in the rover beeped. Jeff answered the call, a transmission from Utopia. The entry station confirmed their arrival. A voice chatted with Jeff in a familiar way about conditions at the colony. Jeff drove to one of three doors at least twenty meters across. Each had a number above it. He explained that large equipment could be brought in via these doors. The first section was an airlock. They waited five minutes. A series of vents hissed air while fans pulled out dust. Only then did a second door roll up with a rumble. A woman used a light wand to direct Jeff to a parking lane. She wore a life support helmet but the glass shield was flipped up. The process reminded Zen of landing at an airport on Earth.

"What up, Jeff? Didn't expect to see you so soon." The woman popped a mint in her mouth. She eyed Zen and Wyvette with frank curiosity.

"Yeah, station biz never stops. The big companies are hot to suck profits from this place," Jeff called back with good-nature.

"And we'll never see any of it. Let's have a drink if ya got time." She winked at him with a grin.

"We'll see. Lots to do." Jeff waved at her. He watched her stroll off to another vehicle bay. "Rumors about you being here have started."

"How can you tell?" Wyvette followed his gaze to study the employee.

"She's hoping to finesse some gossip from me over bourbon," Jeff quipped. "C'mon. Let's check in and get this party started."

Wyvette exchanged a glance with Zen before they trailed behind him. Doors slid open automatically as they approached. Zen gaped at the scene before them. People milled around as if it was a shopping mall. She immediately realized most of them were humanoids. They had the distinctive smooth skin created to make them look more human.

"Mostly manned by robots?" Wyvette blurted out. She looked around with wide eyes.

"Some hybrids. Worker bees I call 'em. The scientists are all human though. Oh, and watch the language. We don't say words like bot to refer to them. Considered offensive to this new breed of fancy walking AIs. Times have changed, huh?" Jeff did a subtle nod toward the crowd.

"You're right. I didn't think," Wyvette replied.

"Hey, don't apologize to me. I'm with the crowd that thinks the use of robots will bite us one day. I've read *Rise of the Machines.*" Jeff grunted as he led them through the crowd.

"Isn't that the racist, anti-tech book nationalist crazies use as almost a bible?" Wyvette whispered aside to Zen.

Zen nodded, still looking around. "Hmm. If you consider humanoids a new race, yeah. I don't think the secret colony on Earth's moon reassure folks like Jeff."

They walked on, increasing their pace to catch up to Jeff. He seemed confident they would follow because he didn't glance back. He led them to the security station. Space Command and Black Rock officers manned the only police-type presence at Utopia. Jeff introduced them to the local officer. She gave them directions to the sector where Sela was last seen.

"Dr. Xavier is at the Tethys camp closer to one of the small rivers that feed into Ligeia Mar. I don't think Ms. Hahn left town though," the young woman said. She nodded to Wyvette. "You were LMPD back on the moon. I trained there."

"One of the cadets. A lot of them came through. Did we meet?" Wyvette shook hands with her.

"Nah. You spoke to our class a few times though." The woman seemed more comfortable seeing a familiar face. "So, is Hahn dangerous?"

"We honestly don't know, officer. But we should be prepared," Zen said.

"Lucky for you Utopia is quiet for the most part. Now, with extra boots on the ground, we got you covered," the officered replied.

"So, you won't be spread thin?" Zen glanced around. A few civilian employees bustled around performing tasks.

"Not at all. I sent the officers out to the general area where Ms. Hahn should be. She hasn't checked out a vehicle or life support gear."

"Pull them back."

"Ma'am?" The officer blinked at her with a surprised expression.

"I don't want her to see officers and know we're looking for her. It might push her to do something desperate," Zen said.

"If you say so..." The young officer tapped the Bluetooth headset in her ear. She moved aside and quietly talked to her fellow officers.

"We have to assume that Sela already knows Alex hasn't returned to Utopia. My guess is she's arranging a discreet way to reach her." Zen nodded when the officer gestured confirmation her instructions had been followed.

"Leaving Utopia isn't a big deal. I mean, she could hitch a ride with just about anybody going out," Jeff put in. "Folks go out to the camps all the time."

"I didn't realize the colonies had developed this much." Zen frowned and turned in a circle. "Could there be more people here than you think?"

Jeff frowned in a thought for a few seconds. "Possible. One of the big rival companies might have settlements, too. It's not like they have to get permission from Crius Space Command. Or anybody for that matter."

"NASA and the UN have been more focused on the science. They've left the business side to private companies," Wyvette said.

"We have to move fast. Get to Sela before she leaves. Jeff, get us a vehicle and—"

The Utopia officer strode over to them. "Ma'am, no need. One of the officers talked to a surface hiking outfit. Ms. Hahn tagged along with some guys going out to kayak."

"Shit," Wyvette hissed. "We gotta climb into suits and go after her."

"It's not bad with the new lightweight gear. I'm more worried about civilians getting hurt," the officer said.

"We best get moving," Jeff said. "I'll get the rover ready. Meet me back at the entry sector."

"Ten minutes," Zen called after him as he strode away.

"Our helmets will help you move faster. The air system converts the hydrogen of Titan's atmosphere to generate oxygen. Of course, the humanoids and even some of the hybrids don't need to breathe. That's the big advantage they have."

"They built Utopia and the main colony, right?" Wyvette asked.

"Yep. Hey, I didn't mention it in front of Jeff, but three of our officers are locals. Humanoids trained in policing. What with how he feels..." The young officer shrugged and heaved a sigh. "Some of the older space folks are still back in the last century."

"Yeah." Wyvette pulled Zen aside when the officer walked away. "Maybe we should leave Jeff behind. Be easier if it's just us. It's a straight shot to Tethys. I can drive a rover."

"You're worried his attitude will be a liability." Zen glanced over her shoulder in the direction Jeff had gone.

"I bet that's why he isn't sent to Utopia more often. Goddard doesn't want the blow-back from folks on Earth who think like him." Wyvette broke off when the young officer returned carrying equipment.

"Here you go." She nodded and stepped away as if acknowledging they wanted privacy to talk.

"Thanks." Wyvette smiled and then turned her back to whisper. "Plus, you don't want chatter about Dr. Xavier's identity getting back. Jeff doesn't impress me a guy who can keep his mouth shut."

"It won't matter if she's dead, Wy. We need to go." Zen accepted a life support pack adapted for Titan's atmosphere.

The officer walked over to them again. "Your heat pack is the most important next to the oxygenator. I have a two-seater rover with everything you need. Just saying."

Wyvette turned to Zen. "Well?"

Zen hesitated only a moment. She turned to the officer and nodded. Then she radioed Jeff through her headset to tell him the change in plans. He debated with Zen for a few minutes before yielding to her authority. Wyvette, fully outfitted, waved her readiness a few yards away. Zen never stopped moving during her brief talk with Jeff. True to her word, the officer got them to the nearest vehicle pool. Fifteen minutes later they were cruising toward Tethys. The outpost wasn't the small, crude tent Zen had imagined. A large cream-colored geo-dome grew larger as they traveled the six kilometers to it. Two smaller domes sat to the side on the dirt road along the way.

"Emergency stops outfitted with life support, first aid kits, and food. In case of dust storms," Wyvette said. "Akon, Akon Mehmood, the officer we were talking to? She told me about them as I got ready."

"You make friends quick." Zen glanced at her sideways and then at her tablet.

"Got to out here. Loners don't do well in space. What are you reading?"

"I've been thinking. Why was Navalny doing work that day? The local report says he got a last-minute work order."

"Part of his regular duties. Everybody said he liked extra orders. More money."

"Look." Zen held up her small tablet. "He was off that day. Which meant double pay for the hours he'd put in. Someone knew he loved money. That he would respond. I wonder..." The rover hit a dip and Zen almost dropped the tablet.

"Sorry, boss. Tried to miss that pothole." Wyvette steered around a small boulder.

"No worries. I—" Zen gasped. "Shit, shit, shit! She felt wrong the whole time."

"What is it?" Wyvette looked from the road to Zen several times.

"Sela Hahn set up Navalny. Damn it." Zen stared at the tablet and shook her head.

"But why? Based on Ms. Hadley's report, we know she's not a member of Vlast. Zero connections to any crime syndicate that does business with them," Wyvette said.

Zen scrolled through more pages looking for answers. She hissed out more expletives when she found none. "I don't know."

They drove on in silence, both thinking over what they knew about the case. A trip that would have taken minutes on Earth took longer on Titan. The thick atmosphere meant slower progress traveling. Something extreme sports enthusiast relished. Likewise, kayaking required special boats with small engines. Pushing through liquid methane required more than arm power. Not to mention the lake being poisonous to humans.

"We're here," Wyvette said. She pulled the rover close an entrance.

"First, we have to get Sela away from Lexi."

Zen stepped down to the surface of Titan from the rover. She had no time to savor the experience. Her heart thumped at the thought that they might be too late. As they entered the geodome airlock anteroom, a hissing sound greeted them. Two minutes ticked by before a green light flashed that the air was safe. Wyvette and Zen entered the dome. People milled around laughing and talking.

"Well, doesn't look like anything has happened. That's good news. Officer Mehmood said there's a popular café over..." Wyvette consulted a nearby colorful map. "That way."

Zen and Wyvette scanned the crowd from different angles. Dressed in dusty camouflage that matched Titan's colors, they talked excitedly about their adventures. Zen spotted Lexi's familiar gait fifty feet away across from the café. Lexi put on her helmet and stepped through a door.

Another person, also dressed like an adventure tourist, followed her a few moments later.

"Wyvette, there. Move!" Zen raced to catch up to Lexi and her stalker. People moved out of their way, looking at them in surprise.

"Boss, wait," Wyvette yelled.

Zen increased her speed to a dead run. She shoved her way between two women, ignoring a blonde's angry yelp. Ahead, a sliding door had a sports company logo on it. A tall man blocked Zen's path. She slid to a stop.

"Move!" Zen started to push past him when he grabbed her.

"Hey, boss, don't." Wyvette grabbed her arm just as Zen drew back to punch the guy.

He let go of Zen and scuttled away, both palms up. "I'm trying to save your life, lady. This exit goes straight to outside with no breathable atmosphere. At least not for real people."

"Two women just left. Which way did they go?" Wyvette asked as Zen hurried to look out of a window of thick glass.

"Down to one of the docks. Or to a popular hiking path. Could be either one," the man said. Then he paused. "Though I think the one chick might go parasailing. Hey, you need to buy a ticket. This ain't no free—"

"Police business. Stop us and get arrested," Wyvette snapped.

The man scowled at them both. He grumbled as he watched them snap their helmets in place. He offered no help as they hurriedly checked their power packs. Seconds later they entered the lock. Air hissed to seal the anteroom.

Then a light flashed "Go!" in bright colors matching the sports company logo. Beyond the second exit, a smooth path had been created. Distance markers showed how many meters led to the lake. Another sign pointed to the parasailing station. Zen was about to turn left to follow it when Wyvette pulled at her. She pointed. Two figures stood on the lake shore.

"I'll follow these tourists, blend in and approach from there," Wyvette said. She fell in step with a group of four.

Zen nodded, her heart thumping. She headed toward Sela and Lexi.

Chapter 13

Zen pushed through Titan's heavy air. Each step felt as if ten-pound weights were strapped to her feet. Still, her physical training kicked in. Her body adjusted, aided by the lighter equipment the young officer had provided. She searched the three frequencies on the headset's communication channels. She whispered a prayer that she'd get Lexi first.

"Can you hear me?" Zen whispered, as if that might help.

Sela Hahn answered instead. "You're annoyingly clever, Special Agent Batiste. So, you figured out who she is and who I am. Correct?"

"Think about what you're doing, Sela. How will going to prison help your family?" Zen shot a glance to her left without moving her head. She didn't want to draw attention to Wyvette.

"Tell me her name. Her *real* name. I deserve to know." Sela's tone matched the freezing Titan temperature.

"What?" Zen stopped about ten feet from the two women.

"I have to give the Lodestone Project credit. Even I couldn't dig up her true identity. Though the records did verify she was a student with my niece. I didn't find her old identity, but I learned the new one." Sela backed away enough that she could watch Zen and Lexi.

Zen heaved out air. "Then you know there wasn't solid evidence against Dr. Xavier."

Sela let out a dry laugh empty of humor. "Two students are killed. A year of investigation. Their classmate, a brilliant young woman, goes through treatment reserved for criminals and then disappears off the face of the Earth. Literally. You really underestimate me, Special Agent Batiste."

Zen took a step toward Sela but stopped when she fired the gun, the report muffled in Titan's thick atmosphere. A burst of dust went up near Alex's left foot. The tourists near Wyvette didn't seem to notice anything unusual.

"The justice system—"

"In America is corrupt. She obviously comes from a powerful family. And they've sent *you* to protect her." Sela's thin lips curled up in contempt when she glanced at Zen.

"You would know about corruption," Alex said. "Your entire family has profited off misery for generations. Your precious Tuva thought she could steal my work."

"Arrogant to the end," Sela snapped.

"Her sense of entitlement was off the charts. Katrin thought she could take whatever she wanted," Alex went on.

"Lexi..." Zen shook her head.

"What? Don't tell the truth? She raped a fellow student. Got her high on a designer drug. I walked in on Tuva with her hand down the girl's—"

Sela fired another shot. Alex grunted and grabbed her right thigh. Zen cried out at the grimace of agony on Alex's face. Sela smiled at them both. A movement to west of their position distracted Sela. Zen trudged closer to Alex, pushing hard with each step. Before she could reach her, Sela fired another shot.

"Move again and I'll kill her and then you," Sela shouted.

"Tuva's parents went along with a quiet investigation and my treatment. Mostly because..." Alex panted for a few seconds.

"Deep breaths. Let me patch the tear." Zen fumbled with the small pocket. Each suit contained an emergency repair kit.

Alex waved her away and stood straight despite obvious pain. "Because there wasn't enough evidence. And they didn't want the truth to come out about their little darling."

"Shut your filthy lying mouth," Sela screamed and aimed again. A shot rang out, but not from her. A burst of rocks sprayed Sela's suit, which caused her to stagger for a moment.

"You can't kill us and get away with it. Witnesses." Zen worked to keep her voice calm. She jerked her head to the west. Wyvette, carrying a short rifle, stopped walking forward when Sela turned to look at her.

"She's still far enough away." Sela sounded less confident. Her gaze flickered between Wyvette, Zen, and Alex.

"Stop and think, Sela. Dr. Xavier is banished from Earth. Her entire life wiped clean. She's lost her family, even most of her memories." Zen pointed to Alex.

"Bullshit. She's having a grand old time. Screwing around, getting high praise for her 'groundbreaking innovations.' Don't waste time trying to sell her new life as *punishment*," Sela hissed.

"You can't escape." Zen broke off when Alex groaned and clutched her leg. "We can still fix this. Dr. Xavier needs medical attention."

"Get away from her or I'll shoot again." Sela pointed the weapon at Zen. She glanced at Wyvette and used her free hand to warn her off. Wyvette froze.

"Forget trying to reason with her, sis. She's a psycho, like crazy Tuva," Alex said through gritted teeth.

Sela looked from Alex to Zen. "Sisters?"

"Sela, calm down." Zen looked held out both palms.

"I should have known," Sela shouted.

"Listen, it's not what you think." Zen tried a calm, reasoning tone but Sela's tirade drowned her out.

"You helped her run, spread ugly lies about Tuva." Sela's voice grew strangled with rage as she walked toward Zen. "And then you came here to *save* her, pretending to investigate a crime."

Before Zen or Wyvette could make another move, a gust of wind blew them almost off their feet. Still at least twenty yards away, Wyvette struggled to wipe her faceplate clean so she could see. Then rain, liquid methane and hydrogen, pattered down. Alex yelped and staggered. She almost went to one knee but managed to recover her footing. Another blast of cold air pushed Zen away from the two women. Sela alone seemed unaffected.

"I've been coming to Titan for months now. This is nothing to me." Sela let out a cackle.

She rushed Alex, forcing her onto the short dock built to launch kayaks. Zen's head filled with the chatter of voices. Wyvette and Officer Mehmood engaged in a rapid-fire exchange. All of it came through as garbled noise. Zen watched in horror as Sela reached to shove Alex into the lake. Freezing liquid methane would kill Alex. A saturated suit wouldn't protect her for long. Another shot rang out and Sela jerked around. In that second of distraction, Alex rose to her feet in a smooth movement.

"Thanks for coming to my little party," Alex said.

She knocked Sela's weapon arm aside. The shot went wild into the lake surface. Then Alex slammed a fist into Sela's abdomen. When Sela doubled over, Alex delivered a solid blow with one foot to Sela's left knee. Sela screamed and tried to recover, but Alex held a camping knife to her throat, one hand ready to rip through her life support unit.

"Since you like the lake so much, I'll let you take a dip. Don't struggle. You'll contribute to valuable research. I'll write a paper about the effects of liquid methane on the human body." Alex's voice sounded composed despite her labored breathing. "Don't struggle, dear. You see, I've been training for this day, too."

"Lexi, listen to me..." Zen cursed at the Titan weather.

"Boss, the rain will be over soon." Wyvette's voice crackled over a different frequency.

"Yes, ma'am. We're close." Officer Mehmood was several yards beyond Wyvette.

"No, stay clear. Both of you." Zen turned her attention back to Alex.

"Now you're going to explain that killing her will destroy my new life." Alex tightened her grip on Sela when she struggled. Then she rested her helmet against Sela's. "I'll yank the capacitator if you don't keep still."

"Lexi—"

"My name is Dr. Alexandra Xavier, Special Agent Batiste. You know what's funny? You didn't mess up Sela's plan. You messed up *mine*." Alex gasped as she forced Sela to turn in a circle to face Zen.

"Your plan?" Zen felt a chill go through her that didn't come from Titan's weather. The ice in Alex's tone scared her more than any danger from the lake.

"You wrapped up your cases. I knew you would. I also knew Sela would use the distraction to cause my 'accidental' death. Catching me out here with few witnesses would be too good for her to resist. I just didn't think you'd catch on to who she was, what with so much on your plate. No wonder you're famous." Alex looked at Sela and back to Zen.

"Sela was close to her niece—"

"Like sisters. I know. I'm just as good as getting information as OSI. Hey, in another life we could have been working together." For a moment, Alex's callous expression softened. "Remember our tree house days?"

"Yes. And all the things Daddy did for us. Then you understand grief is driving her irrational behavior. Look, you've won. She'll face disgrace, prosecution. While you can continue your work," Zen said.

"You can't be naïve, Special Agent Batiste." Alex let out a sigh as if disappointed in Zen.

"I know you're angry she attacked you, but killing her—"

"This isn't about me. This is for Mika." Alex spat out the name, anger in her tone for the first time.

"What..." Zen's mind spun as she fought to catch her breath. "Navalny?"

"She put in the work order luring him to the quadrant.

"I don't... How would..." Zen stared at her sister for a few seconds.

"We were supposed to spend the day together. I got called to work last minute, too. Mika never could resist double overtime pay. A perfect cover. The hitter wouldn't leave me as a witness. Something Sela knew. Vlast would think I was acceptable collateral damage. Like Mika was acceptable collateral damage for *you*. Right, Dr. Persson-Hahn?" Alex slapped the side of Sela's helmet.

"I don't care about what happens to me. Not if you die, bitch!" Sela shouted and twisted in Alex's grip.

Sela used one hand to grab at Alex's helmet. Then she raked her gloved hand over the ceramic headpiece toward Alex's life support connections. They both stumbled until they plunged off the dock. Liquid push up in a thick splatter that surrounded both figures. Zen raced forward against the restraint of the suit and atmosphere. Hands grabbed her before she jumped in after them. Wyvette yelled at Zen. Her voice penetrated the helmet's face plate and rang through the comm speaker.

"Let them do it!" Wyvette pointed up.

A hover craft hummed as it glided overhead. Seconds later it eased down to rest on the surface. Two figures emerged. Using what looked like grappling hooks, they threw one at a time. Alex grabbed on but slipped backward.

A figure managed to clutch her outstretched hand. Only the top of Sela's helmet appeared, bobbing like a small buoy. A second rescuer pulled Sela's limp body from the lake. The hover craft then lifted up. Moments later it landed near a large rover with a giant red cross painted on the side.

"Ma'am, I alerted the team of a possible medical emergency," Officer Mehmood panted.

Zen made her way over to where Alex had been placed on a floating stretcher. "Is she..."

"Breathing? Yeah, but we gotta move. The other one is worse off. Got a leak in her helmet or suit somehow. Crazy tourists. Gotta get these two in the rover." The EMT pushed Zen aside without ceremony and helped his colleague. They worked to seal the breaks in Sela's suit. Then they hooked her up to oxygen through a tube.

Zen crouched next to the stretcher. "Le... Alex, you're going to be okay."

"I died once. Doing it again will be a breeze," Alex croaked, forcing a cheeky grin. Then she shuddered hard until the stretcher shook.

"We're on the move," the EMT said.

Zen stood and stepped clear. Both electric stretchers rose. They slid smoothly into place onto a platform of the ambulance rover.

"She's gonna be okay, ma'am." Wyvette placed a gloved hand on Zen's shoulder.

"Yeah. Dr. Alexandra Xavier is a survivor. With killer instincts." Zen watched the ambulance roll away at top speed.

Three hours later, Zen, Wyvette, and Officer Mehmood sat in the waiting room of Utopia's medical unit. Three doctors, one a frostbite specialist, worked on both patients. Nurses scurried back and forth to help with dressings and IVs. Opaque partitions prevented them from seeing into the actual treatment rooms.

Jeff strode in and clapped his hands together. "I outfitted a cabin to hold the prisoners. Not that we need to worry since they're both banged up. That's if they survive."

"We got a great medical team, ma'am. Have to with all the ways you can die out here. Not to mention extreme sports tourists taking dumb chances." Officer Mehmood spoke in a reassuring tone. She glared a mean looked at the older officer.

"Hey, falling in a liquid methane lake is no joke. Freeze human flesh like that," Jeff snapped his fingers. "The suits give you some protection but..."

"Everything good for the trip back to Crius then?" Wyvette cut in.

"Oh, yeah. Solid. Hey." Jeff lowered his voice, glanced around, and leaned forward toward the three women. "Those docs are humanoids. Hope they don't have a glitch or something."

"Humanoids are statistically less likely to make a medical error. And they do better in hostile alien environments," Officer Mehmood snapped.

Jeff's eyes narrowed as he stared at her. "Is that so? Look who's been cozying up to bots. Best remember I'm your senior officer, lady."

Wyvette stood and stepped between them. "OSI is lead on all law enforcement actions, *Officer Kingston*. Officer Mehmood was instrumental in apprehending the two subjects and saving lives."

"I would have been, but she sent me off to do errands." Jeff stabbed a thick forefinger at Zen.

Zen only heard their exchange as background buzz. She couldn't take her eyes off silhouettes moving behind the partitions. Wyvette placed a hand on Zen's shoulder after she sat next to her. It took ten seconds for Zen to register Wyvette's effort to get her attention.

"Ma'am, Akon is going to supervise the other officers, securing their suits," Wyvette said low.

"What?" Zen massaged her forehead as if to clear her mind.

"Forensic evidence. We need to tag everything. Insure chain of custody."

"Right. Go with her." Zen glanced at Jeff. He stood away from Officer Mehmood, arms crossed in a defensive posture.

"I should stay with you in case..."

"In case the doctors come out with bad news? I'm good, Wy. Your new friend will need backup in case she's challenged."

Wyvette followed Zen's gaze to Jeff. She grimaced. "Yeah. He's going to make trouble for Akon, I bet."

"Go on. Getting everything tagged and bagged is important," Zen replied. "Imagine how bummed he's going to be once he realizes her fellow officers are humanoids."

"And to think he thought he was hot. For an old guy, I mean."

"Get out of here and get to work, youngster." Zen playfully swatted her on the forearm.

"Yes, boss. For real though, Akon says they have the most advanced treatment here."

"I know. I can handle whatever happens." Zen smiled at Wyvette and sat straight. The young woman wouldn't follow the order to leave if Zen looked fragile.

Wyvette turned to look at Jeff. With a sigh, she strode over to stand in the space between him and Officer Mehmood. Zen watched Wyvette take charge with confidence. Wyvette gave Zen a parting wave before all three left. Assured things were in hand, Zen turned back to the treatment area again. Moments later, she stood when a tall doctor walked out of one room. He spoke briefly to a male nurse before heading for the waiting area.

The doctor nodded to her. "Special agent. In lieu of family, I'm told you can receive updates on the two patients. I'm Doctor Lemma."

Zen resisted the urge to identify herself as Alex's sister. "I, um, that's right, doctor. What is Dr. Xavier's status?"

"Freeze burns on both legs. We wrapped her in a medical warming blanket. Fortunately, her suit didn't have major damage. Thanks to self-repair xenbots in the fabric. We've developed topical meds that heal *homo sapiens* flesh quickly."

Dr. Lemma had ice-blue eyes and blond hair. He looked like an early model humanoid.

"Is she conscious?" Zen looked past him briefly and back at his pale face.

"You mean for questioning, I suppose." Dr. Lemma shrugged, which made him look very human. "You can talk to her, but not for too long. No interrogation to stress her. It inhibits healing. Stress, not questions."

"Sure." Zen started off but his voice stopped her.

"You haven't asked about the other patient."

Zen blushed at her oversight. All she'd been able to think about was the dread of telling her parents Lexi was really dead. "Oh, right. Of course. Ms. Hahn. How is she?"

"Her life support connections were pulled loose. One section of her suit was ripped. A clean cut. Didn't the first reports say she accidently fell into Ligeia Mar?" Doctor Lemma raised two artificial eyebrows at Zen.

"There was a struggle, yes," Zen said, her tone neutral.

"Ah, hence the police presence. I'd say Ms. Hahn's opponent got the better of her." Dr. Lemma wore a placid expression as if he wasn't describing a violent encounter.

"Right. Right. May I?" Zen nodded toward the treatment bays.

"I approve fifteen minutes with Dr. Xavier. No more." Dr. Lemma beckoned to the male nurse. He stepped forward to direct Zen to another small room. She washed with a special soap and put on a paper jumpsuit. The nurse explained it was required to keep the treatment module as sterile as possible.

"This way, Special Agent Batiste."

The nurse, with dark brown hair and brown skin, spoke in a more natural voice than Dr. Lemma. He led the way back to Alex's bedside. He raised his hand to press a thumb to an access panel but stopped at a signal from the doctor.

"Fifteen minutes." Dr. Lemma gazed at Zen pointedly.

Zen realized he was waiting for her to indicate compliance. She nodded. "Understood."

Dr. Lemma glanced at the nurse, who then touched the scanner. A section of the panel slid open. Zen paused on the threshold. Alex lay on a bed with her eyes closed. Hyperbaric-ozone units attached to both legs and one arm seemed to pin her in place. Warming sheets had been draped over the rest of her body. Alex looked younger somehow, more vulnerable. Then she opened her eyes.

"I'm not asleep or dead, so come on in," Alex said in a scratchy whisper. "If you ask something silly like how I'm feeling..." Her eyes drifted shut again as the sentence trailed off. She seemed to have run out of energy. She inhaled and then slowly exhaled.

"Take it easy," the male nurse said quietly before he let the panel close.

"I don't have to ask. I can tell you feel like shit, but the doctor says you'll recover just fine." Zen found a cushioned stool in a corner out of the way. She pulled it near the bed and sat.

"Hmm." Alex roused after a few seconds and looked at Zen. "You have questions."

"I can wait. I just wanted to make sure you were okay."

Alex wore the ghost of a smile. "Liar."

"Lexi, I care about you. I felt so lost, so miserable after—"

"I know. I meant about the questions." Alex opened one hand, her smile still in place. She sighed when Zen closed her own hand around it gently.

"Relax and heal. Besides, Dr. Lemma will ban me from this place if I don't follow his orders. I get the feeling people out here don't give a damn about Earth authority figures," Zen quipped. She swallowed hard and worked not to let a tear spill down her cheek.

Alex gave Zen's fingers a weak squeeze and let go. "We have cutting-edge treatments. My work contributed to at least three. Besides, humanoids are famous for being blunt. No sugar-coating. I'll recover in a few days. Ask away."

"I meant it, *Alex*. Your recovery is the priority," Zen said. She reminded herself to use her sister's new name from now on.

"The famous space super cop is itching to get answers. Admit it." Alex's hazel eyes twinkled with mischief.

"You lied about having a relationship with Navalny." Zen said.

"A combination of pride and rebellion. I was a bit embarrassed that Mika's corny charm worked on me. Not a relationship though. He was fun and the sex was good. Great, in fact. When he didn't turn up, I didn't think much of it. Mika had lots of playmates. He would disappear sometimes." Alex shifted in bed.

Zen rose and fluffed the pillow beneath her head and neck. "Don't fidget."

"Bossy big sis," Alex whispered. "Raise me up a little. What did you find out before you came to Titan?"

"Sela's maiden name matched one of the girls killed. I thought about how easily she'd become Lewis's informant. Then I wondered who put in the work request that brought Navalny to spot where he died." Zen filled a small cup with water, put a straw in it, and helped Alex sip.

"Later than me, but you got there," Alex teased.

"What made you suspect her?" Zen dabbed Alex's mouth and put the cup down.

"I learned to watch my back. Her name kept popping up every time I got a new job or moved in space. Process of elimination. Took a while to dig into her background. I don't have your unchecked government resources." Alex seemed to perk up. She gestured for more water.

Zen retrieved the cup for her. This time Alex held it on her own. "So, you figured out she was after you."

"One thing about Ms. Hahn, she's patient. Which meant she intended to kill me, not report my location to detectives on Earth," Alex replied and handed the empty cup back to Zen.

"The court and district attorney have to be included in the decision to provide treatment. And..." Zen stopped when Alex shook her head.

"There's backlash, especially from cops."

"Wealthy and connected people get the majority of Lodestone treatments instead of prison sentences," Zen said.

"Or those with skills that make the wealthy even more money," Alex added. "More and more judges are being persuaded Lodestone treatment isn't justice."

"Sela didn't report you to them. She just kept pursuing you." Zen looked at a wall as if she could see into Sela's treatment bay.

"Yes. Anyway, she knew I was Mika's latest lover. We spent our days off together. When I saw she originated the report about the unit needing to be checked, I knew. Look into her digital trail. I'll bet she told those criminals about Mika's side hustle."

"His grand crime boss ambitions."

"He was greedy and talked too much. But he didn't deserve to die. Sela exaggerated the threat he posed to the gang." Alex wore an angry scowl.

"You knew I was here, Alex. You should have told me about Sela."

"And you would have done what? Arrest her for a crime she hadn't committed yet? Force her to leave Crius? How?" Alex raised an eyebrow at Zen.

"You lured Sela to Titan. I just..." Zen blew out a sharp breath.

"She chose to follow me. She attacked me first," Alex said, her voice stronger. She leaned forward as if to emphasize her argument.

"Her suit and life support were intentionally damaged. You didn't have to kill her," Zen insisted.

"The Persson family is large, and just as relentless. You think Sela won't tell them who you are? If they can't get to me, they'll see hurting my family as a fitting act of vengeance. Think about Astra and Brianne. No, my original plan still works for me." Alex sank back onto the pillow again with a soft grunt. She looked frail again.

"No more talk about revenge and the past."

"Better get your answers from me. I doubt Sela will be talking." Alex gazed at Zen with a coldness in her eyes.

Zen stepped away from the hospital bed. The panel slid open automatically at her approach. "I'll, uh, look in on you later."

Alex's eyes drifted closed. "Don't have to worry about me. I'll be well taken care of here. We look out for each other."

Zen gazed at Alex. The faint traces she'd imagined seeing of her little sister were gone. Any resemblance she had seen had been the result of Zen's wishful thinking. Did she really expect Alexis Batiste to be reborn? The panel closed and a voice just over her shoulder made Zen jump. She turned to find the doctor standing close by. Dr. Lemma held a digital notepad in one hand. He glanced up from writing notes with a stylus and then down again.

"Did you get what you expected?"

"I'll see Ms. Hahn now," Zen replied.

"You won't get any information. She's in an induced coma. You should contact her next of kin. She won't survive. And Dr. Xavier won't be cleared to travel for another three weeks. I don't think you'll be staying on Titan or even Crius that long." Dr. Lemma tapped the notepad one final time and slipped it into his white coat pocket.

"Oh really?"

"Your reasons for coming here—both cases have been resolved, I hear. And Dr. Xavier hasn't committed a crime, so you can't take her into custody," Dr. Lemma said in a mild tone.

"Are you her doctor or her lawyer?" Zen studied him with interest. He seemed oddly protective of Alex.

"Simply making a logical observation. I won't clear Dr. Xavier for travel anytime soon. Good-bye, Special Agent Batiste." Dr. Lemma stuck both hands in his lab coat pockets and smiled at her.

"I'll be in touch." Zen gave him a chilly smile and spun around.

A different nurse helped her dispose of the jumpsuit and shoe coverings she wore. Moments later Zen joined Wyvette and Officer Mehmood in the clinic lobby. Wyvette met her halfway, an anxious frown on her smooth face.

"Boss, is she..."

"Dr. Xavier is going to make a full recovery. As for Sela Hahn, the doctor says her chances are slim. Her suit was damaged." Zen looked at Wyvette for a few seconds of silence.

"Okay," Wyvette murmured.

Officer Mehmood cleared her throat. "Excuse me, but a first examination of Ms. Hahn's suit suggest it was tampered with, damaged on purpose?" She glanced from Zen to Wyvette and back again.

"Ms. Hahn and Dr. Xavier struggled." Zen stopped and rubbed her forehead.

Wyvette spoke up. "Yeah, Akon. Hahn attacked Dr. Xavier and she fought back. Ms. Hahn came out here to confront her. That's all we can say."

Officer Mehmood studied Wyvette for a few seconds. "I saw her pull a weapon on Dr. Xavier. Clear case of self-defense if anybody asks me."

"I saw the same." Wyvette clapped Officer Mehmood on the back.

"Look, I got paperwork. Second Lt. Kingston has complained about my 'insubordinate' attitude. My captain ordered me to respond." Officer Mehmood shook her head when Wyvette frowned with anger. "Don't worry. He knows Jeff. It's just for the record."

"Let me know if you need a statement from me," Wyvette said.

Wyvette and Officer Mehmood exchanged a firm handshake. With a quick nod to Zen, Officer Mehmood strode off. The clinic hummed with activity behind them suddenly. Zen and Wyvette turned to see three nurses and Dr. Lemma rushing to the treatment area. Zen's heart slammed against her chest for a moment. Then she realized they were going to Sela Hahn's treatment bay. Ten minutes ticked by. Wyvette and Zen stood rooted to the spot, neither able to look away. Silhouettes of the medical team moved with urgent efficiency. Another ten minutes passed and the male nurse who had helped Zen get outfitted came out. He glanced at them but his expression was blank. Then the doctor emerged. He approached them.

"It was close, but Ms. Hahn is hanging on. Strong human, that one." Dr. Lemma hurried off when a nurse called to him.

"Relentless," Zen murmured, echoing Alex's description of her.

"Alex, Dr. Xavier," Zen added, conscious of Dr. Lemma's observant presence behind her. "We're leaving now. You haven't been cleared for travel yet."

"Sela?" Alex looked from Zen to Dr. Lemma.

"Only a matter of hours at best," Dr. Lemma replied.

"Obviously we can't transport her either. Do you want to file a criminal complaint?" Zen studied her sister for a reaction.

Alex didn't respond immediately. She looked away as if pondering her decision. Then she blew out a soft breath. "Sela was known to have a temper. We had a disagreement and she couldn't let it go. She's got a tough road ahead."

"She won't recover from her injuries," Dr. Lemma added, his voice devoid of emotion.

"Anyway, I think she's learned her lesson." Alex's smile lit up her pretty face.

Zen shivered as she gazed at her. She turned to Dr. Lemma. "I need a moment alone with Dr. Xavier."

Dr. Lemma exchanged a look with Alex. He nodded to her and slipped from the room without another word. Zen turned back to find Alex gazing at her with an impassive expression.

"I'm going to be fine. I've got my work. And so do you. My life is here now," Alex said.

"You don't see yourself ever coming back to Earth?"

Zen stepped close to the bed. She felt a distance from her that had nothing to do with inches or feet. Still, she wanted to feel her sister, maybe for the last time. She grabbed Alex's left hand, looked into her eyes, and sighed. She saw the answer to her question.

"Doubt it. But hey, never say never," Alex said softly.

"Right."

Zen swallowed against the swell of emotion in her throat at the old quote from their father and his father. She leaned forward, hesitated as she studied Alex's reaction, then hugged her tightly. Alex placed her uninjured left arm around Zen's neck. She held on for a few seconds and let go.

"Tell that sexy major-general of yours I said hello. And he better treat you right." Alex grinned at Zen's shocked expression.

"I'm going to give Daddy hell for telling my business!" Zen pretended outrage and then grinned back at her. She pecked Alex's forehead. "I'll see you later. One day. I know it."

They looked at each other in silence for a full minute. Then Zen backed out of the room. She waved good-bye as the panel slid open behind her. Zen checked one last time with the nurse that Alex was recovering well. A code blue was called, interrupting their talk. Five minutes went by before Dr. Lemma emerged. He shook his head at Zen. Moments later she was on her way to the *Dragonfly*.

The trip back to Crius was smooth if tense. Jeff brooded, giving clipped replies when Zen or Wyvette spoke to him. Wyvette raised an eyebrow at Zen but said nothing. They arrived back at the Crius docking port to an illustrious greeting party. Ambassador Abramov, Commander Gusev, and General Blanc were visible through the ship's porthole.

Peter stood a distance from them. Then a handsome, commanding figure with his back to the group turned around.

"Major-General Ramirez! What the hell has happened now, boss?" Wyvette blurted out and twisted to look at Zen.

Zen checked her smartwatch. "No messages. But we're about to find out."

"Cleared to exit my ship," Jeff announced through speakers overhead.

Wyvette snorted. "Oh, now it's *his* ship. What an asshole."

"Let it go, Wy," Zen said. "We got other priorities."

"Crap. Look who else is out there." Wyvette pointed. "Jacques smells a story light years away."

"Hmm." Zen squinted at the various expressions of their welcome committee but got no clue.

She and Wyvette strode down the ramp with Jeff behind them. A senior officer left Commander Gusev's side. The man, a lieutenant-colonel based on the insignia on the shoulders of his blue shirt, pulled Jeff aside. They had a terse exchange. Jeff marched off behind him, a stiff expression making his square jaw tight.

"Malone!" Zen gave a short nod to the others before she hurried past them. She wrapped both arms around his muscular body, not caring about appearances. "I'm so glad to see you."

"Do you go anywhere without turning Earth upside down?" Malone whispered close to her ear. His lips brushed her cheek, an imperceptible kiss, before they separated. "We need to talk."

Zen nodded and followed him to a UTV motorcade. Commander Gusev drove ahead of the group. They pulled up to a contingent of waiting Space Command officers. After a flurry of two-sentence reports, they were ushered into the main incident room. Wyvette followed close on Zen's heels. Despite her junior rank, none of the commanders asked her to leave. Ewan and Imirah quietly entered through a side door. Both seemed content to stand against a wall out of the way.

"We have a situation," Ambassador Abramov intoned once they were seated around a crescent table.

General Blanc alone had remained standing. "The humanoid community assisted Special Agent Lewis in securing the weapon system. A system only the US government knew about." He switched a stony stare between Zen and Malone.

Commander Gusev cleared his throat. "They also used their expertise to gain control of access to the so-called Outernet. We gained valuable information to root out members of Vlast."

"Great. Two murders solved. Crius can contain the criminal activity. An international crisis averted." Zen looked around at the tense faces. "This doesn't look like a celebration."

"They have a demand. The humanoids." Commander Gusev gestured with one hand.

Imirah stepped forward. "They have presented a formal request to the United Nations to be declared a sovereign space nation. The first of its kind in history. Dr. Alexandra Xavier is their representative."

"Say what now?" Wyvette gawked at Imirah with wide eyes and her mouth hanging open.

"They're a loose-knit entity, a community with no government. No territory," Zen said.

"Most of the inhabitants on Titan are humanoid or hybrid. They're physically able to live on alien planets and satellites not easy for humans. Some don't breathe oxygen at all, others—"

"Yes, yes. We know about robots and AI humanoids," Ambassador Abramov broke in with an annoyed grimace. She turned to Zen. "The humanoid community has submitted a formal request that we can't ignore."

"With Titan as their home world. I understand this is a novel development, but it's not surprising given how advanced they've become." Zen glanced around the room.

"Do you have any idea the uproar this request has caused? Jacques Clairmont broke the story before the UN Council of Nations would even review the request. Never mind meet with various governments or craft a series of careful press releases. The paranoia, wild conspiracy theories... it's a diplomatic and global nightmare." Ambassador Abramov huffed in frustration. Then she seemed to recover. "But, as you said, they have advanced."

"And no nation or corporation can claim Titan as its own. In other words, who can stop them from making Titan theirs?" Malone said. He raised both eyebrows at Zen.

Zen gazed back at Malone for a few seconds. Her mind clicked pieces into place. Alex's words "new worlds" echoed in her mind. "Especially since they have a weapon system to defend themselves and a space-connected digital network. The Outernet."

"They'll take responsibility for the creation of both," Malone said.

"Letting the White House and certain other governments off the hook," General Blanc said with a sardonic grin.

"In exchange for global recognition of their sovereignty," Commander Gusev said in a mild tone.

"Extortion," General Blanc grumbled and rocked back in his seat.

"A solution to a dangerous situation on Earth. We have straightforward answers to two crimes. Neither had anything to do with spying or international intrigue. Once those on Earth realize we in space simply want to exist in harmony, things will die down." Commander Gusev shrugged and looked at the others.

"Easy for you to say. We'll both return to Earth to a shit-storm," General Blanc snipped. Then he flinched at the fiery look Commander Gusev shot at him. "Apologies for the strong language but the situation—"

"Was caused by Earth governments and solved by space residents. Rather neatly, I might add." Commander Gusev wore a satisfied expression.

"I'd hardly call blackmail and a new global crisis 'neat'," Ambassador Abramov said. "But dealing with anti-humanoid sentiments present a lesser challenge than stopping a world war. At least this new nation is millions of miles away from Earth."

"A point I'm sure the media will be happy to include in future stories. Mr. Clairmont is thrilled to have a front seat to and an exclusive," Imirah said.

"Okay, so the UN has its work cut out for it." Zen looked around, letting the question of why she was in the room hang in the air.

"The UN and the White House need OSI to redact your final reports. Leave out mention of a weapon system or the Outernet. We've already spoken to Director Anderson." Ambassador Abramov's tone implied the matter had been settled.

"Agreed," Zen said and stood. "Now, if you'll excuse me."

"Of course, you must be tired and hungry." Colonel Smith spoke for the first time. "Check the amenities app in your living quarters. Menus of all restaurants are available. Your meals will be delivered to avoid curious crowds."

"Thanks," Zen replied with a grateful smile. She glanced at Malone. "I'll see you later?"

"Much later by the looks of it," he said quietly, nodding at the group talking to each other in low tones.

Zen and Wyvette left, going their separate ways once out of the room. Still full of energy, Wyvette went off to find her new pal Officer Turner. They would share celebratory food and drinks. Zen wanted more than anything to see her daughter. She checked the satellite connection first and then put in a video call to Astra's smart tablet. Minutes later the call bounced back. Astra's nervous young face appeared on Zen's screen.

"Mama, are you alright? It's one o'clock in the morning. You're not hurt or anything? The stories about Crius are wild." Worry made Astra sound like her seven-year-old self again.

"I'm fine, sweet girl. I just wanted to hear your voice and see you. I should be home in a few weeks, thanks to the EmDrive. How are things with you?"

Astra smiled with relief, blew out a sigh, and then yawned. She launched into a spirited description of her studies. Zen was sure the account of her new social life was edited to exclude boys and partying. But she was just as sure Jordan was keeping a close eye on their daughter.

"Enough about my boring life. You're back in the news big time. Whew! And you got to visit Titan. The media can't stop talking about you and Dr. Alexandra Xavier. She literally cheated death to escape a crazy lady. You helped save them both. Amazing adventure."

"So, that's how they're spinning it," Zen mumbled.

"What?" Astra blinked at her rapidly.

"I said my head is spinning I'm so exhausted. I'll be glad to get home," Zen replied with a tired smile.

"The Global Press article says Dr. Xavier is brilliant, helping develop planets for human habitation. She discovered a previously unknown exoplanet. It might lead to colonization even farther in space. What's she like up close?

"Like you said. Amazing."

"Yeah. Guess Brianne and me will never get to meet her. Oh well." Astra shrugged.

Zen wondered how much time would pass before she told them about their aunt. "Never say never."

Don't miss out!

Visit the website below and you can sign up to receive emails whenever Lynn Emery publishes a new book. There's no charge and no obligation.

https://books2read.com/r/B-A-YISG-LDZXB

BOOKS 2 READ

Connecting independent readers to independent writers.

Also by Lynn Emery

Dr. Zen Mystery
The Lodestone Puzzle
The In Situ Murders
The Titan Paradox

Joliet Sisters Psychic Detectives
Smooth Operator
Hunting Spirits
Dead Wrong
Dead Ahead
Die Trying
Spirited Sisters

LaShaun Rousselle Mystery
A Darker Shade of Midnight
Voodoo Lily
Between Dusk and Dawn
Only By Moonlight

Into the Mist
Third Sight Into Darkness
Devil's Swamp
LaShaun Rousselle Mysteries Books 1-3

Triple Trouble Mystery
Best Enemies
Devilish Details
Pretty Dangerous

Standalone
After All
Louisiana Love City Girls Boxset
A Time to Love
One Love
Sweet Mystery
Night Magic
Good Woman Blues
Gotta Get Next To You
Soulful Strut
Tell Me Something Good
Tender Touch
Louisiana Love Box Set

Watch for more at www.lynnemery.com.

About the Author

Mix knowledge of voodoo, Louisiana politics and forensic social work, and you get a snapshot of author Lynn Emery. Lynn has written over twenty novels so far, one of which inspired the BET made-for-television movie AFTER ALL based on her romantic suspense novel of the same name. Holly Robinson Peete and DB Woodside starred as the lead characters.

Her romantic suspense titles have won and been nominated for several awards, including Best Multicultural Mainstream Novel by Romantic Times Magazine.

Get exclusive offers each month in Lynn's newsletter and a free short story when you sign up! Go to:

https://www.subscribepage.com/s1y8j8

Visit www.lynnemery.com to see a full list of Lynn Emery novels.

Read more at www.lynnemery.com.

www.ingramcontent.com/pod-product-compliance
Lightning Source LLC
Chambersburg PA
CBHW061310190726
48288CB00002B/437